Moon Rise

By Marilee Brothers

Dedication
This one is for the boys.
To Tim, Mark, Todd, Brandon,
Eric and Blake Brothers . . .
love you guys!

Smyrna, Georgia

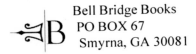
Bell Bridge Books
PO BOX 67
Smyrna, GA 30081

Bell Bridge Books is an Imprint of BelleBooks, Inc.

ISBN: 978-0-9821756-9-9

TITLE: Moon Rise

We at BelleBooks enjoy hearing from readers. You can contact us at the address above or at BelleBooks@BelleBooks.com

Visit our websites,www.BelleBooks.com
and www.BellBridgeBooks.com.

10 9 8 7 6 5 4 3 2 1

Cover design: Debra Dixon
Photo Credits:
Orchard - © Kathy Gold - Fotolia.com
Moon/clouds - © chrisharvey - Fotolia.com
Girl - © Chaoss Foto - Dreamstime.com
Interior design: Linda Kichline

Chapter One

"Ouch!"

The butt pinch happened when I bent over to pick up the quarter I'd dropped on the gym floor. I shot up, looking for the guilty party as a bunch of guys, high on hormones, drifted by. Oh, they were good . . . no fist bumps . . . no high fives. Nothing but smirks and sneaky, sidelong glances. What else could one expect from a group including Cory Philpott, official school bully and my number one suspect?

Someone *had* pinched my ass. It wasn't the first time, and I wasn't the only one. And it wasn't a gentle pinch followed up with a tender little pat signaling, *Wow! You're hot. Maybe we can hook up later.* No, it was nothing like that. It felt like a vicious Chihuahua had latched onto my right bun with razor-sharp teeth.

Yes, it's true. A serial ass pincher roamed the halls and gymnasium of John J. Peacock High School of Peacock Flats, Washington. But, not to worry. I, Alfrieda Carlotta Emerson Purdy, aka Allie, was determined to discover the identity of the perpetrator and make him accountable for his deeds. I had to. I am the fighter of evil, the girl with the star on her palm and the magic moonstone around her neck. And I was in a nasty mood these days, talking tough and snappin at my friends and family. Not like me at all..I was scared, and worried. But hadn't I vanquished two nasty Trimarks single-handed? Well, almost single-handed. Never mind that my supernatural powers were acting up at the moment. With time, I'd sort it out.

It was Halloween night. I straightened, rubbing my offended butt cheek and checking out the crowd at the

Halloween party our school hosted each year in an effort to keep roving bands of teenagers off the highways and byways of Peacock Flats. Its purpose was to cut down on egg-coated cars, bottle rockets whizzing into hay fields and sacks of burning dog poop placed on *Welcome* mats. In that last scenario, the prankster rings the doorbell, hides in the bushes and tries to stifle his/her laughter as the homeowner stomps on the burning paper sack, only to end up with a shoe caked with smelly, brown stuff. Don't ask me how I know this.

"Allie! What's wrong?" Kizzy, the star attraction at our fortune-telling booth, peered at me over the top of the murky crystal ball resting on the table in front of her. Kizzy and I shared a secret. We were bound together by the moonstone she'd given me. She said it was my *destiny* and, oh yeah, that *destiny* had almost gotten both of us killed. Even though I'd assured her I was fine, she continued to worry about me, just as I worried about her, even though she'd recovered fully from the beating the Trimarks gave her. Bottom line: we both knew the supernatural wasn't about cloudy crystal balls and party tricks. Right now, despite the comical tilt of her turban and smile, she was in full mother hen mode.

I agonized over my answer. Kizzy was an elderly woman, at least fifty or sixty. I struggled to find the appropriate term to describe what had happened to me just now. What did people from her era call that part of their anatomy? Buttocks? Bottom? Rear?

I needn't have worried.

"Did one of those boys pinch your ass?" Kizzy asked, one corner of her mouth curled down in disgust.

I hid my smile and nodded.

"If there's one thing I hate, it's an ass pincher!" Kizzy declared.

My friend and neighbor, Mercedes Trujillo, giggled in agreement. Mercedes is a huge daytime drama fan and hopeless romantic. Swear to God, she sees love in all the wrong places.

She and I were dressed in long, colorful skirts, white, scoop-necked peasant blouses and lots and lots of beads. Mine, of course, included the above-mentioned moonstone. We were Kizzy's assistants, manning the most popular booth in the gym. Kizzy, also known as the town witch, was the head fortune teller. She's not really a witch. She's the descendant of a Romany gypsy. At least that's what she claimed. Me? Not sure I really believe that. More than once, she'd looked at me and known exactly what I was thinking.

But, tonight, she wasn't really telling fortunes. At least, not truthfully.

Our act went something like this:

Kizzy (staring into the crystal ball and speaking with a cheesy gypsy accent): "Ah, yes. Now I see vhat lies ahead. Something vonderful, I believe."

Her beautifully manicured fingernails would flutter over the crystal ball like pale, pink butterflies before she paused and gazed up at Mercedes and me with sparkling turquoise eyes. "Vhat do you think, my ladies?"

I could always count on Mercedes to clasp her hands over her heart, beam happily and say, "Love. I see love in your future. All your romantic dreams will come true."

That left me as the bearer of bad news. I'm sorry, but most of our teenage clients needed a reality check. I'd say something like, "If you don't study harder, I see a D in geometry." Or . . . "You'd better quit screwing around in class or you'll be in trouble with Mr. Hostetler."

Before I could say, "Next!" the kids at our booth suddenly turned as one and stampeded to door leading into the foyer. Curious to discover who had spirited away potential customers, Mercedes and I trailed behind. An unruly mob of guys—the very group I suspected of harboring the ass pincher—were now lined up at a dunking booth which had been placed on the vinyl floor of the foyer.

Mr. Hostetler, our principal, sat high above the water. He was dressed in navy blue gym shorts and a Green Bay Packers tee shirt. Originally from Wisconsin, Mr. Hostetler was a huge Packer fan. He had, wisely, removed his glasses and watch. Blinking nervously at the gathering crowd, he managed a weak smile. "Now boys, be nice."

They weren't, of course. They could hardly wait to hand over their money to get even with the guy who stood between them and their atrociously bad behavior. (*Atrocious* was this week's vocabulary word. I tried to use it as much as possible.) Mr. Hostetler had a lot of enemies, and they were elbowing each other for the opportunity to be the first. They only got to throw the baseball three times. Three must be a lucky number, because the third guy in line was the winner.

Bam! The ball hit the magic spot and down went our principal, a look of sad resignation on his face. As he hit the water, a geyser shot up and a great cheer rang through the foyer. It made me feel a little sad. Poor Mr. Hostetler. Apparently, Mercedes felt the same way.

As we meandered back into the gym, she said, "I really hope this doesn't affect his relationship with Miss Yeager."

"Are you talking about the new school counselor? *That* Miss Yeager?" I said.

"Yeah." Mercedes shook her head sadly. "Hostetler just got divorced. I've seen the way he looks at her, that counselor woman. He's definitely got the hots for her. Haven't you noticed?"

I waved my hand dismissively as we approached our fortune telling booth. "You're nuts, Mercedes. Mr. Hostetler is nice to everybody."

"No, no," she insisted. "He looks at her exactly like Junior looked at you. Remember, I was the first one to notice Junior liked you. But, did you believe me? No! And, who was right?"

A stocky fake blond, standing at our booth, whirled at

the sound of Junior's name. She raked me with a murderous glare. "What about Junior? Don't think I've forgotten you took him away from me, Emerson!"

I'd failed to notice that the person awaiting Kizzy's fictional fortune was Sonja Ortega, one of the toughest girls in Peacock Flats. Not that I recognized her. She was decked out in the blond wig, fishnet stockings and four inch heels, Sonja's version of an appropriate Halloween costume. The hostility in her voice communicated her real meaning. *Come on, give me an excuse so I can beat the crap out of you.*

"Oh hi, Sonja," I said as Mercedes and I slipped behind Kizzy. "Cool costume," I added. Yeah, I was being a total suck-up, but I liked the shape of my nose and didn't want it flattened. I bumped Mercedes with my hip, hoping she could somehow distract Sonja with her usual rapid-fire dialog.

"Oh yeah, Junior," Mercedes said. "I was just saying . . . Sonya, you know how he'd give you that look, and you could tell he was interested? Kinda like this . . . " With her eyes half-shut in her version of lustful longing, Mercedes leaned toward Sonja and allowed her sleepy brown gaze to wander over Sonja's ample form. "Then he'd wink and say, 'Oooo, girl, you are *so* hot!'"

A dreamy smile appeared on Sonja's face. She murmured, "Yeah, that Junior Martinez was something else."

Sensing we could use some help, Kizzy jumped in. She examined Sonja's costume and waved a hand over the crystal ball. "Ah, yes, I believe I see you standing in front of an audience. They're on their feet, clapping, calling your name. Tell me, darling, do you sing?"

Apparently, Kizzy was interpreting Sonya's outfit as "rock star" not "hooker."

"Yeah," Sonja said. "And I can bust a move, too."

"That's nice, dear," Kizzy said. She turned to look at Mercedes and me. "*Vhat* do my lovely assistants see?"

Mercedes quickly said, "Someone far away is thinking of you, Sonya."

Before I could open my mouth to add my bit, Sonja stabbed a long, black fingernail toward my heart and jeered, "Yeah, he's thinking about *me*, not *you*, Allie."

Sonja stomped away, her spike heels torturing the wooden gym floor. Kizzy turned to me, a look of consternation furrowing her brow. "Is Junior gone?"

Mercedes and I exchanged a glance. Last May, Kizzy had been attacked and left for dead. She'd mostly recovered from her injuries but her memory faded in and out like an out of range radio station. I hadn't yet told her about Junior.

"He's in Mexico, Kizzy," I replied.

Mercedes, of course, had to embellish it. She stood and rolled her eyes heavenward.

"It was sooo sad," she said. "Allie and I were working at her uncle's fruit stand. Let's see . . . we were sorting peaches. Right, Allie?"

"Whatever," I mumbled. I knew there was no stopping her.

"Well, anyway," she continued breathlessly, "Junior drove up, and he looked hot, you know, all that and then some. Allie looked good too, dressed in her Daisy Dukes. Junior said his Tia Rosa's daughter was getting married in Mexico City, and he had to drive his mama there.

"Couldn't she fly?" Kizzy asked. She was caught up in the story.

"Exactly what Allie said. But Junior's mama is afraid of airplanes, so he had to drive her. He promised he'd be back by the end of September but . . . guess what?"

I looked into the distance like I didn't give a rip, even though Mercedes' dramatic rendition of my last moments with Junior was painful to relive.

"He's still not back, and it's the end of October," she finished.

"Oh my, what a shame," Kizzy declared.

Mercedes looked around for Sonja, then leaned close to Kizzy and whispered, "Here's the best part. Junior got out of the car that day. He and Allie went behind the fruit stand and he laid the goodies on her."

"Mercedes!" I yelped. "Kizzy doesn't want to hear that."

"Oh, but I do." Kizzy pulled Mercedes into the chair beside her. "What kind of goodies?"

"The kissin' kind," Mercedes said. "Let me tell ya, I watch a lot of soaps and I've never seen anything like *that*. Man, oh, man!"

"It's not nice to spy on people." I tried to be mad, but now I was the one with the sad, dreamy smile on my face. Junior Martinez had been my sort-of boyfriend. Sinfully handsome, with charm up the wazoo, Junior had cut quite a swath through last year's crop of Peacock Flat girls. Up to the moment he'd left town, we'd shared only a few chaste kisses. Not by my choice. Junior had some weird idea I needed protection from my baser self. But our farewell kiss was a real doozy. A tongue-tangling, tonsil-tickling, heavy-breathing, toe-curling kiss that would live forever in my memory.

Mercedes sighed deeply. "Now he's gone, and Allie's heart is broken. Right, Allie?"

Before I could answer, I heard the unmistakable sound of high heels clicking on the wooden floor. I knew the sound and it was too late to run. It was her . . . that counselor woman.

"Allie!" Jeanette Yeager screeched. Her eyes, slightly bulging on a good day, almost popped out of her head as she checked out my costume. "Aren't you just adorable!"

I pulled Mercedes out of her chair and pushed her forward. Miss Yeager squealed again and waved at Mr. Hostetler, who was trudging toward the boys' locker room in rubber flip flops. Despite the towel dangling from one hand, he was leaving a trail of wet footprints on the gym floor.

"Herb! Herb! Come see these darling girls!"

Mr. Hostetler, still without his glasses, squinted over at us. He didn't look happy, but obediently changed course. I guess if you're the principal, you have to do stuff you don't want to do.

Miss Yeager squealed again and flapped her hands. In my opinion, her reaction was way over the top. But that's how she was . . . half-hysterical most of the time. I knew, because I was her pet counseling project.

"Aren't they precious? They look like cute little, fortune-telling twins, one Hispanic and one Caucasian," she gushed.

Mr. Hostetler went, "Heh, heh, heh. Yep, they're cute all right," and squished away. Miss Yeager clasped her darting hands together and watched him go.

Since my almost fatal encounter with the Trimarks last May, I'd come up with sure-fire techniques to check people's palms and look for an inverted triangle, the sign of a Trimark. Since Miss Yeager didn't have it, I believed her obnoxious qualities were just part of her personality. She'd heard about my "trauma," as she called it, and insisted on meeting with me once a week.

Mercedes nudged me and whispered, "She's checking out Mr. Hostetler's butt."

A huge snort-laugh burst from my mouth. Miss Yeager looked at me curiously, and I snapped my mouth shut.

She leaned toward us and frowned. "Something funny, Allie?"

"No, no!" I gazed around the gym, looking for something to distract her. She had a very short attention span. It was then I spotted Beck Bradford, who was new to our school this year.

"Oh look," I babbled. "There's Beck."

It worked. Miss Yeager's head swiveled to the right,

and she was off and running, allowing me to study the hottest guy at John J. Peacock H.S. Funny how things work out. Last year, the old Bradford place was the scene of my near-death experience. But now, I couldn't take my eyes off Beck Bradford, grandson of old Mr. Bradford and son of Melissa Bradford, who'd returned to the family place with her son and daughter. Maybe with his family back in residence, old Mr. Bradford's ghost would take a hike. I didn't like thinking about the Bradford place and what happened there so I focused on Beck. Yum!

He trailed behind a gaggle of chattering girls who, just my luck, were the coolest girls at school. Beck was tall and lean with tousled, dark-blond hair, sensuous lips and unusual hazel eyes that looked golden in the harsh gym lights. He wasn't wearing a Halloween costume, just jeans with holes in the knees—lookin' good on Beck—and a form-fitting black tee shirt that showed off his well-defined biceps, triceps, pecs, abs and all that other stuff. Somehow, he looked bigger tonight. How could that be?

His twin sister, Nicole—real twins, not pretend Mexican-American twins like me and Mercedes—was smack dab in the middle of the cool girls. Nicole had fit in from the minute the Bradfords enrolled in school. Cute, bubbly, popular, an instant hit with both guys and girls. Unlike her brother, Nicole was short, curvy and brunette. The only characteristic the twins had in common was their unique golden eyes.

Beck's personality was nothing like his sister's. Stand-offish and aloof, he was a real brain in math and science and no slouch in his other classes. French class is where we crossed paths. My favorite teacher, Mrs. Burke, talked me into taking French.

She said, "Allie Emerson, as smart as you are, you'll get a scholarship for sure. You *must* take two years of a foreign language. I absolutely *insist* you sign up for French."

Beck spoke French fluently and was Mrs. Burke's class assistant.

I watched Miss Yeager scamper up to Beck, who looked down at her with a puzzled expression.

"Oooo, girl!" Mercedes gushed. "That Beck guy is so hot!"

True, I'd rid myself of one irritant—Miss Yeager—but, as I'd learned in science class, nature abhors a vacuum. Mercedes filled the void. Determined not to encourage her, I reluctantly pulled my gaze from Beck Bradford and watched Medina, our janitor, mop up the trail of water left by Mr. Hostetler. Medina was muttering oaths and shaking his fist.

"Allie! Allie!" Mercedes urgent whisper was not to be ignored. "Beck is totally checking you out!"

When I looked at Beck, the intensity in his eyes slammed into me like an unexpected blow to the gut. Unable to look away, I gasped in surprise. Here's the weird part. I'd seen this guy every day in French class, and he'd never so much as given me an interested glance.

Why now? Was it my fetching costume? My Mexican twin? The moonstone pendant?

My money was on the moonstone. The scoop neck of my peasant blouse suddenly felt like a neon sign flashing, "Hey, look at my chest!" Sadly, the most interesting thing about my chest was the moonstone. I felt my cheeks growing hot as he continued to stare into my eyes. Instinctually, my right hand flew up to cover the gem.

I felt the heat of another gaze and glanced away from Beck. Nicole Bradford had joined the staring contest. She stood apart from her friends, her eyes narrowed in suspicion. While Beck looked intense, Nicole simply looked hostile. This was getting stranger by the minute.

Suddenly Kizzy's voice broke the spell. "Allie! Is that the Bradford boy?"

Startled by the sudden interest in her voice, I turned to face her. "Yes," I said. "His name is Beck."

She pushed away from the table and stood. "Beck Bradford," she called. "Come over here."

Beck jerked, as if waking from a dream. He gave Kizzy a puzzled look. "Excuse me?"

Nicole re-joined her friends, but her gaze remained fixed on Beck. Mercedes and I exchanged a worried glance. Was Kizzy having one of her bad moments?

I tugged at Kizzy's sleeve and whispered, "I don't think he's into fortune-telling, Kizzy."

She patted my cheek and smiled. Her bright, turquoise eyes sparkled with mischief. "Who said anything about fortune-telling?"

Kizzy bustled around the table and approached Beck, who took a tentative step toward her. She reached out and grasped his hands. He looked startled but didn't pull away. Kizzy leaned close and began speaking to him in low tones, unfortunately way too low for me to eavesdrop. How did she know he was a Bradford? Why didn't she want me to hear what she was saying? Questions without answers made me crazy, but I knew one thing for sure. This was the Kizzy I remembered before the Trimark assault. Strong. Determined. Ready to take on the world and straighten it out.

I poked Mercedes with my elbow and smiled. "Yes!" I said. "She's back."

Mercedes, still drooling over Beck, nodded absently. "Oh, my God, did you see the way he looked at you? He thinks you're a fox."

I knew better. Mercedes had no knowledge of my paranormal abilities. But I'd seen the look on Beck Bradford's face. The hostility radiating off Nicole. Were they Trimarks? Was that what grabbed Kizzy's attention? It had to be about the moonstone.

And, oh yeah, tomorrow I was traveling to the Seattle area to be the honored guest at a Star Seeker's meeting. Every person in this ultra-secret society wanted to meet the girl in the moonstone prophecy. The girl with the star on her palm, who had the psychic ability to make bulls trot backwards and read minds. The girl who was destined to seek out Trimarks and put a stop to their evil plans.

I had just one teensy problem. Destiny was flipping me the bird.

My paranormal powers were gone.

Chapter Two

"I don't know why you're going. Purdy doesn't care about you," Faye said.

My mother and I were engaged in a squinty-eyed, visual smackdown, neither of us willing to blink. I gripped the edge of the table and glared at her.

"Just because you're bitter and spiteful doesn't mean I have to be."

My voice was shrill with anger. "Besides, half of me came from my dad, whether you like it or not."

Faye was sitting at the dinette in the twenty-four-foot travel trailer we called home. "Brain Dead Roy," an underwater welder and Faye's current boyfriend, sat between her and the wall, probably so she could wait on him.

"Yeah," Faye said with a bitter smile. "And I'm seeing his half right now. The half that always has to be right, the half that won't listen to reason, the half . . . "

I released my pent-up breath. It whistled through my teeth making a noise that sounded like, *Phhhhtttuuuiii.*

Faye popped up, danger signs flashing in her eyes. "What did you say?"

Apparently, she'd heard some kind of "f" word in that gibberish and, combined with the *uh* sound, it wasn't looking good for me.

I raised my hands and backed away. "Nothing. No way. I wouldn't say that to you. You heard wrong."

"Hey, ladies. Take a chill pill."

Roy said lame stuff like that all the time. He stood, stretched and gazed at us through heavy-lidded eyes, Roy's version of a look so compelling, so sexy, we would stop fighting and focus on him. Maybe it worked for Faye. It definitely didn't work for me. If I hadn't been in the middle of a fight with my mother, I'd have busted out laughing.

Faye and I spoke in unison. "Shut up, Roy!"

He smirked and pointed at the door. "I'll wait outside . . . *ladies*."

The word *ladies* was dripping with sarcasm, another one of Roy's specialties.

Faye stepped back to let him by. I retreated to the couch and drew up my feet, unwilling to let a single Roy molecule touch my person. Faye rolled her eyes. After Roy stepped outside, she hissed, "Why are you so mean to him? He's always nice to you."

I hissed back. "Oh, are we talking about Roy, now?"

The sound of a car coming down Uncle Sid's driveway put a stop to our bickering.

Faye flapped her hands in a dismissive gesture and plopped down on the bench seat. "Your ride's here."

Her voice was dull and she wouldn't look at me. I started to flounce off and then reconsidered. Visions of a bloody car crash and Faye weeping over my flower-draped casket flashed through my mind. Our relationship had been upside-down for as long as I could remember. It was about *me* taking care of *her*. But, in the last few months, Faye had pulled it together. She'd left her fake sick bed and gotten a job. She was trying. Now would be a good time to remember that. Plus, it was hard to ignore the little voice whispering, "She's your mother, you jerk."

I crossed to the dinette and dropped a kiss on top of her head. "Bye, see you tonight."

When she looked up, her eyes were still angry. "Yeah, just don't forget where home is."

I smiled. "As if."

When I stepped outside, Roy was sitting in a lawn chair,

cleaning his fingernails with a Swiss Army knife. He smiled. "See ya, AC. Have a good time."

"Whatever." I headed for the limo. I would always be AC to Roy. It wasn't short for Alfrieda Carlotta. In Roy's world, AC stood for *Angry Chick*.

Kizzy didn't drive, so when she wanted to go somewhere—usually every day—she hired Charlie to drive her. And today, she had decided, she and Charlie would deliver me safely to and from the Star Seekers meeting

Charlie grinned and winked as I approached the car; he opened the door and stepped back with a slight bow. "As I live and breathe, I do believe its Miss Allie Emerson. Your chariot awaits."

I gave him a wan smile. "Thanks, Charlie."

Kizzy took one look at my face and said, "Fight with Faye?"

"Yeah."

I gazed out through the tinted window as Charlie executed what the drivers education manual called a three-point turn and headed down the driveway toward Peacock Flats Road.

Our trailer was parked next to a cow pasture behind the big house belonging to Sid and Sandra McNeil. Sid was Faye's step brother. No blood involved. When Faye's mother died, Grandpa Claude hooked up with Sid's mother, who, according to Faye, died a few years later of terminal meanness. Last year, I'd had a mad crush on Matt, Sid and Sandra's seventeen-year-old son, but when the moonstone let me peek into his mind, I'd discovered his thoughts didn't match his friendly, private-Christian-school image.

We were approaching the house when Matt and his younger sister, Tiffany, came through the back door. Tiffany was wearing a pink tutu, black tights and a ferocious frown. Aunt Sandra desperately wanted Tiffany to become the next Little Miss Maraschino Cherry, junior princess for the

Peacock Flats Fruit Bowl Festival. A very big deal in our little corner of the world. She'd enrolled Tiffany in dance lessons to teach her poise and grace and hopefully burn off ten extra pounds of blubber. Only problem was, Tiffany hated physical exercise of any kind. She bitched and moaned constantly about how her mother was torturing her. Apparently Matt had been volunteered to take Tiffany to her dance lesson.

As we rolled by, I zipped the window down so they could see it was me in the limo. Matt smiled and waved. I ignored him and called to Tiffany. "Have fun, Tif. No pain, no gain."

Tiffany stuck out her tongue. Maybe I deserved it.

Kizzy watched this exchange in silence. After we turned north on Peacock Road, she said, "What's going on with you and Faye?"

I shook my head. "It's my dad. She hates him. I tried to tell her, it's the Star Seeker thing. He knows about it. I *don't,* and I need to learn from him." I sighed and settled back into the cushions. "It seems like she's mad all the time."

"That's because she's scared."

"Scared? I don't think so."

"Oh, Alfrieda," Kizzy said, shaking her head. "Don't you see? She thinks you'll choose your father over her. She's afraid of losing you. Beneath the anger, she's scared to death."

"Well, she's got a funny way of showing it."

I gazed out the window and thought about what Kizzy said. Maybe I was acting like a self-centered little jerk. Dealing with Faye's emotions had never been easy, and when her boy-toy, Roy, invaded our little family circle, I'd looked for every excuse to avoid both of them. It's not that I didn't want my mother to be happy. I was all for happiness. But she had a habit of picking losers who cheated on her, stole her life savings . . . well, you get the picture. If Roy was like the others, it was just a matter of time before the big crisis hit. Faye was in a good place now and I didn't want to see her knocked down again.

A sudden thought flashed through my mind. Could I use what Kizzy said to find out what I really wanted to know?

I turned to Kizzy and gave her a bright smile. "I'll bet you're right. Faye probably *is* scared. You know what scares *me*?"

"No, tell me."

"Not knowing what you said to Beck Bradford."

Kizzy laughed and shook a finger at me. "Nice try, Allie," she said and clammed up.

Dang! Last night, after Mercedes took off, I'd peppered Kizzy with questions. How did she know he was a Bradford? Did she think Beck was a Trimark? Was she talking to him about *me*? Okay, that last question sounded a little self-centered. She'd just looked at me and smiled. When she had enough of my pestering, she lifted a hand and said, "Stop! You'll find out soon enough."

Since nothing had happened to change her mind since last night, I stayed quiet for the rest of the two-hour trip, responding with nods and smiles as Kizzy filled me in on the shopping she planned to do while I was at the Star Seekers' meeting.

We were headed for the Paul and Patricia Sugden Institute for Scientific Learning in Bellevue. Bellevue was a large city separated from Seattle by Lake Washington. It was there I would join my newly-discovered father, Mike Purdy. We'd met once before, but this would be our first face-to-face meeting since he'd reluctantly copped to donating the sperm resulting in Alfrieda Carlotta Emerson. The closer we got to our destination, the more jittery I became.

Normally, I'm not too concerned about my appearance. Remember, I'm from Peacock Flats, Washington, population

852. But when Bellevue's high rise buildings came into view, I blurted, "Do I look okay?"

Kizzy ran a practiced eye over my attire. "Alfrieda, you look lovely."

Without turning around, Charlie raised a thumb in the air and said, "Hubba, hubba," which apparently, in the olden days, meant, "You look hot!"

I'd worked in Uncle Sid's fruit stand all summer and saved my money. A nice pair of stone-washed jeans and dressy black boots burned through most of it. I'd found the scoop-necked, white silk tee and fitted black blazer at a yard sale. The moonstone pendant was my only accessory and another reason for the anxiety attack.

The star on my palm and my status as the keeper of the light, as per the moonstone prophecy, were my ticket in the door. I had a horrible feeling I was expected to perform a minor miracle, like make all the Star Seekers float in the air above their seats or read the minds of the entire front row. I'd had nightmares for a week. I decided to broach the subject to Kizzy.

"What if they want me to—you know—do something?"

A look of confusion bloomed on Kizzy's face. "Do something?"

"The Star Seekers know about the prophecy. They know I'm 'the maid who's strong of mind.' Purdy said they all want to meet me. I'm thinking they'll want a demonstration of some kind."

The frustration I'd experienced for the past few months boiled up and added a bitter edge to my voice. "I've tried and tried but it's *gone*. The telekinetic power."

I clutched the moonstone. "It's like somebody pulled the plug and the magic just drained away. Maybe the prophecy was wrong. Maybe I'm not the right girl."

Kizzy patted my arm. "No, the moonstone is exactly where it belongs. Think about it, Alfrieda. You've been through a lot. You were seriously injured."

"So were you," I added.

Kizzy nodded. "It takes energy to heal the body. There's nothing left for anything else. Severe trauma injures the mind as well as the body. For me, it's blank spaces in my memory. In your case, something is blocking your power. Give it time. The magic will return."

I gave her a shaky smile. "Today would be nice."

Charlie pulled up into a curved, sweeping drive and stopped in front of an impressive building that occupied an entire city block. Made of stucco and topped with a red tile roof, it was unlike anything I'd seen in the modern, rainy part of Washington. It looked like pictures I'd seen of the dry Southwest and somehow felt friendlier than the sleek high rises surrounding it.

Broad stairs led to a spacious paved area in front of the building where people were clustered in small groups. I spotted my father, Mike Purdy, deep in conversation with another man who seemed to be guarding the door. It's hard to describe what I felt. Part of me hoped he wouldn't be there so we could turn around and drive back to Peacock Flats.

The other part said, Geez, you're such a wuss!

Charlie jumped out and opened the door. Purdy gave us a dismissive glance, returned to his conversation, then looked back a second time when he realized it was his love child stepping out of the limo, the daughter of his baby mama. Would have been downright funny if I hadn't been so nervous.

"Good luck, dear," Kizzy called before Charlie shut the door.

As the car pulled away from the curb, I felt like running after it, screaming, "Wait! Wait! It's all a big mistake."

Purdy wore jeans, a black windbreaker, athletic shoes and a black baseball cap emblazoned with a gold starburst.

With his carpet-salesman smile firmly in place, he walked up to me, thrust out his right hand and said, "Hi, Allie."

Okay, we were going to shake hands, not hug. That felt right. I put my hand in his and said, "Hi, uh, Mr. Purdy."

"Mike," he said. "Call me Mike."

After giving my hand a teensy squeeze, he grasped my elbow and guided me toward the building. "A lot of people want to meet you."

I had a feeling this was a big ego trip for him. Mike Purdy, father of Allie Emerson, the chosen one and keeper of the moonstone, whose light would reflect and enhance *his* light. I hoped I was wrong.

Red brick steps led to the entry way, double-doors set into a rectangle taller than the rest of the building. To the right of the doors, an oblong wing stretched to the end of the block. Behind its façade, I spotted a domed roof.

The guy I'd seen talking to Mike—I found out later he was Larry, an off-duty policeman—was checking people as they filed through the door. It looked like they were doing some weird, high-five thing, but before I could figure it out, another man took his place. Larry walked toward us, a big, burly guy with keen blue eyes and a bushy, black mustache flecked with gray. He, too, wore a ball cap with the star burst.

Mike made the introductions. No smile or handshake from Larry. Just an appraising look and a curt, "Pleased to meet you."

He ushered us through the door. "I'll take it from here, Mike."

My father shrugged. "Oh, yeah. Orientation. See ya inside, kid."

He strolled away and left me with Big Scary Guy.

Orientation? Oh, geez, did I have to pass a test? What if I didn't pass? Would they toss me out? Would I be lost and alone, wandering the streets of Seattle, a little country bumpkin abandoned in the big city? My heart began to pound.

Before I could fake a bathroom emergency, Larry said, "Follow me."

Because I didn't know what else to do, I trotted behind him like a faithful dog. He led me into a small, windowless room and switched on the light. When he shut the door, it felt like all the air had been sucked out of the room. I must have looked as scared as I felt, because his mustache twitched and his eyes warmed up.

A small table and two chairs were placed in the center of the room. He waved me into a chair and sat across from me. "I don't know what your dad told you about the Star Seekers . . ."

I looked down at my hands, clenched tightly in my lap. "Not a lot." I glanced up at him. "Just that it's made up of people like me who are, well, different. Maybe they have certain psychic abilities like, uh, uh . . ."

If this was a test, no way was I acing it.

Larry leaned toward me. "Relax, Allie. I'm here to help you."

I managed a weak smile.

Larry lifted his right hand, fingers pointing up, palm facing me. I spotted the star in the middle of his palm. Was I supposed to show him mine? Damn, I needed a rule book.

Larry lowered his hand and stared intently into my eyes. "Star Seeker history dates back to the twelfth century. Back then, psychic abilities were thought to be signs of witchcraft. The Star Seekers met secretly and formed a common goal: To use their powers to fight the evil in the world. Understand so far?"

I nodded.

He continued, "All Star Seekers have a star located somewhere on their palms, an indicator of psychic powers. Their secret is still closely guarded. Nothing is written down.

Ever. Even today, we have legitimate cover. To the outside world, we're just everyday folks with an interest in astronomy, meeting here at the institute. Let me see your hand."

I thrust out my hand, palm up. He checked it and nodded. "The Star Seekers' oral history includes the story of a powerful gemstone and the maid who is meant to have it. Your star, because it's in the exact center of the lunar mound, is extremely rare. You know lunar refers to the moon, right?"

"Yes." I knew where he was going.

"Along with the moonstone, that mark means you possess powers far beyond the rest of us. It means you're the girl from the prophecy."

Should I tell him my power cord had been yanked from the outlet? That I was out of juice? I gripped the edge of my chair and looked at the ceiling, hoping for some sort of divine intervention.

Fortunately, Larry had a further agenda. "Trimarks. I understand you've met a couple of those bad boys."

I didn't like to think about Chris Revelle and Baxter. "Yeah."

"We'll cover the Trimarks later, during the program. Now, you need to know the sign and the greeting."

Much better. "You mean we have a secret handshake?"

Larry showed me his frowny face. "This is no joking matter, Allie. If it isn't done properly, you will not be admitted."

I sobered quickly and followed his instructions. At every checkpoint, I was to present my palm, facing out, fingers up so the sentry could see my star. He/she would do the same. We would then join palms, interlace our fingers and say, "*Stella potenza.*"

"Means 'Star power' in Italian," Larry told me.

"Why Italian?" I asked.

Larry shrugged. "Who knows? Maybe that's where it

all started. Maybe they were in a country that didn't speak Italian and it was a secrecy thing. Doesn't matter."

He made me practice for a while until I could flash my palm, slap it against his and spit out "*Stella potenza*" like a pro.

Larry stood and opened the door. "You're ready. Good luck."

On dragging feet, I exited the small room. I'd never felt more *unready* in my life.

Chapter Three

I scoped out the people milling around the foyer, hoping to spot Mike. He was nowhere to be seen, so I wandered around the exhibit hall and picked up a brochure that showed the position of the stars for tonight, November 1st. Then, I read about the Sugdens, the filthy-rich couple who'd endowed the building. At one time, Paul's family owned most of what would become downtown Bellevue. When they sold the property, they'd kept a full city block. Patricia missed her home in New Mexico. Paul, a devoted husband and lifelong astronomy buff, built the Southwestern-styled institute for two purposes: to encourage the study of the heavens and to make his wife happy.

A fleeting thought darted through my mind. Was Patricia a Star Seeker? Did she have supernatural powers? Really, how many husbands would run out and erect a multi-million dollar stucco, red-tiled building to keep their wives happy? Maybe Patricia had tons of supernatural charm oozing out her pores and poor Paul couldn't resist. The thought made me smile. If I ever got my powers back, I'd give that kind of man-control a try.

I felt a tap on the shoulder. I spun around to see a sweet old geezer dressed in a white shirt with a bolo tie, faded jeans and cowboy boots. We eyed each other's palms, clasped hands and exchanged a *stella potenza*.

He studied my face. "I'm Hank. You're the girl we've been hearing about. Right? Alice? Allison?"

"Allie," I said. "My real name is Alfrieda."

Hank's eyebrows drew together, and he frowned. "No

such name. You sure it's not Elfrieda . . . with an *E*?"

I forced a smile. "It's kind of a long story. When I was born, my grandfather paid the hospital bill so he got to name me. His mother was called Alfrieda Carlotta and so am I."

I hoped he wouldn't ask why Purdy, my father, hadn't paid the hospital bill. I had an answer, but this wasn't the time or place.

Hank checked his watch. "Time to go. Follow me."

He turned and strode toward the door leading to the domed section of the building. He moved pretty fast for an old guy. I had to run to catch up with him. A solemn-faced woman was posted outside the door. Once again, we did the hand thing and the greeting. No way was a Trimark going to sneak into this meeting!

I followed Hank into the dome-shaped room and gazed around in wonder. Above me, stars were scattered across a midnight blue sky. A circle of light leaked in from the horizon, bathing the room in a rosy glow. The circular wall was lined with a dark red padded bench. Hank stopped and pointed at a bank of controls in the center of the dome.

"See those levers? They're used to simulate the night sky hour by hour. What you're looking at right now is the coming of dawn. Every time we meet, it's the same . . . dawn breaking. It's a Star Seeker thing, you see. You know, hope for the future."

"Cool," I said, smiling at Hank.

I was tempted to plop down on the bench and watch the night fade away. Chill out until the Star Seekers meeting was over. But Hank wasn't going to let that happen.

"This way," he said, looking back to make sure I was following him. We passed through another set of doors into a large auditorium with a stage at one end.

"There's your daddy," Hank said, pointing toward the stage. "Front row, center."

Sure enough, Mike was right up front, looking over his

shoulder, scanning the crowd. When he spotted me, he waved and pointed at the seat next to him. I stifled a groan. So much for blending into the crowd.

"You go on down, Allie," Hank said. "I'll grab a seat back here. See you later."

I thanked him and trotted down the aisle, amazed by the size of the crowd. The place was literally packed with Star Seekers. I sat down next to my dad.

"All set?" he asked.

Struck dumb, I just stared at him. Did *all set* mean I'd passed my orientation session with Larry? The secret handshake and *stella potenza*? I had a horrible feeling it didn't. *Now would be the time to tell him about your little problem, Allie.*

I'd just opened my mouth to speak when the lights dimmed. Was it too late to make a run for it? It was. Larry strode onto the stage and tapped the microphone. His voice boomed from the speakers.

"Welcome, fellow Star Seekers. Before we welcome our special guest, we have some business to take care of."

I gave a little yip of alarm. Mike looked over at me and raised an eyebrow. Oh my God, was I embarrassing him? Already?

I murmured, "I'm fine, I'm fine," all the while thinking, *Idiot, just tell him your powers are gone!*

When Larry started the program, I tried to relax, drawing in huge, gusty breaths and blowing them out, earning another puzzled look from Mike.

First, the lights came up and we all clapped and cheered for our benefactor, Patricia Sugden. Paul was nowhere to be seen—probably back at the family manse getting his nails buffed or whatever it is rich people do—which meant Patricia *was* the Star Seeker, as I'd suspected. She stood and blessed us with a diamond-twinkling wave of the hand and a smile.

Next, we looked at pictures of Trimarks projected on a large movie screen positioned behind Larry. Close-ups of Trimark faces flashed on the screen, one after the other. Pleasant looking, ordinary people, much like my fellow Star Seekers.

Larry warned, "Trimarks are experts at worming their way into your circle of friends. Almost instantly, they figure out what you need and become that person. They can be charming, vulnerable, compassionate . . . whatever it takes to earn your trust."

A Nazi concentration camp flashed onto the screen followed by a close-up of Adolph Hitler.

"Trimark," Larry said.

New faces flashed on the screen, one after another. Larry recited their names and deeds. "Ted Bundy, serial killer . . . Trimark. Timothy McVeigh, Oklahoma City bomber . . . Trimark. Saddam Hussein, cruel dictator . . . Trimark."

After a dozen more, he said, "Here's the bottom line: Trimarks are attracted to evil like moths to the flame. Our job as Star Seekers is to stop them."

He leaned closer to the mike and lowered his voice. "I can't stress this enough. You must find a way to palm-check for the inverted triangle. If you need help with that, see me after the meeting. For you new people, we have no handouts. No brochures. We write nothing down."

Just as Larry said, "Remember, the inverted triangle may not be fully formed . . ." Chris Revelle's face flashed on the screen. The air whooshed out of my lungs like I'd taken a punch in the gut.

Immediate flashback: Revelle gluing Faye's hand to a table. Baxter standing over her with a razor-sharp hatchet. Me, tied up and helpless. I must have made a sound because Mike murmured, "You okay, Allie?"

Unable to speak, I nodded my lie.

What Larry said next snapped me out of my emotional

meltdown.

"Okay, people. Listen up. This is important. New information about the Trimarks has come to our attention. They've had a defector."

An excited murmur ran through the crowd. I was doing more than murmuring. I was doing imaginary cartwheels of joy! Maybe the special guest was the defector, not me.

Larry lifted a hand. "A Trimark with a conscience? I know it sounds impossible, but it's true. Security reasons prevent me from sharing the particulars, but, because of this man's actions, his only son was killed. Grief-stricken, he sought out one of our members and shared some vital information."

People began shouting questions.

Larry lifted a hand for silence. "We all know Trimarks love to do bad things to people. Right? That's what they live for. But, we didn't know they have supernatural abilities."

Someone shouted, "Like what?"

"Here's where it gets confusing," Larry said. "Our informant would only tell us it has to do with triangulation and that Trimarks are forbidden to use it unless something extremely important is at stake."

Like the moonstone, I thought. Then, why hadn't Revelle and Baxter used their magic to take it from me? Very curious.

"The Trimarks have in their possession, a dark crystal that infuses them with limited power. According to their oral history, it comes from the dark side of the moon," Larry continued.

Star Seeker hands were waving all over the auditorium. Larry pointed at a woman in the third row who stood and asked, "Is the informant here?"

"No. We offered him sanctuary, but he refused. He was a no-show for our second meeting. He's either scared or the

Trimarks took care of him."

His comment caused another ripple of alarm, times two for me, since I was now certain about the identity of the special guest.

Larry rapped his gavel. "Quiet, please. I have one more point to make."

He paused for a moment and looked around the room before his gaze settled on me. "If it's true that the dark crystal originates from the dark side of the moon, the moonstone reflects the opposite, the visible or bright side of the moon. In other words, the moonstone and dark crystal represent two halves of a whole, which is why the Trimarks want the moonstone so badly. If the two halves were joined, the full power of the moon and its magic would belong to the Trimarks."

An eerie silence followed. Slowly, I became aware that everyone in the audience was staring at me. Under the heavy weight of their scrutiny, I broke out in a clammy sweat. I clutched the moonstone pendant and turned to look at my father, whose face had turned chalk white. My deep breathing morphed into hyperventilation.

Larry's words faded in and out as I tried to get my troublesome emotions under control. The next thing I heard was, "Thanks to our special guest, we've learned Trimarks can be deterred by a crucifix. And now, here she is, the girl we've been waiting for, Allie Emerson."

Oh. My. God. Not now. Mike catapulted from his seat and all but yanked me out of mine. He clamped an arm around my shoulders and began to march me toward the stage.

"Mike!" I cried. "It's not my time."

But, I was unable to stop the irresistible force that was my father on a mission to deliver his oh-so-gifted daughter for show and tell.

No need to go into all the sordid details of the most

humiliating experience of my life. Okay, maybe just a few.

Picture this: Allie walking onto the stage to a standing ovation. Mike beaming with pride. Allie's knees knocking together as the audience settles into their seats. Two-hundred pairs of eyes following Allie's pitiful and fruitless attempt to use telekinetic power to make a No. 2 pencil roll across a perfectly flat surface. Murmurs of disappointment from the crowd. Mike looking embarrassed.

But, as bad as that was, worse happened during the after-meeting social, where Star Seekers mingled, guzzled purple punch and ate cookies shaped like stars and crescent moons. Everybody, and I mean *everybody,* felt compelled to offer words of advice, comfort and excuses for my failure.

"You just need to relax!"

"You're trying too hard!"

"Too much pressure!"

"Don't worry, we believe in you." (That one made me sad.)

And, of course, the old standby—"You're young. There's time."

All I really wanted to do was crawl in a hole and die, but I choked down a few cookies that turned to sawdust in my mouth, listened and nodded.

By the time Kizzy and Charlie picked me up, I was shaky and exhausted. Kizzy took one look at my face and gathered me into her arms, where I sobbed out my misery.

Later that night, I turned out the lights in the trailer and opened the blinds so I could lie on my couch bed and look at the sky. Faye was sound asleep in her room. I thought about the start of it all: My fall off the ladder onto the electric fence of the pasture outside the trailer's yard. How the telekinetic power kicked in when I needed it the most, because a bull was about to trample me. How I was able to use the moonstone to read minds. And now all those powers were gone.

Here's the funny part—last spring, when my powers were alive and well, all I wanted was to get rid of them. Now they were gone and I wanted them back. Could it be I was a serial worrier? Was I a malcontent, destined to undermine each and every bit of happiness coming my way?

I fixed my gaze on the North Star and said my prayers. I've repeated the same prayer every night since the afternoon when Jesus opened his eyes and looked at me. Yeah, I know it sounds crazy, but that really happened.

I was cowering behind the drapes at Junior's house— long story—and Chris Revelle was about to discover my hiding place. One of my hands held the moonstone. With the other, I lifted my hand, palm out, toward the crucifix hanging on the wall above Junior's TV. The cross began to glow and Jesus opened his eyes. Swear to God! Would I lie about something so weird? Revelle and his buddy got scared off and I escaped with my life.

I've never been sure who or what saved me. So, to cover all the bases, every night I clutched the moonstone, looked at the sky and said, "Hello, Jesus. It's me, Allie. I'm still here. Thanks."

I lowered the blinds and tried to clear my mind. That's when I remembered something Kizzy said when Charlie pulled next to the trailer to drop me off.

She lifted a hand and laid it on my cheek. "Don't be afraid, child. Your healer is coming."

At the time, I'd been so upset, I'd stared at her dumbly and repeated, "My healer?"

"Soon," she said.

Did I need a healer? Apparently, Kizzy thought I did. I was too heartsick and tired to think about it tonight. Maybe it would make sense tomorrow.

Chapter Four

It was back. My big, ugly, hairy nightmare had its brawny arms around my body and wouldn't let go. It was always the same. I was invisible, sitting in a small living room. A woman dressed in dark slacks and a pink sweater paced back and forth between the kitchen and living room. Her eyes were puffy from crying and, as she paced, she gnawed on a thumbnail. Two little girls knelt by the front window, peering out at the passing cars. Every few minutes, one of them would turn and look at their mother. Waif-like, both of them had abnormally huge, sad eyes like the picture our art teacher used as an example of how not to draw eyes.

"Mommy, when is Daddy coming home?" The girls would say, in tiny, pitiful voices, tears spilling out of their enormous eyes.

Mommy never got a chance to answer, because Chris Revelle would burst through the front door and say, "He's never coming home! Allie Emerson killed him."

The woman and two little girls would begin to sob and wail. I'd shout, "I didn't mean to kill him! I'm sorry. I'm sooo sorry!"

"Allie, wake up! You're yelling again."

I struggled to fight my way out of the nightmare. Faye's insistent voice finally penetrated my foggy mind. I woke up, face down on a soggy pillow, my heart bumping up against my ribs like it was trying to get out.

"Okay, okay," I groused. "I'm awake. Is it time to get up?"

I rolled over and tried to focus. The glowing red numbers

on the clock flashed 6:45. The bus came at 7:15. Startled, I shot up to a sitting position. I was groggy and it was dark so, really, it wasn't my fault. I hadn't realized Faye was hovering directly above me. Our foreheads collided with a sharp *crack.* I moaned and sank back onto the bed.

Faye screeched like she'd been stabbed through the neck with a butcher knife. "Ow! Ow! Damn, that hurt. Oh my God, I can't see. I'm blind!"

I sat up and switched on the light. "All better?"

She rubbed her head and glared down at me. "I'm going back to bed."

I pushed back the covers and swung my legs to the floor. "What about work?"

Faye had a part-time job, waiting tables at Bea's Honey Pot Diner. Good tips. Awful food. I knew because she brought leftovers home. The diner was shaped like a giant bee hive and attracted tourists who took pictures out front and ate there once.

"I'm working dinner, not breakfast. I'll be gone when you get home, so call me."

Before she closed the door separating the bedroom from the living room/kitchen, she said, "You really need to do something about your nightmares. Are you talking to the school counselor?"

"Yes, Mother."

Faye sighed and slid the door shut. I heard the rustle of sheets as she settled back in bed.

"Leftover biscuits and gravy in the fridge," she called.

The image of congealed, gravy-coated biscuits lurking in the refrigerator triggered an instant gag reflex. I swallowed hard. "Oh, yum."

It's possible Faye may have picked up a tinge of sarcasm in my tone. Even though she mumbled her reply, I clearly heard the words, "Smart ass."

I got ready for school quickly and smeared peanut butter

on a slice of leftover toast from the diner. As I munched, I thought about my dream. It was just plain wrong on so many levels. First of all, despite having a picture-perfect family in my nightmare, Baxter was a creepy Trimark who wanted to chop off my mother's fingers one-by-one before he killed us both in a slow, painful way. No woman in her right mind would marry him, much less risk bearing his children. Furthermore, when he died, nobody had come forward to claim his body.

My intention had been to merely disable him so Faye and I could get away. I didn't mean to kill him. Okay, I *did* use telekinetic power, and I *did* make a bunch of heavy apple bins fly through the air and land on top of him, but I was tied up at the time. Literally. The only weapon available was my mind.

So why did I feel so guilty? Why did I keep dreaming about Baxter's wife and big-eyed children? My only conclusion was . . . nightmares aren't logical, so using logic won't make them go away.

I brushed my teeth, grabbed my backpack and ran down Uncle Sid's driveway just in time to climb onto the school bus behind Manny and Mercedes.

Manny turned and gave me his shy grin. Mercedes said, "Hey, girlfriend!"

I followed them down the aisle toward our usual seat. Cory Philpott, a bully I thought I'd vanquished, but who'd grown bolder without Junior around to beat the crap out of him, sneered, "Hey, Algae. You got slimy, green stuff growing on your face."

Unfortunately for Cory, I was still out of sorts, big time. Also, unfortunately for Cory, he needed a hair cut.

I grabbed a handful of greasy hair and yanked. Instant facelift for Cory. I looked deep into his eyes and snarled. "Do . . . Not . . . Mess . . . With . . . Me . . . Today!"

Cory started flapping his arms and hollering, "Hey, let

me go! Dammit, that hurts!"

Kids at the back of the bus starting chanting, "Fight, fight, fight!"

I was so angry I didn't realize our driver, Patti, was standing behind me.

"Allie, let him go!"

Patti's raspy voice broke through the red mist of my rage. I released Cory and looked down at the top of Patti's head. Short, but fearsome, she had a black belt in karate, claimed she had a closed-circuit camera tucked inside her bleached-blond pony tail and smoked nasty, unfiltered Camels during her breaks. Nobody sassed Patti.

She thrust out an arm and pointed at the seat across the aisle from the driver's seat. "Go! Sit!"

The "Bad Kid" seat. Biting my lip and avoiding eye contact with my classmates, I slunk down the aisle, plopped myself down and stared out the window.

Patti pulled out onto the road and started in on me. "What the hell's the matter with you, girl? You're mad all the time. You used to handle Cory with your mouth, not your fists."

"I didn't hit him," I protested.

She shook a finger at me. "Be quiet and listen!"

I hung my head in shame while Patti lectured me. She was right. My emotions were on the ragged edge, as raw as an open sore. It was like an evil Allie twin lived deep inside me and popped out every so often to call the shots. I knew I was screwed up. I just didn't know what to do about it.

When we pulled up in front of the school, I grabbed my backpack and stood, preparing to bail out quickly. I leaned close to Patti and whispered, "Thanks for not turning me in."

She glanced back at Cory. "No blood, no broken bones, no problem."

As the doors hissed open, Patti said, "Hang in there,

Sweetie. Things will get better."

I nodded, then shot down the steps and headed for home room, where we spent the first twenty minutes of each school day, listening to announcements and catching up on homework required for graduation. As I trotted down the hall, a sense of calm settled over me. I've always loved school. The prescribed routine allowed me to feel *normal*. For at least seven hours a day, I knew what to expect, unlike the rest of my messed-up life.

My French teacher, Mrs. Burke, was also my English teacher and home-room teacher. As usual, she was delighted to see me.

"*Bon jour*, Allieeee!" she exclaimed in her fake French accent then stared at me expectantly until I responded, "*Bon jour*, Madame Burke."

The rest of the class straggled in, trailed by Sonja Ortega, who accidentally on purpose stepped on my foot. I'd already had one confrontation today, so decided to let it slide. Shortly after the bell rang, the intercom crackled to life and our principal, Mr. Hostetler said, "Good morning, students and faculty. I have an important announcement."

He paused and cleared his throat. I heard papers rustling. "A certain matter has been brought to my attention. It seems we have a male individual here at John J. Peacock High School who is, shall we say, invading the personal space of other individuals of the female persuasion, inflicting pain and suffering upon said person's lower regions."

He paused and rattled his papers again. I noticed Mrs. Burke's face was a study in confusion. We all looked at each other and went, "Say, what?"

Sonja, who was no dummy, said, "He's talking about the ass pincher."

"Ahhh," we chorused.

"Let it be known," Mr. Hostetler continued "this person *will* be apprehended and *will* be suspended. Such actions *will not* be tolerated in my school. Whoever you are, take heed. This is your warning!"

I saw a couple of boys squirm in their seats, leading me to believe my theory about an individual serial ass-pincher was wrong. Apparently, we had an ass-pinching *gang*.

After Mr. Hostetler signed off, the breathless voice of Miss Yeager, the school counselor, came over the speaker.

"Hey, all you awesome dudes and chicks!" she began.

Everybody rolled their eyes and groaned.

"Do you sing, dance, do magic tricks, perhaps play the flute? Run, do not walk to my office and sign up for the first ever John J. Peacock High School talent show. Think you're not good enough? Well, think again. Who knows? This could be your springboard to success . . . the launching of your star!"

As she rattled on and on, Mrs. Burke's pleasant smile began to fade. I tuned out and checked my geometry homework. Half way through the pitch, Sonja hollered, "Hey, I can sing and dance. I wanna sign up."

Mrs. Burke nodded, and Sonja tromped out of the room on her three-inch wedgie slides. It was then I remembered Halloween night and Kizzy's comment to Sonja, something about her singing in front of an adoring crowd. Oops.

*

The rest of the day passed without incident. In my last class of the afternoon, French, Beck Bradford was back to his arrogant self, ignoring me, as usual. Not so much as a glance. He even waited until I was at the board, conjugating verbs, before placing last week's work on my desk. So, what was the deal the other night? Why had he stared at me like I was the eighth wonder of the world? Not that I cared. Okay, maybe I cared a little.

Beck Bradford was still on my mind when I got off the

bus and trudged down the driveway toward the trailer. Let me say, up front, I've never been a big believer in coincidence. At least, not until I read the note stuck to our trailer door.

"Allie. We got our backpacks mixed up. I've got yours so apparently you have mine. Bring it to my house at exactly 7:30 tonight. Don't knock on the front door. Go around to the back."

It was signed, "B. Bradford."

My first reaction was . . . *No way*! I unzipped the backpack. It looked exactly like mine except for the physics and calculus textbooks lurking inside. He was right, but how could we have switched bags? We hadn't been within six feet of each other.

I studied the note again, more than a little ticked off at his demanding tone and strange message. Why exactly 7:30 p.m. and no front door knocking? Did I have to use the servant's entrance? Even stranger, why was I being summoned to the Bradford place at all? Beck had a car. He obviously drove to our place and stuck his stupid note on the door. Why didn't he wait until I got home to drop off my backpack and pick up his?

If Beck was a Trimark, I'd be putting myself in grave danger by going to his house. Besides, the Bradford place was the scene of my almost-fatal encounter with Revelle and Baxter. Of course, nobody was living there at the time, at least nobody *living* was living there. I'd never seen the ghost of old Mr. Bradford, who hung himself in the warehouse, but plenty of other people had. So what if old Mr. Bradford's daughter, Melissa had moved back and was fixing the place up? The thought of returning there, especially after dark, made goose bumps pop out all over my body.

Decision made. Even though I couldn't do my homework, no way was I going to Beck Bradford's house.

I went inside and called Faye, letting her know I was home. At loose ends without my backpack full of homework, I flopped down on the couch. It was then I heard the tinkle of wind chimes, a sound I hadn't heard for six months. Not like this: Loud. Louder than the windchimes could possibly ever sound.

So this could only mean one thing . . . Trilby, my ditsy spirit guide, was back.

Chapter Five

"It's about time you got out here, girl! Seems like I've been ringing these damn chimes for hours," Trilby scolded.

I'd stepped outside and found her perched on a thick branch about half way up the gnarled, old apple tree next to Blaster the bull's pasture. My mouth dropped open when I saw what she was wearing. A tailored gray skirt and white blouse topped with a dark blue blazer, pantyhose and sensible, low-heeled pumps. Her wildly curly dark hair was slicked back into a neat bun.

My hippy-dippy Trilby? Dressed like a real estate agent?

Teetering precariously, she muttered curses and yanked on her blazer, which was snagged on the branch directly above her.

"Careful!" I called. "You'll fall."

She scowled down at me. "In case you haven't noticed, Sherlock, I'm already dead. It's this damn jacket! Trust me, if I tear it, there'll be hell to pay in heaven."

"Want me to get a ladder and help?"

She ignored me and gathered herself for one last assault. First, I heard "Stupid tree!" and then the sound of a breaking branch. The jacket popped free and Trilby plummeted to the ground. I felt a familiar icy chill as she passed through my body.

"Boo!" she said from directly behind me.

I turned and grinned at her. "Still working on that 'scary' thing, huh?"

I was no longer freaked out by the fact I was the only one who could see or hear Trilby. A hippy during what she called "the days of peace and love," she'd smoked a lot of weed before passing on. Consequently, she usually forgot her instructions, forcing me to read between the lines. Irritating? Yes. Scary? No.

She'd first appeared last spring, the day my telekinetic power kicked in. I was her special project, she'd told me, her ticket to a better place. The last time I saw her, I'd passed the tests and she'd made it to heaven, but only to the first floor . . . the "pink gown level," she'd told me..

I looked her over. "I see you got rid of the pink thing. What floor are you on now?"

The corners of her mouth turned down. She smoothed a hand over her skirt. "Second. They make us dress like this."

"How many more to the top?"

She shrugged. "Hell if I know. You'd think they'd have hand-outs or public service announcements, but . . . noooo." (Huge eye roll) "That would be too easy."

"What about that guy with the long, golden hair from the first floor? The one you had the crush on?"

Her eyes turned dreamy and she smiled. "He was hot. Micah, with the big, old . . . uh . . . "

"Furled wings?" I supplied, helpfully.

"Yeah." Suddenly, her mood changed and she snapped, "No Micah now. No men at all. Second floor is all women. Dress code? 'Business casual.' It sucks, big time!"

Whoa, my idea of heaven had just been altered forever. But, then again, maybe it takes time to let go of one's physical body and its needs. I decided to keep an open mind.

"Why are you here? Do you have a message for me?"

Trilby sat down on a nearby stump, hoisted her left leg and examined it carefully. "Damn tree! Ruined my pantyhose."

She lowered her leg and glanced out at Blaster's pasture. "Hey, where's the farting bull?" Your uncle make hamburger outta him?"

Last week, Uncle Sid loaded Blaster into his special trailer and delivered him to a dairy farm in the lower valley. "Off impregnating cows. Trilby. Focus."

She gazed up at me, puzzled, clearly trying to remember her mission.

Finally, she snapped her fingers. "Okay, I've got it. It's all connected . . . my moving to the next level and you screwing up."

"Hey, I couldn't help it! My telekinetic power's gone."

Trilby shook her head. "Not that. Here's the deal. To get to the next floor, I have to memorize a bunch of stuff. That's kinda hard for me, so they gave me another option. It has something to do with a hot guy who's supposed to heal you, but you're being a big weenie and won't go. If I send you on the right path, I get to move up. So, don't mess it up! Okay?"

"Are you talking about Beck Bradford?" I asked.

She punched a fist in the air. "Right on, sister! That's the guy. Scoot your ass over there and get healed."

"But, he might be a Trimark," I protested.

"News flash from the top." She jerked a thumb skyward. "He's not. See ya, kid."

She shot up and away before I could ask her about my troublesome Jesus/moonstone problem. Not that she'd have an answer, but it was worth a try. Maybe next time.

*

"You sure you want to go there?" Manny glanced over at me. His hands were positioned at ten to two on the steering wheel of his 1985 Chevy Impala. The car had once belonged to his dad, Pedro. After the birth of his sixth child, Pedro parked it behind Uncle Sid's barn and purchased a mini van. Manny was totally in love with the old clunker. He was in the process of restoring it and talked endlessly about the car's throttle body fuel injection and 5.0 liter V-8 engine. Like I knew what that was! The car was covered in primer and full of dings, but hey, it beat walking along Peacock Flats Road after dark.

Manny was seventeen, and because his driving record was spotless, he was now allowed to transport people other than family members in his car.

"Do I want to?" I repeated. "No, but I need to get my backpack. I'm having some problems in French. Beck said he'd help me with my homework. If I need a ride home, I'll call you."

I said this to squelch Manny's natural desire to serve and protect. He was determined to wait and drive me home. But, I figured this "healing" thing could take a while so I had to come up with a good excuse.

His chubby face was filled with concern. "You're not scared? After what happened? You almost got killed there. I heard the place is haunted. You know, when people kill themselves, they can't go to heaven. That's why Mr. Bradford's ghost is hanging around."

Manny and Mercedes were real superstitious. That's why I didn't dare tell them about my paranormal abilities or, my lack thereof.

"I'm not scared," I lied. Actually, I was trying to ignore the butterflies fluttering around in my belly.

"All that stuff happened when the place was deserted," I said. "I heard Ms. Bradford fixed the house up real nice. She even hired a foreman to take care of the orchard. I sure didn't see any ghosts when I was there."

Okay, maybe I saw a few Trimarks.

Before we reached the Bradford property, Manny pulled onto the shoulder, put the car in neutral and revved the motor.

"You know what that is?" He turned and looked at me. In the dim light of the dash, I could see his blissful smile. Without waiting for an answer—good thing, because I didn't have one—he said, *"That* is the sound of 165 horsepower!"

I murmured something like, "Um . . . that's nice. Can we go now?"

Manny eased the Impala into gear, carefully checked the rearview mirror for oncoming traffic and pulled slowly onto the road.

When we hit Bradford property, I noticed several new *Private Property, Keep Out* signs posted next to the road. "The driveway's up ahead."

Manny gave me a disgusted look. "I know where I'm going, Allie."

"Okay, okay, just trying to be helpful," I muttered and came up with the following conclusion: *Guy plus Car plus Helpful Suggestions from Female Passenger equals Snarly Response from Guy.* Live and learn.

He turned right and we proceeded, at a snail's pace, up the long, gravel driveway. The house was set well back from the road. At the rate we were traveling, it would be morning before we arrived.

"You sure you don't want me to wait? I don't mind," Manny said.

"I'll be fine."

As we drove through the night-shrouded orchard, my heart began to pound. Maybe I wouldn't be fine. What if Trilby was wrong? What if I was about to deliver myself into the hands of a Trimark? Because I still had my suspicions about Beck, I'd left the moonstone at home for safekeeping.

A sudden gust of wind danced through skeletal branches, setting the few remaining leaves aflutter. Clouds, heavy with rain, obscured the moons and stars. The twin beams of the Impala's headlights revealed nothing but row after row of trees. I peered through the murky darkness, trying to spot the house on a hill to our left. If we continued to follow the driveway, we'd end up at the warehouse where Faye and I were held captive. I really, really didn't want to end up at the warehouse. The pitch-black night had me spooked and disoriented. A few more turns and I caught a glimmer of light filtering through the trees.

"There! The turn-off's just ahead."

Manny gave me another look, but refrained from comment as he turned onto the spur that led to the old, two-story house. Another hundred feet of bumpy driveway and we'd arrived. Manny turned off the ignition. We studied the house in silence. Surrounded on both sides by overgrown shrubs and trees, the house loomed like a tall, dark specter.

"Victorian," I murmured.

"Huh?"

"Kizzy told me this is an old Victorian farmhouse. She said you can tell by the curlicue designs around the overhang and roof. 'Gingerbread,' she called it. And look . . . "

I pointed at the second story. "See that round thingy hanging out over the porch? It's called a turret."

"Don't see nothin' but a creepy, old house," Manny said, squinting through the darkness.

The porch light was off and the curtains drawn, but strips of dim, yellow light leaked from three bay windows set to the left of a double door. Wind stirred the scraggly branches of a tall tree next to the house. Icy pellets of sleet bounced off the windshield. An eerie pattern of shadow and light danced across the front of the house.

I reached for the car door, my heart in my throat. If Manny knew how scared I was, I'd never get rid of him. *Just do it, Allie!*

I grabbed Beck's backpack, jumped out of the car and gave Manny a big, brave smile. "Thanks. See you tomorrow."

He frowned and made no move to start the car. "I'll wait until you're inside the house."

I flapped my hands like I was shooing chickens. "Don't

be silly. Go! Go!"

"Your mom know where you are?"

"I called her."

Not a total lie. I'd told Faye I was studying with a friend.

Manny folded his arms and stared straight ahead. *Okay, now what, Allie?*

I trotted across the lawn and up the creaky steps to the front porch. I pretended to knock then called out to Manny, "Somebody's coming. You can leave now."

I heard the motor start but the car didn't move. The front door was unlocked. I opened it a crack, hoping I wasn't breaking some cardinal Bradford rule about front door usage. I slid the backpack inside, turned and gave Manny a merry wave.

Yes! The car backed slowly down the driveway. When his lights disappeared, I closed the front door, walked to the corner of the house, took a deep breath and stepped into a pool of darkness.

Chapter Six

After a few steps, I stopped, allowing time for my eyes to adjust. As I stood in the utter blackness, my other senses kicked in. Night sounds . . . the hooting of an owl . . . the sound of wind sighing through the trees and something else . . . voices floating on the wind. A burst of high-pitched laughter. A deeper voice responding.

Slowly, I began to see shapes as my night vision improved. The peaked roof of the house. The outline of a detached garage. A wheelbarrow and push lawn mower a few yards to my right. I crept along the side of the house, staying close to the shrubs. When I tripped on something and landed face-down in the dirt, my fear turned to anger. This was bull! I assessed my body for damage and yelled, "Hey! Turn on the lights!"

I stood perfectly still, waiting for someone to respond. No answer. No lights. Muttering, I made my way to the corner of the house and stopped. A screened porch stretched across the back of the house, illuminated by a single bulb hanging from the ceiling. The dim wash of light extended only a few feet from the house, into a large grassy area. Beyond the splash of light, in the deep shadows, I saw something that made me gasp and dart behind a bush. I tried to comprehend what I was seeing, but my brain said, *Does not compute.*

Two pairs of golden orbs floated above the ground, glowing in the darkness, moving toward me. Closer. Closer. Then, suddenly, they disappeared. I shook my head in denial. No way! I had to be hallucinating. Crouched behind my bush, I breathed deeply, trying to slow my racing heart. When I looked again, I sensed movement and sound just beyond the pale slash of light. Curiosity overcame fear. What was I seeing?

I stood. Took a couple of steps and peered into the shadows. I saw the outline of two individuals, one bigger than the other. They kicked and spun, throwing punches, ducking and dodging in a blur of motion, faster than any mortal could move. The smaller person stepped away from a roundhouse kick before leaping effortlessly over the taller one's head. Not possible. Not *humanly* possible.

The tall person whirled around and the two faced each other again, both inching toward the light. Could it be . . . ?

Before my shocked gaze, Beck and Nicole Bradford appeared in the light, eyes fixed on each other, engaged in a silent, deadly skirmish, with moves so incredibly swift and powerful they defied description.

Nicole, dressed in knee-length exercise pants and a midriff-baring tee shirt, took a step back as Beck advanced. In spite of the weather, he was naked from the waist up. His shoulders were broad and gleaming with sweat, his chest and arms ripped with well-defined muscles. A pair of faded jeans rode low on his hips and clung to muscular thighs. Whoa! Where did this guy come from? The Beck I knew was lean and sinewy.

Mesmerized, I watched the ritualistic pattern of advance and retreat, feeling the tension build between them, each waiting for the other to make a move. Nicole made a little growling sound, her lip curled into a sneer. Beck's face lit up in a savage grin. Caught up in their game, I was unprepared for what happened next. They turned and began walking toward me, their golden eyes glowing with anticipation.

I didn't stop to think about it. Instead, I listened to the voice inside my head, screaming, *Something's very wrong with this picture. Run, Allie, run!*

I'm pretty fast on my feet. Especially when chased by a set of twins with glowing, golden eyes who looked like they wanted to toss me back and forth to tenderize my flesh before throwing me on the barbeque. Never mind, I could hardly see my hand in front of my face, much less the various garden implements scattered in my path, I took off like the Road Runner pursued by Wile E. Coyote. Eyes fixed on the front of the house, I'd sprinted maybe six steps when . . . *Whomp!* I hit a brick wall. At least that's what I thought. Turned out, it was Beck Bradford's chest.

Steely arms held me tight against his body. Frantic to get away, I kicked and screamed and tried to sink my teeth into Beck's chest. Through it all, I heard the murmur of his voice, deep and soothing. In my panicked state, the words became meaningless, nothing more than garbled sound. In our struggle, I must have nipped him in a sensitive place, because I heard a grunt of pain followed by, "Allie, stop! Listen to me!"

He released me and cupped my face. His hands were warm, his touch soothing. "You're safe here. We won't hurt you."

A little hard to believe when you're standing in the dark and all you can see is a pair of glowing eyes. Make that *two* pair. Nicole stood behind Beck. As I calmed down, I became aware of my breathing. Each inhalation was accompanied by a rhythmic squeak. I sounded like a terrified mouse cornered by a cat. Very embarrassing. But, hold on! Why should I be embarrassed? I was the victim, here. Beck was the aggressor.

I put my hands on my hips and glared up at him. "You know what! You're a jerk! First, you tell me to come over and get my backpack and, oh, be sure not to use the front door. Then, I practically kill myself stumbling around in the dark and see you and Nicole doing…whatever you were doing. I have one question. Why? Okay, make that two questions. How? How did you get from point A, the backyard, to point B, here, so fast? Fly?"

I stopped my squeaky tirade and gulped air.

Beck took my hand. "I don't blame you for being mad, but I needed you to see what we are. Nicole and me. We're . . . well, we're different. You're different too, aren't you, Allie?"

Struck dumb, my mouth opened and closed, unable to formulate an answer. How did he know about me? Should I trust him? Trilby seemed to think so. More importantly, she thought I needed him to restore my missing powers.

"Let's go inside. We'll explain everything," Beck said.

Followed by Nicole, he led me to the back of the house and through the enclosed porch into the big farm kitchen. A wooden table and four chairs were placed in the center of the room. Beck pulled out a chair and guided me into it. He turned one of the chairs around, straddled it and studied my face like I was a science experiment gone wrong.

Nicole gave me a disinterested glance and turned to her brother. "Is that it? I've got stuff to do."

"Stick around a while, okay?" Beck said.

Nikki heaved a sigh but flopped down in the chair across from me. She ran a practiced eye over my outfit (jeans and sweatshirt) and my hair (wild, frizzy, escaping from a pony tail) before saying, "It was Beck's idea. I told him you'd be scared. Hope you didn't pee your pants."

I leaned across the table and narrowed my eyes at her. After what I'd been through, I didn't need attitude from cute, little, I-can-kick-my-brother's-ass-without-breaking-a-sweat, Nicole Bradford. "I wasn't *that* scared."

"Yeah, right."

"What's your problem, Nicole? What have I ever done to you?"

She glared right back at me. "Nothing. I just don't want

you here."

I shot up so fast the chair crashed over. "Fine. I'll get my backpack and leave."

Beck took hold of Nicole's arm and gave it a little shake. "Come on, Nikki, Allie needs help. You know I have to do this."

Nicole looked down at the table. I saw her lower lip quiver. "But then she'll know about us." She pulled away from Beck. "This is the first time I've had friends. Cool friends." She glanced at me then back at Beck. "What if she tells them about me? About us?"

"She won't," Beck said.

Even though I was still ticked off, I was intrigued by Nicole's comments. I picked up the chair and sat down. I tried to focus on Beck's face but it was hard. Think about it. Me, Alfrieda Carlotta Emerson, sitting next to a hunky, bare-chested, totally buff Mr. Beefcake centerfold. A feast for the eyes. To hold on to my anger, I thought about Beck's little plan, how I'd played right into his hands. "Was all that really necessary? The mysterious note . . . 'Come at exactly 7:30 . . . don't use the front door?'"

Beck sat. "Yes, call it a demonstration. Now that you've seen what we can do, you're ready to hear the rest."

He looked at Nicole and waited.

She examined her nails then said, "We're Cambions."

Okay, now I was *really* screwed. But no way was I going to let Nikki get the best of me.

I nodded. "Oh yes, from Cambia. What's so different about that?"

Nicole smirked and Beck fought to keep a straight face. "So, if you know so much, tell me where is Cambia located?" Nicole asked me. She looked at her brother and grinned.

"Um . . .I think it's in Eastern Europe. Oh, I know! It's one of those little countries with weird names like

Uzbekistan or Herzegovina. Right?"

"Wrong." Nicole looked at Beck. "Tell her."

Beck leaned toward me, his face deadly serious. "Don't say anything. Just listen."

I nodded, silenced by the sudden pain in his eyes. He took a deep breath and began, "Nicole and I are half-mortal, half-demon."

I bit my lip to keep from crying out. I wasn't sure what he was talking about, but it didn't sound good.

Except for the beating of my heart, the house was quiet. I wondered if Beck and Nicole's mother was home and if she was human. I'd seen her at the diner and she *looked* human. Of course, Beck and Nicole looked human too. If their mother wasn't human, did that mean the whole Bradford family was a pack of demons? A covey of demons? That might explain Beck and Nicole's grandfather's suicide and subsequent so-called ghostly appearances.

It was like Beck knew what I was thinking. "Our mother is human, our father isn't."

Because I was embarrassed, flustered and in way over my head, I almost said something lame, like "Bummer." I resisted the urge. Instead I glanced toward the front of the house. "Is your mother here?"

Beck said, "She's with her critique group. She writes Christian fiction. You'll be gone by the time she gets home."

I felt hysterical laughter bubbling up in my chest, and tried, unsuccessfully to disguise it as a coughing fit. When I was able to speak again, I said, "So, your father was a demon and your mother writes about angels? Anything else?"

"For obvious reasons, Mom doesn't want it to get around she has half-demon children," Nicole said. "That's why we had to talk to you tonight, while she's not here."

Beck's gaze was so intense I had to look away. Nicole looked like she was spoiling for a fight. I assumed they were waiting for me to ask questions. Believe me, I wanted answers, but had no idea how to ask them without treading on half-human, half-demon toes. I especially didn't want to put their mother down for hooking up with a demon.

Thankfully, Beck noticed my dilemma. "What do you know about demons?"

"Zip," I said. "I'm a newbie in the hocus-pocus world."

"Demons are fallen angels who got kicked out of heaven for rebelling against God."

Suddenly, I wanted to know the whole story. The questions burst out of me like water out of a fire hose. "Where did your mother meet your dad? Did she think he was human? Have you met him? Do you call demons 'it'?"

I knew I was babbling, but, really, I don't think the smartest person in the world would know what to say in this weird situation.

Nicole gave me another of her superior looks. "You make it sound like they went to prom together. No, we haven't met dear old Dad. Demons don't stick around. They just like the baby-making part."

Beck's face darkened. The black pupils in his amber eyes increased in size. "Our mother was in a convent in Northern California. She had a year to go before her final vows. But that all changed when she got pregnant with us."

"Our mom is super religious," Nicole said. "She'd never been with a guy when she entered the convent."

"This demon, what was he doing hanging around a convent?"

"Good question." Beck said. He went to the refrigerator, snagged three bottles of water and returned to the table. He handed one to Nicole and me then twisted the cap off his and drank it down without taking a breath. He glanced at Nicole.

"You want to tell her?"

Nicole shook her head.

Beck turned his chair around and pulled it up next to me. I could feel heat radiating off his body. "I swear what I'm about to say is true. The demon visited our mother at night. All she remembers is having a series of really hot dreams."

He looked at me, but not with the knowing smirk I was anticipating. He just looked at me. "You know about those kinds of dreams . . . right?"

Flames licked at my cheeks, and I studied the tops of my shoes.

Nicole snickered.

"Yeah," Beck continued. "But in her case, they weren't dreams. Three months later, she figured out she was pregnant. She left the convent, moved to Europe and had us."

I thought about Faye and me and our constant struggle to stretch our money to the next pay day. "But how did she live? Did she have a job? Why did she move to Europe?"

"She had family money," Nicole said. "Then she started writing and selling books. Have you heard of the *Hell Bent or Heaven Bound* series?"

"Sure, everybody has. But some *guy* writes that series."

Beck shook his head. "She writes it under a man's name. Nobody knows but her publisher. She writes other stuff under her real name."

The *Hell Bent or Heaven Bound* books were a huge hit, so apparently money was no problem for Beck's family.

Nicole added, "We were born in Europe because she wanted to get away from everybody who knew her past. Five years later, she brought us back. She told her family she married a guy in France, that it didn't work out and she took her maiden name back."

"So nobody knows the truth about your real dad?"

"Now *you* know. That makes four of us," Beck said.

At his words, I felt the hum and whirr of gears meshing

somewhere deep inside my brain. At some level, I knew exactly why I was there. We were "different." Beck and Nicole and me. All the old feelings rushed back. Was I a freak? Who could I trust? Maybe Beck and Nicole felt the same way. Food for thought.

Nicole rose. "I'm outta here. You'd better get on with it before Mom gets home."

She grabbed a package of cookies off the counter and sauntered out of the room.

"What's she talking about? Get on with what?"

He pulled his chair closer to mine, invading my space. Spooked, I fought the urge to shrink away from him. *What's your problem? Just a minute ago, you felt sorry for the guy!*

Beck said, "Give me your hand."

My hands were tightly clenched in my lap. Did I want to hold hands with a demon? Had I made a terrible mistake coming here? Wary and filled with doubts, I slipped into a familiar mode . . . hostility. "Why should I?"

"Don't be afraid." Beck's voice was smooth, silky and seductive. He was so close, I felt the warmth of his exhalations against my skin. I'd thought I'd never stop missing Junior Martinez, but now . . . . Unwilling to meet his eyes, I studied the dark stubble on his chin. He trailed his fingers along the contour of my cheek. I shivered as delightful sensations spiraled outward from where he touched me, pouring through my body like liquid fire. His fingers settled around my chin, tilting it back until I met his gaze. The black pupils had grown larger still, with only a slight rim of amber showing. Unable to look away from the pools of darkness in his eyes, I felt my tension drain away. As if it had a will of its own, my right hand rose from my lap. He wrapped his hand around mine, the dry heat of his touch creating another firestorm of pure energy zinging through my blood.

When I was able to speak, I whispered, "Why am I here?"

His face was just inches from mine when he replied. "You know why. Your powers are gone. "

Chapter Seven

A sudden gust of wind rattled the windows, the sound jerking me out my trance and back to real time.

Whoa! What just happened here? Was I really so screwed up I needed healing by a half-demon who probably wanted to steal my soul or, at the very least, my first-born child or whatever it was demons were always stealing in movies and books?

I snatched my hand away. "How do you know my powers are gone? Who told you?"

Beck planted his feet on the floor and rocked back until his chair was balanced on two legs. For a demon, he seemed pretty relaxed. "Your friend, the witch."

"What? Are you talking about Kizzy?"

He nodded.

"Kizzy's not a witch," I said, glaring at him. "She's a Romany gypsy and . . . "

Beck shrugged. "Call her what you want. She seemed pretty witchy to me."

"Why? What did she tell you?"

"That you were hurting and I could help you."

I felt like a little kid who'd been sent out of the room so her parents could discuss her "problem." I didn't know who to be mad at, Kizzy or Beck.

Beck studied my face, now hot with anger. "Why are you freaking out? Was it the 'witch' comment?"

"No. But she should have told me what was going on."

"She didn't think you would accept it. It had to be this way."

I folded my arms and stared at him. "Why you?"

"She sensed I was a psychic healer. When she took hold of my hands, she knew for sure."

When I heard *psychic healer*, I barely resisted the urge to roll my eyes and say, "Yeah, right." But then, I remembered why I was here. Kizzy, who loved me unconditionally. Kizzy, who always had my best interests at heart. Out of respect for her, I should at least listen to what Beck had to say. Not that I totally trusted him. In my world, it paid to be cautious.

"Halloween night in the gym," I said. "You stared at me. I thought you were a . . ." My voice trailed off. Before this went any farther, I had to make sure he wasn't a Trimark.

The front legs of his chair crashed down. Beck's gaze pinned me to my chair. "A what?"

"I need to see your hand."

He looked surprised but extended his right hand, palm down. I turned it over and tilted it toward the light. No inverted triangle, but something didn't look right.

"Now, the other one," I said.

I frowned in concentration, trying to remember everything Kizzy had taught me about palmistry.

"Something wrong?"

I released his hand. "Your fate line isn't solid at the end. It splits into three lines."

Beck said, "Like a pitchfork."

I squirmed a little. "Well, it's probably nothing. It's just that I've never seen one like it."

"Nicole has it too."

He showed me his palm again, this time cupping his hand slightly. Sure enough, it looked exactly like a pitchfork. "Demon mark," he said.

I stared at him in disbelief. "No way!"

"Way," he said, solemnly. "Our mother researched it. According to her, Cambions can choose their own fate.

Hence, the three lines signifying three different paths."

"Like good, evil and . . ." I stopped, not able to come up with a third option.

"Doing nothing at all," he supplied. He crossed his arms over his chest and leaned back again. "Of course, in our case, our mother drags us to church a lot. She says it's to make sure we're on the right path."

I wanted to ask if that plan was working. Since I had no clue about half-demon etiquette, I thought it might be rude and maybe I wouldn't like the answer.

He scrubbed a hand across his bristly chin. "So, what were you looking for on my palm?"

I breathed a little easier knowing Beck wasn't a Trimark. Okay, so he had a demon mark but it was open to interpretation. I could live with that.

I sighed. "It's a long story."

He made a *lay it on me* motion with his hands. I gave him a quick history of the Star Seekers and Trimarks. Nothing I said seemed to shock him.

When I paused for breath, he nodded and smiled, "Any more questions?"

I nibbled a hangnail. "Yeah, you look bigger tonight than you did at school today."

One corner of his mouth drew up in a brief smile. "I'm a creature of the night."

I blinked at him.

"Our powers don't kick in until after dark. During the day, we're just like everybody else."

I was skeptical. "Nicole doesn't look bigger at night."

"Our powers aren't the same. She's stronger at night, of course, but she also has some abilities during daylight hours. My mother thinks Nikki has more human qualities than me."

"Meaning you have more demon qualities?"

"Yeah. Which bugs the hell out my mother. She thinks

Nikki is perfectly fine, but she worries about her bad old demon boy."

I thought about Nicole and her snotty, self-centered attitude. Maybe Melissa Bradford was worried about the wrong twin. "What's the deal with your eyes?"

"When we're outside at night and other people are around, we wear special glasses that keep our eyes from glowing. If anybody asks, we tell them we have problems with night vision. That's bogus, of course. Our senses are more animal than human."

His nostrils flared as he leaned toward me and inhaled deeply. "You smell like pine needles and rose petals with a dash of Juicy Fruit gum."

"Huh? What?"

"In fact," he continued. "I knew you were here the minute you stepped out of the car."

"You could smell me?" My voice squeaked in surprise.

He nodded and grinned. "Yeah, and you smell damn good."

Thank God he didn't say "Good enough to eat." Just thinking it gave me the willies. A good reminder, though, that I was dealing with someone not fully human. To me that meant visions of hungry werewolves or vampires. Time to change the subject.

"What exactly did Kizzy tell you?"

"That you had special powers. You'd had a setback, but were okay physically."

He paused. I knew what was coming next.

"She said you hadn't recovered emotionally, and it was robbing you of your powers. According to Kizzy, I'm the one who can restore them."

I could have worked myself up into a righteous snit. I could have stayed deep in denial, grabbed my backpack and demanded a ride home. But, then again, my trusted friend Kizzy *had* set this in motion. Trilby, as well, had popped in to say, "Scoot your ass over there and get healed."

I'm not a genius, but I had learned a thing or two in the last six months. Life—especially *my* life—doesn't always make sense. Sometimes you have to suspend belief and go with the flow. I said, "What exactly does healing involve?"

He glanced at the kitchen clock and stood. "We've got forty-five minutes. Follow me."

Without checking to see if I was behind him, he went through the back door and into the covered porch where he flipped on a floodlight, illuminating the back yard.

I couldn't resist saying, "I could have used a little light when I was stumbling around out here."

He looked over his shoulder and grinned. "Not part of the plan."

I followed him down the steps and into the yard, hurrying to keep up with his long strides. Freezing rain, whipped by a gusty wind, peppered my face, chilling me to the bone. Geez, did I have to catch pneumonia to get healed?

"Hey!" I yelled as I scampered after him. "Can't we do this in the house?"

He muttered something I didn't catch and disappeared behind a black Ford Ranger parked next to the garage. I heard the jingle of keys. A light flicked on in the detached garage. I scooted around the corner to see Beck standing in the open doorway, his muscular body outlined in a halo of light. He stepped back and waved me in.

"I'll get some heat going." His voice was husky as he closed the door behind me. He crossed the room to a gas fireplace and flicked it on.

I stood, my back pressed against the wall, scarcely believing my eyes. What I assumed to be the garage was a cozy apartment, complete with a small kitchen, table and chairs, overstuffed couch and gas fireplace. A narrow, neatly-made bed hugged the far wall.

"You live out here?"

"Yeah, pretty much." Beck pulled on a black tee, then crossed to the table and picked up a chain with a silver cross. He slipped the chain over his head and tucked the cross inside his shirt. *A demon wearing a cross couldn't be all that bad . . . could he?*

I felt like the chick with the blindfold who holds the scales of justice. But, in my case, I wasn't weighing right and wrong. My dilemma was this: Trust a demon and maybe get healed or . . . run like hell! I decided to trust a demon.

Chapter Eight

Beck busied himself clearing books and papers off the table and stacking them on the floor next to the couch. "I like to do experiments and stuff. My mom doesn't like me messing up her kitchen."

His small kitchen counter was cluttered with bowls of colorful stones and dried plants. Open shelves above the sink held fruit jars filled with liquids and candles in a variety of colors. Pots and pans hung from an overhead rack. A dish drainer filled with inverted glass beakers sat on the counter. Next to it was a Bunsen burner like we used in science glass. The air was fragrant with a mixture of odors. Pine. Sage. Lavender. I inhaled deeply and felt the soothing aroma coil through my body, easing my tension.

I pushed away from the wall and picked up a bundle of dried weeds tied with string. "What do you do with this?"

He took it from me and set it in an earthen bowl. "It's called a smudge stick. White sage and pine."

He struck a match and set the bundled weeds on fire. The flame died back quickly, leaving only a curl of fragrant smoke. Beck set the bowl on the table. "It helps the healing process."

He turned to face me. "When's your birthday?"

"Huh?" I said, confused by his abrupt question.

He glanced at his watch. "Just tell me."

"May fifth."

"Okay, you're a Taurus. Your element is earth, so you need to face north."

He put the smudge stick on the table and pulled out a

chair, gesturing for me to sit. Stepping to the stove, he said, "While I get stuff ready, tell me what's bothering you."

He poured liquid into a small pan and set it on the stove to heat. When I didn't answer, he turned and raised a quizzical brow.

I looked away, ashamed of my weakness.

"Talk to me, Allie. Let me help you."

I didn't see him move, but suddenly, he was standing over me, cupping my face in his hands. Once again, I felt the strength and power of his touch singing through my veins. It was too much, too soon. I pulled away.

Beck folded his arms across his chest and stared down at me. "Okay, I get it. You don't trust me. Problem is, if we're going to do this, I need a starting point."

"Of course I don't trust you. I don't even know you!"

"Guess what? I don't know you either, but it looks like this is supposed to happen, so maybe we should just chill out."

Okay, new information. Sounded like Beck wasn't too psyched up about this healing thing either. I glanced up at him. He smiled and gave me a nod of encouragement.

Should I stick a toe in the water and see what happened next? Was it possible to trust someone just a little? Just enough to get healed? Did I have any other option other than to cut and run?

I sighed. "What do you need to know?"

"Start at the beginning."

By the time I finished, I'd told him everything. The fall off the ladder. The telekinetic power, the moonstone prophecy. My ability to read minds with the moonstone. Make that my former ability to use TKP—telekinetic powers, meaning I could move stuff just by thinking about it—and read minds. Caught in his hypnotic golden gaze, I described my recent humiliation at the Star Seekers meeting. Finally, in a voice choked with emotion, I told him about killing Baxter with the apple bins, and about my nightmare.

When I ran out of words, he nodded and went back to his preparations. I watched him digging through a container of stones and felt a spark of hope flicker to life. Sharing my burden with another living, breathing person—even though he was only half human—seemed right. I felt like I needed to hang on to the table to keep from floating up to the ceiling.

Beck selected a stone, frowned and held it to the light.

"What happens next?" I asked.

"Have you heard the term 'shaman'?"

"I think it has something to do with Indians . . .Native American Indians?"

Beck nodded and dropped the stone into the pan. "A shaman is a healer who believes in the old ways. I was trained by one."

Beck glanced over at me. "When we came back from Europe, we lived in a remote area close to an Indian reservation. My mom home-schooled us. After our lessons, we had lots of time to wander around. One day, I found an orphaned, half-dead fawn. I knew where the shaman lived so I took the fawn to him. His name is Jed Nightwalker. I came back every day and watched what Nightwalker did, how he healed the fawn. From that point on, I hung out there as much as I could. He said I was a natural healer."

"Did this Jed guy know you're part demon?"

"Oh yeah, he knew," Beck said. "That first day, he wouldn't let me inside his house. But, I kept coming back, day after day. Finally, he accepted me for what I am. Every time I found an injured animal, I took it to him. We became friends."

"Your mother's okay with this shaman stuff? Her being so religious and all?"

His mouth turned down in disgust. "She doesn't like it, but she can't stop me."

I thought about his rush to get me out of there before

his mother returned. Seemed like half-demon Beck had a few demons of his own.

"So what if she comes home early?"

Beck selected three more stones and placed them in the liquid, wiped his hands on his jeans and gave me a grim look.

"She would assume the worst. Like I said, she got pregnant by an incubus, a male demon who has sex with sleeping women. Sometimes I see her watching me and she looks terrified, like she's waiting for me to be like him. Like it's just a matter of time."

Eyes flashing in anger, he turned back to the stove. I studied his profile. His body was stiff with outrage. A knotted muscle twitched in his tightly clenched jaw.

"So, that's why she makes you go to church so much?"

"Yeah, she thinks she can pray the demon out of me." His voice was bitter, and he wouldn't meet my eyes.

And I thought *I* had problems. Suddenly, all I wanted was for him to feel better.

"Hey, demon boy, lighten up!" I said, with a grin. "You are what you are. Sure, your eyes glow in the dark, and you can jump really high, and you're stronger than the average non half-demon guy, but you seem okay to me."

His shoulders relaxed and he gave me a quick smile.

"Besides which," I added. "Most of the girls at school have the hots for you." I felt myself blush and looked at my feet. "Except for me, of course."

In a blur of movement, Beck was there beside me, lighting a fat, white candle. He removed the pan from the stove and set it on the table. Its fragrance wafted upward and mingled with the smoke from the smudge stick. Somehow, somewhere in the last few seconds, he'd managed to dim the lights. Damn! How did he do that?

"Except for you, huh? Guess I'm losing my touch," he said.

His tone was light, but when I looked up, his eyes were intense and focused. Caught up in his gaze, I was unable to look away. He leaned over me, his palms flat against the table, his face bisected by the flickering candle into light and shadow. Half-human, half-demon. Time was measured by the thudding of my heart as I wavered between fear and fascination. Beck moved closer. The heat from his golden eyes poured through my body like molten lava. I gasped in surprise.

"Keep looking at me, Allie. Let me into your mind."

No problem. I couldn't *not* look at him. I heard the splash of water and felt his finger brush the center of my forehead with warm liquid.

Beck's voice was deep and whispery. "May this healing water rid your mind of pain and distress."

Still gazing into his eyes, I allowed his words to wash over me. I wanted to be healed, didn't I? I visualized my mind as a clenched fist. I willed each finger to relax and extend outward, to release the guilt and pain I'd been clinging to. I jumped in shock when I felt a burst of pure energy arc from his body to mine.

Beck murmured, "It's working. Stay with me, Allie."

He dipped both hands into the liquid and stroked my temples. "May your mind be filled with peace and harmony."

Drawn into his hypnotic gaze, I allowed my heavily-guarded heart to unfurl like a rose in time-lapse photography. From tight bud to full-faced glory. Bathed in sunlight, open and trusting. Again, Beck's power slammed into me. Again, I emitted a little squeak of surprise.

"Almost done," Beck whispered, dipping into the water one last time.

His warm, wet fingers stroked the length of my neck and stopped at the hollow of my throat. He leaned closer and blew a puff of air into my mouth which was, quite conveniently, hanging open.

"Allie Emerson," he said. "Bathed in pure white light, you are restored in mind and spirit." The deep timbre of his voice poured over and through me like warm honey, permeating every cell in my body.

Beck cupped my face in his hand and stroked my eyebrows with his thumbs. My eyes grew heavy and I let them fall shut. As if from a great distance, I heard Beck say, "So shall it be."

We stayed like that for a long moment. I felt the warmth of his hands against my face, the strong pulse of his heartbeat against my skin, his inhalations catching the rhythm of mine until we breathed as one. When I opened my eyes, his face was just inches from mine. His gaze had softened. His eyes were filled with a yearning that sparked across the short distance between us, morphing into a physical hunger I felt clear down to my toes. His lips were inviting and only a few inches from mine. The dark centers in his eyes grew larger. Oh, yeah, he felt it too. All I had to do was move a little closer and . . .

Stop! With great effort, I pulled away and listened to Faye's voice in my head. *What are you thinking? Beck's a half-demon. The other half is horny teenage boy. He has magic abilities you've never dreamed of. Sure, he looks like a lost little boy, but damn, girl, don't be so trusting. Did you forget my lecture on the one-eyed trouser trout?*

I caught Beck's fleeting look of disappointment. He knew. I hadn't said a word or moved a muscle but he knew I'd moved out of the moment. And I knew he would have taken that kiss in another second. Maybe Faye was right, even though she was consorting with Brain Dead Roy. I gave him a shaky smile. "Are we done? Am I healed?"

He looked startled, like he'd been jerked out of a dream. I knew how he felt.

"It's the first step. Right now, I'm trying to block the nightmare." He scrubbed a hand across his face looking embarrassed. In fact, the heat from both our faces could have lit the Bunsen burner at forty paces.

Okay, this was really awkward and time was ticking away. I had no desire to face the wrath of Melissa Bradford. In spite of what Beck had told me, she'd probably think I was bringing out the beast in her son. I decided to kick it into gear.

"Great!" I chirped. "What's next?"

"We have to bless the stones." He fished around in the pan and extracted four gemstones, wiping them carefully on his shirt before setting them on the table. He selected one I recognized as an agate and set it in his palm. "The energy from the agate will give you strength and courage."

He held up a brilliant yellow-green stone. "The citrine will protect you from harm and enhance your powers."

Next came the turquoise. According to Beck, it would "relieve my guilt." I was all over that. The final stone was a rose quartz "for strength and emotional healing."

Beck reached in his pocket and pulled out a small silk pouch with a drawstring top. He dropped the stones into the tiny bag, pulled the drawstring tight and placed it in my hand, clasped both of his around mine and said, "Mother Earth and Father Sky, bless these stones. May their healing power restore balance to this child of the universe."

An involuntary shiver danced down my spine as I felt the stones warming in my hand. Beck smiled. "Keep them with you all the time. Put the pouch under your pillow when you sleep."

He stood, stretched and checked his watch. "I need to get you home."

The ride home was filled with comfortable silence, the awkwardness between us gone, blown away like a whisper on the wind. I turned slightly to study Beck's profile. His tawny hair was shaggy and curled down the nape of his neck. When he glanced over at me, a wayward lock fell across his forehead. I wanted to reach over and brush it back. Before I could act on my impulse, he gave it an impatient swipe with his fingers.

"Feel okay?" he asked.

Good question. How *did* I feel? The anger was gone. True, I wasn't giddy and jumping up and down with joy, but it was a good start.

"I'll find out tonight." At his questioning look, I added, "You know, the dream."

He nodded and pulled into Uncle Sid's driveway. The trailer was dark and the truck was gone. Faye would be home any minute. Beck stopped and cut the lights. I reached for the door.

"Allie, wait."

He reached under the seat, pulled something out and thrust it into my hands. "I made you a dreamcatcher . . . to stop the nightmare."

The dreamcatcher was beautiful, a work of art. Three pieces of woven rawhide hung from the round hoop, each decorated with turquoise beads and feathers. An intricately-woven web studded with beads filled the inside of the hoop.

I stroked the feathers and thanked him. He looked so serious I couldn't resist saying, "What about the good dreams?"

He smiled. "Test it out. Maybe you'll dream about me."

I blushed and reached for the door again. Once again, Beck stopped me.

"I've been thinking about school, you know, in case we need to talk or something."

"I figured you'd just go back to ignoring me like always."

Okay, that sounded a little snotty. Snotty but true.

Beck cleared his throat and stared straight ahead. "Maybe we could be like pretend girlfriend and boyfriend when other people are around."

Was he serious? He removed the night glasses he wore so he wouldn't freak out oncoming motorists and peered at me with dancing, golden eyes.

"You up for that?"

He acted like it was the most natural thing in the world instead of the wackiest idea I'd ever heard. But two could play that game.

In my calmest voice, I said, "Sure. See you tomorrow."

"One more thing," Beck said, one hand slipping around the back of my neck. "Since we're sorta going together—not really, but sorta—I thought I'd kiss you good night."

I smirked at him. "Oh really? A pretend kiss?"

Beck's voice was husky. "Call it whatever you want."

He stroked my cheek with his free hand. I shivered. I knew what would happen if I looked in his eyes, so I clamped mine shut. His scent filled my nostrils. Fresh air. Sage. Pine. I sensed him coming closer. When his mouth touched mine, it was hot and insistent. My lips parted and, blindly, I reached for him, my arms encircling his neck. I felt his heated breath mingle with mine, coiling deep in my belly. I ignored my troublesome brain shouting, *Danger! Danger!* and leaned into him.

He groaned and pulled away, his eyes showing just a tiny rim of gold around enlarged dark pupils.

"Enough pretend kissing?" I gasped, grateful he'd been strong enough to break the spell.

With a bark of laughter, he said, "Makes me wonder what a real one would be like."

Before I was tempted to find out, I grabbed my back pack and slipped out of the car. "See ya, Beck."

He raised a hand in farewell and watched me walk to the trailer before he backed down the driveway.

My mind was busy making up a story for Faye. She would want to know who gave me the dreamcatcher. I decided to tell her I had a new friend from the Cambion

Indian Reservation who heard about my nightmare and made the dreamcatcher for me, my theory being, a half-truth is better than an outright lie.

Faye had been home. I found a note stuck to the fridge "Back at nine," and, inside the fridge, today's leftover Blue Plate Special, greasy chicken-fried steak from Bea's. I used a thumbtack to fasten the dreamcatcher over my couch bed and retrieved the moonstone from its special hiding place. I slipped it over my head and settled in at the table with my homework. Processing the strange events of the evening would have to wait.

Pouring over a geometry problem, I started to move into my usual thinking pose . . .chin in hand, elbow on the table. When I raised my hand, I caught a glimpse of my palm. My heart stuttered in fright and I gasped.

I'm very familiar with the lines on my palm. God knows, it was the subject of many a Star Seeker conversation. I know what the fate line looks like. Where it starts and where it ends. Mine has always ended cleanly in the center of the Apollo mound, the mound below the longest finger. But now—I gazed in horror at my suddenly shaking hand—now it split into three lines.

Somehow, during the course of the evening, I had acquired a demon mark.

Chapter Nine

"Mr. Boswell?" Miss Yeager, our school counselor, screeched through the intercom. "Is Allie Emerson in class today?"

I groaned and slumped down in my seat, wishing I could slip through a crack in the floor.

"Yes, she is," Mr. Boswell said.

"Send her to my office, please."

"Mr. Boswell!" I said in a loud whisper. "Tell her we're taking a test."

He lifted his hands helplessly. "You know that won't stop her. Sorry. "

Since I sat at the front of the row, everyone in the room watched as I closed my geometry book, stuffed it in my backpack and slouched out of the room.

It's not like I didn't have enough to worry about already. Now I'd have Miss Yeager probing my mind, trying to get me to tell her more about my "trauma." Just because I'd spent a few days in the hospital with my head cracked after a couple of vicious Trimarks tried to off me. Swear to God, the woman wouldn't be happy until I was sobbing in her arms.

I dawdled down the hall, resolutely *not* looking at my palm. I'd awakened that morning, blissfully nightmare-free and feeling all warm and fuzzy toward Beck Bradford until I remembered. A quick peek assured me it was still there. The split lines were much shorter than Beck's, but what if they grew? Starting the day by checking out your demon mark is a real bummer. I'd made the illogical decision not to look at it again, hoping it would spontaneously disappear.

Beck had some explaining to do. Did the mark mean I was in debt to him? Did it mean he owned part of my soul? Was I now a demon's plaything?

I whispered to myself as I walked, Stupid! Stupid! Stupid! What part of the word 'demon' don't you get? Granted, Beck doesn't have horns and a forked tail but sometimes demons look like hot teenage guys. That's why they're called demons, dummy! And, last night in the car . . . what's up with that? He had you under his spell. Don't deny it!

I slipped into the library to check out the computer stations, but I kept thinking about Beck. He'd blown his breath into my mouth. We'd exchanged a really hot and heavy kiss. He must've given me some of his demon stuff . . . DNA or whatever. I needed to go online and do some research. Our librarian, Mrs. Moats, looked up from her post behind the counter and called, "Can I help you, Allie?"

Somehow, I just knew she'd be looking over my shoulder when I Googled, *How to obtain a demon mark* or, worse yet, *Effects of swapping spit with a half-demon.* I'd have to wait for another opportunity.

I gave her a casual wave. "I'm on my way to the counseling office."

When I arrived, Miss Yeager was standing in the doorway, looking annoyed. She waved me through the door. "Did you forget our appointment?"

I gave her a big, fake grin. "Sure did."

The door was open. I could still make a run for it. She must have noticed, because she reached over and slammed it shut. My heart sank.

She sat on her swivel chair and fingered the necklace she wore every day. It grabbed my attention the first time we met, because the clear, pink stone outlined in black was shaped like an equilateral triangle. In the center of the stone was the letter "J" for Jeanette. It hung from a gold chain, pointy side up. Since pointy side down indicated a Trimark affiliation, I was nervous until I got a look at her palm. She wasn't a Trimark, but her overly bright smile and intrusion into my personal space set my teeth on edge.

I put down my stuff and crawled into the over-sized bean bag chair, Miss Yeager's idea of a cozy nest, where troubled teens could curl up and pour out their problems. I hated it.

There are only two ways to enter a bean bag chair: plopping or crawling. Once before, I tried plopping, but the trapped air whooshed out and made a hideous farting noise. This time, I crawled in on my hands and knees, flipped over and squirmed around to make an indentation for my butt. Helpless as a turtle on its back, I waited for Miss Yeager to begin her interrogation.

She perched on the edge of her chair and peered down at me, her head cocked to one side like a robin about to pounce on a juicy worm.

After giving me her standard intro, about how everything I say is confidential, blah, blah, blah, she said, "So, Allie. How do you feel?"

"Fine. I feel fine."

"Any issues you'd like to discuss? I'm here to help you."

"Well, actually, I do have an issue."

Her eyes practically popped out of her head with happiness, and she clapped her hands. "Oh, Allie, that's great!"

From her reaction, I'd guess she was short on clients. Part of me felt sorry for her, but it didn't stop me from saying, "Geometry's kinda hard for me. I can't afford to miss it once a week. Can we meet at a different time?"

Her right eyelid began to twitch, and her lips compressed into a thin, pale line. She leaned forward, her long neck stretched out like an angry goose. "Allie. I sense a definite lack of cooperation on your part. Counseling is a two-way street. You insist you're fine."

Oh, no. Here it comes! The "T" word.

"However, you've been through a severe trauma."

I heaved an irritated sigh.

She glared and continued, "As I was saying, you've been traumatized! You may not know it, but you need my help. May I express my true feelings?"

I heard the tension in her voice and looked at her madly twitching eyelid. "Sure."

"I find your resistance to counseling extremely frustrating."

Sometimes I'm impulsive. Make that most of the time. I should have bitten my tongue and nodded. Instead, I said, "May I express *my* true feelings?"

"Of course. That's why you're here."

I rolled onto my stomach and began to crawl backward out of the bean bag, my butt in the air. "I feel I'm missing something important in geometry."

I struggled to my feet and looked down at her. Her eyes sparked with anger. When she spoke, her mouth barely moved. "Are you mocking me?"

"You said you wanted me to express my true feelings."

She inhaled deeply and exhaled through her nose, the air making a whistling sound. She grabbed a tissue out her pocket and blew. I edged toward the door.

Before I could make my escape, she said, "Hold it! Your case worker, Susan Wright, dropped in to see me. She told me you and your mother had some issues with Child Protective Services last spring."

Her words flew past my defenses and struck my heart. Direct hit. I started to bristle up, but thought better of it. "My mother's working now. We don't have any issues with CPS."

She folded her hands and placed them on her desk. "It seems everyone involved in your case feels you and your mother would benefit from family counseling."

I barely controlled my urge to groan. Wisely, I kept silent.

"Furthermore," Miss Yeager said. "Since our counseling sessions—if you can call them that—are going exactly nowhere, I tend to agree. Ms. Wright thought it would be best if you and your mother didn't have to drive to Vista Valley for counseling, so from now on I will be working with you both."

She sat back in her chair, looking pleased.

I glared down at her. "My mother isn't going to be happy about this."

Talk about the understatement of the century. If Miss Yeager thought *I* was uncooperative, wait until she got Faye in her bean bag chair.

Miss Yeager beamed happily. "I guess I'll cross that bridge when I come to it."

*

I didn't catch up with Beck until later that morning. I stiffened when he threw an arm around my shoulders. "Any bad dreams?"

The hall was crowded with students changing classes. I pulled him over to a bank of lockers and held my palm up in front of his face. I tried to control my outrage as I spoke through tightly clenched teeth. "No bad dreams, just a real, live demon mark."

His eyes widened in shock. "No way!"

He took my hand in both of his, examining it carefully. I snatched it away. "I assume you've kissed other girls. Right?"

His gaze rolled upward like he hoped to find the correct

response spray-painted on the ceiling. When he finally met my eyes, he had that trapped look guys get when you ask them about former girlfriends. He blustered. "Well, yeah, sure. I bet you've kissed other guys too."

I sighed. For a smart guy, he was really dense. "You're missing the point. This isn't about how many girls you've kissed. It's about the demon mark."

My voice had risen in frustration. We were getting some curious glances. I pulled him closer and whispered, "Come on, Beck. Think. Has this happened before? When you kissed those other girls, did they get the mark?"

His brows drew together as he pondered my question. He must have kissed a lot of girls because he took a good long time to answer. "No, I don't think so."

His eyes slid away from mine, and I thought I detected a teensy smirk. "I wasn't really interested in checking out their palms, if you know what I mean."

If he was lying, he was really good at it. But then, a demon would be good at lying.

"Hmmph," I snorted, not liking the visual I was getting. He was standing much too close, and I felt the same magnetic pull I'd been unable to resist the night before. I took a step back. When I spoke, my voice was shaky. "Does this mean I'm part-demon?"

Beck was totally serious now. He shook his head. "No, no, don't even go there."

He looked around to make sure nobody was listening and lowered his voice. "Allie, please believe me. I'm so sorry. I would never do anything to hurt you. I'm pretty sure the mark means you were *touched* by a demon."

I stared up at him. "Pretty sure?"

Beck took my arm and pulled me into the stream of traffic. "We need to get to class. Let me think about it, and we'll talk at lunch."

His eyes dropped to the moonstone, its bulge obvious

under my shirt. "You weren't wearing the moonstone at my house last night . . . right?"

"No. I thought you might be a Trimark and try to take it from me, so I left it at home."

His eyes gleamed with sudden knowledge. "I think I know what happened. I need to do some research. I'll see you later."

He peeled off and headed toward the library. I watched him go. As he disappeared down the hall, I knew the fragile bond of trust between us was stretched to the max. Did Beck really think I'd sit back and let him tell me stuff that might or might not be true?

Guess what? He wasn't the only one who knew how to do research. My science teacher had a computer in his classroom ,and I was way ahead on my work. I'd do some research of my own. Then, and only then, would I find out if I could trust Beck Bradford.

When the bell rang for lunch, I practically sprinted to the cafeteria. Beck was already there, leaning against the wall, a sack lunch in hand. "Grab some food and we'll go talk in the Ranger."

"I'm not hungry."

We were almost to the door when we ran into Mercedes. Her eyes widened in surprise. I knew how her mind worked and braced myself. Her smile was so big, her eyes crinkled shut. "Oooo, girl! Got a better offer, huh?"

Manny, Mercedes and I always ate lunch together. I leaned close and whispered, "I'll tell you all about it after school."

I didn't have time to enjoy the reaction of my female classmates as Beck swept me toward the parking lot, but I knew the drill.

First, the shocked looks followed by, "He's with *her*?"

Next, shock morphed into downright envy, signaling the unspoken, *It should have been me.*

Lastly, whispering clusters of girls would gather together to analyze the data, speculate on the cause and make dire predictions.

"Oh my God, Beck Bradford is hot!"

"I can't believe he's with Allie Emerson."

"Isn't she still hot for Junior Martinez?"

"What a skank!"

"He'll dump her in a week."

We zipped past Nicole Bradford and her cool friends, heading for the Dairy Queen. She smirked and said, "Hey, Bro, what are you doing with *her*? Nothing good, I bet."

She turned to her friends and murmured something under her breath. They all laughed and gave me knowing looks. I stopped and took a step toward the group, my face hot with anger.

"I didn't quite hear you. What did you say, Nicole?"

Beck ignored his sister and took my arm. "Nikki's just being a twit. As usual. Don't let her get to you."

At Beck's words, Nicole's friends sobered quickly and watched as Beck led me away. I felt Nicole's eyes burning into my back.

"Why does your sister hate me?"

Beck shook his head. "She doesn't hate you, she hates what she is. It's kinda hard to hang with the cool girls when she changes into something not fully human after dark. She acts like a snob because she thinks that's what they want to hear."

My snort of disbelief let Beck know I had a hard time feeling sorry for Nicole Bradford.

He slipped an arm around my shoulders. "I know, it doesn't make sense, but try to be patient. She'll come around."

Yeah, I thought as Beck unlocked the Ranger and opened the door for me. About the same time my mother has a boyfriend with an IQ higher than a mushroom.

Beck slipped into the driver's seat and closed the door. He opened his lunch sack and pulled out what looked like a meatloaf sandwich. He unwrapped it carefully and offered me half.

I waved it away in exasperation. "What did you find out?"

He took an enormous bite and practically swallowed it whole. "Sorry." He chomped down on the sandwich again. "I'm starving."

"And . . .?" I could hardly wait for his answer.

"It's what I thought." He took another big bite.

Boys and their stomachs! It was like he had a ravenous tapeworm living inside him. "Beck. Put-down-the-sandwich. Tell me why I have the demon mark."

"It's because you're wearing the moonstone."

I scowled. "And?"

Beck said, "I remembered reading about demons being driven out of people using exorcism. I looked it up on the Internet. When a demon exited a person's body, it left a mark like a tattoo. An exit mark. In your case, a forked fate line, like mine. It happened when you put the moonstone on after you went home last night. It drove the demon dust, or whatever you want to call it, out of your body."

Next test. I asked, "So, if I take the moonstone off, will the mark go away?'

Beck shook his head. "I don't think so, but you can try if you want."

I removed my necklace and set it on the seat between us, making sure it didn't touch any part of my body. Holding my breath, I looked at my palm. "Nope," I said. "It's still there."

Before he stuffed the rest of his sandwich in his mouth, Beck said, "Yeah, I think it's permanent."

"So, according to your theory, the moonstone drove your demon influence out of my body."

Beck took my hand and skimmed a finger along my fate line. I gave an involuntary shiver. He smiled. "Yes, the moonstone made it happen. The mark means the demon stuff is gone."

Confession time. "Yep, that's what I found out too."

One eyebrow shot up. "You did your own research? You don't trust me?"

"Hey, I'm the one with a brand-new demon mark on my hand. Did you think I'd just sit back and think, 'No problem. I'll let big old hunky Beck handle it?'"

He flushed and dropped my hand. "So, this was like a test?"

"No," I said. "Not *like* a test. It *was* a test. The good news is, you passed. You told me the truth."

When he looked at me, his eyes were filled with regret. "Allie, please believe me. I didn't know that would happen. I'm so sorry."

I looked at my hand, then at Beck. "Do you think the mark will grow? If we . . .you know, get too close to each other like last night?"

Apparently emotion riled up his tapeworm, because Beck opened a plastic bag of cookies. "I don't think so."

"Oh," I said in a small voice. "But, it might."

He popped two cookies in his mouth and pondered my question.

"Because," I said. "I really, really don't think I could handle that along with all the other things I've got going on."

Beck inhaled his last cookie. "Actually, I have a second theory about the moonstone. Wanna hear it?"

I nodded.

"I think the moonstone acts as a shield. Sort of like mosquito repellant."

"Hmmm." I was warming to the notion that the moonstone could protect me. But, maybe that's what Beck wanted me to believe. We were back to the issue of trust. Speaking of which, I had one more question.

"If the mark is left by the demon leaving a person's body, doesn't the mark on your palm mean your demon has left *your* body too?."

Beck said, "No, it's different for me and Nicole. The demon entered our mother's body and left its imprint on Nicole and me . . .along with its DNA, if demons have DNA."

I felt a prickle of apprehension as I stared at my fate line. "So, we don't know for sure if the moonstone will protect me from you."

Beck must have sensed my uneasiness, because he gave me a dark look, full of promise. "We could test it out. Like an experiment. When you're wearing the moonstone and I kiss you, if the line stays the same, we'll know it works. The moonstone keeps the demon out. But if the mark grows, we'll know the demon got a foothold in you."

The funny thing was, I'd been thinking exactly the same thing. However, he didn't need to know that. I smiled. "Dream on, demon boy. Like I'd risk letting you and your demon kiss me again."

He leaned close and handed me an apple. He tilted his head until his mouth was just inches from my neck. If I'm not mistaken, he sniffed me again. I sniffed him back.

A sudden pounding on the window caused me to jump and drop the apple on the floor. I turned to see our principal, Mr. Hostetler, peering in at us and felt as guilty as homemade sin. He made a roll-down-the-window motion with his hand. The engine was off, so the window didn't work. I fumbled with the door handle, frantically scrolling through my mind trying to figure out what rule I'd broken.

I got my answer when I opened the door. Mr. Hostetler said, "Number twelve."

Oh, that one.

Chapter Ten

No PDA. Public Display of Affection. Technically, we hadn't been displaying affection, public or otherwise. After Beck and I scrambled out of the truck, I tried explaining this to Mr. Hostetler.

"I know we were close together, but, swear to God, he was just handing me an apple!"

Mr. Hostetler acted like he hadn't heard me. His steely gaze was fixed on Beck. "Allie, you can go. Mr. Bradford and I are going to have a little chat."

Somehow this struck me as wrong. "Maybe I should stay."

The principal glanced over at me. His eyes were kind, but his tone meant business. "No. I want you to go."

"If Beck's in trouble, then I should be too."

"Relax. Nobody's in trouble." Mr. Hostetler pointed toward the building. "Now, go!"

Beck said, "It's okay, Allie. I'll see you later."

Still apprehensive, I walked across the gravel parking lot toward the school. I glanced over my shoulder and saw Mr. Hostetler right up in Beck's face, using a lot of hand gestures. Beck look unconcerned, leaning against the Ranger with his arms folded. Brimming with curiosity—okay, nosiness—my only hope was that Beck would spill his guts when I saw him later in French class.

The three-minute warning bell rang, and I caught up with Mercedes. She gave me a quick glance then looked away, but not before I saw the hurt in her eyes.

"Guess you won't be eating lunch with us anymore.

Now that you're with Beck."

When I recovered my power of speech, I said, "Are you crazy? In case you've forgotten, Beck and I got our back packs got mixed up yesterday. He still had some of my things in his truck."

Okay, I lied, but my other option was, *We were only talking about my demon mark.*

Mercedes was trying to stay mad, a fruitless effort. The mischief was back in her eyes, and a dimple appeared in her cheek. "Took you all lunch period, huh?"

"Well, uh," I stammered. "We just talked and stuff. You know . . ."

"Yeah, right. Remember, *I* was the one who said Beck was hot for you . . . Halloween night in the gym? Someday, you'll learn not to doubt me. I know these things."

I waved a dismissive hand. "Yeah, yeah. Whatever. Anyway, if Beck wants to eat lunch with me, he'll have to sit with all of us."

We fell into step behind Donna Jo and Dora Jean Hoffman, also regulars at our lunch table. At my words, they stopped, whirled around and peered at us through their thick glasses.

Dora Jean said, "Beck Bradford's going to eat lunch with us?" Her voice was squeaky with excitement.

I groaned inwardly. What had I started? I flapped my hand, "No, no, I just said, *if* he wants to, and I'm sure he doesn't. Let's just drop it, okay?"

When Mercedes giggled, I knew the issue had been resolved. We edged around Dora Jean and Donna Jo, not an easy task, because they were as wide as they were tall, and, of course, the very reason they sat at our table. We were on our way to PE and wouldn't make it on time if we didn't get ahead of the Hoffman sisters.

When we reached the gym, I stopped and grabbed Mercedes' arm. "Nicole Bradford and I had a few words at lunch."

Mercedes' mouth turned down in disgust. "Oh, her!"

"She's in this class."

"Just ignore her."

"Yeah." I wondered if that was possible in a school the size of ours.

It wasn't. Our PE teacher, Miss Miller, was all about fairness. She didn't want anyone to feel left out. When we chose up teams for volleyball, each captain got to pick three people. The left-over people joined the team of their choice. That way, nobody had to be the loser last pick.

After we stretched, Miss Miller appointed two captains. Wouldn't you just know it would be Nicole and me?

I picked Mercedes, Dora Jean and Donna Jo, because I knew Nicole wouldn't. Glaring at me like a rabid pit bull, Nicole picked three of her cool friends, Lexie, Erin and Caitlyn. When the rest of the class sorted itself out, I had three more players: Luella Hoptowit, a Native American girl who was only four-feet-nine and hated white people, Mexicans and well . . .just about everybody else who was taller than she. Maybe she had good reason. Not for me to judge. I also had Jolene, who cringed every time the ball came within ten feet of her and Sonja Ortega, who didn't like me a whole lot, but truly despised Nicole. The rest of Nicole's skinny friends rushed to her side of the net. If the match was based on butt-size alone, we'd win.

The match was for best two out of three. Since we each had one substitute, I put Jolene on the bench for the first game, Donna Jo in the front row and Dora Jean in the back. Sonja and I would spike. I could jump like a deer, and Sonja was just plain mean. She loved to pound the ball through the opposition's front line, preferably off someone's face. The Hoffman twins couldn't move, but took up a lot of space and had good hands.

We won the first game 25-8. Mercedes, who never got

rattled, served the last twelve points. After she served game point, Sonja ran to the net, shook her fist and screamed at Nicole's team, "Losers! You suck!"

The comment earned her a reprimand from Miss Miller and fired up Nicole's team, who tried to intimidate us with dirty looks. Like that would work.

Game Two was a different story. Jolene, who was green with fright, took Luella's place. I tucked her in the back row behind Donna Jo's enormous bulk, thinking she'd be safe. But, Nicole's best server, Caitlin, zeroed in on her. With uncanny ability, she served the ball to the back left corner of the court which forced Jolene to leave the safety of Donna Jo's sheltering body and make a stab at passing the ball. After Caitlin racked up ten points, I called a time-out and tried to convince Luella to take Jolene's place. Luella said, "Screw you, Emerson. Ain't no way I'm goin' back in there."

After the time-out, Caitlin smirked and winged another wicked serve at poor Jolene, who had begun to weep. When the score was 13-zip, a miracle occurred. Jolene closed her eyes and stuck out an arm. The ball caromed off her fist, hit Sonja in the head, bounced over the net and hit the floor between two of Nicole's players. Even though Nicole and her teammates complained loudly, Miss Miller said the ball bouncing off Sonja's head was a legal hit. Point and side-out!

Our happiness was short-lived. After a string of good serves, we lost our momentum. Game Two went to Nicole's team, 25-15. Nicole and her teammates rushed the net, turned around and waggled their skinny little butts, jeering, "Bite me, losers!"

I grabbed Sonja to keep her from charging the net. "It's okay. We'll get them in Game Three. Can you talk to Luella? We need her."

Sonja looked at me through black-rimmed, rage-filled

eyes. "No problem."

Sonja stomped over to a sullen-looking Luella for a pep talk. Because Jolene had fled to the locker room, claiming her period started, we'd be short one player without Luella. No problem. Sonja, through threats or bribery—I didn't want to know which—worked her magic. She threw a beefy arm around Luella and walked her onto the court.

We had first serve. Mercedes floated one in and dropped it between the front and back row. When the ball hit the floor, Sonja screamed, "Ace! In your face!"

Mercedes, pleasant smile firmly in place, followed up with ten more points. Nicole called a time-out. I heard her say, "Come on, you guys! Are you going to let those losers beat us?"

"Hell, no!"

Mercedes' next serve went in the net and Nicole's BFF, Lexie, moved into the serving position. She zinged one into the back row and Dora Jean reacted a little too late. The ball skidded off her arms and fell to the floor. Nicole's team cheered wildly then pointed at Dora Jean and yelled, "Gotcha, Queenie!" (We all knew "Queenie" was their code word for queen-sized, aka "Fat Ass.")

Dora Jean, usually good-natured and placid, narrowed her eyes and growled, "I dare you to try that again, you skinny, anorexic bitch!"

"Language, girls!" Miss Miller cautioned.

Lexie made the mistake of serving the ball in the exact same place. Dora Jean passed the ball to Donna Jo, who made a perfect set. I leaped high in the air and wound up like I was going to smash it into the blocker's face. Instead, I gave the ball a little sideways *dink,* brushing it off the blocker's hands to the floor. Point! Side-out!

After we rotated, Donna Jo's serve ricocheted off the back wall, hit the ceiling, bounced off the net and dribbled to the floor. Nicole's team stomped and cheered. We all dropped back to receive the serve. Caitlin lined up and focused on our right side, Luella.

Caitlin hammered Luella, racking up eleven straight points to take the lead 12-11. Since the third game only went to fifteen points, I called a time-out, trying to ignore Nicole's team who were engaged in a premature, butt-waggling victory dance.

"They're killing us," I said. "Luella, just move out of the way and let us pass the ball."

Luella jutted her jaw and snapped, "I can do it. Give me one more chance."

Sonja heaved a disgusted sigh but, for once, kept her mouth shut. We straggled back to our positions like condemned prisoners facing a firing squad. Caitlin grinned and popped a high floater straight at Luella who was crouched and ready. Without spin, the ball wobbles like crazy. My heart sank as I watched it float toward Luella, then, at the last second, wiggle to the right. *It's all over*, I thought.

"Hiiiiyaaa!" Luella screamed, launching her body flat-out to the right, arms extended in front of her, hands locked together. Somehow she managed to whip her arms up and hit the ball before she crashed to the floor. It flew over the net and landed in the middle of Nicole's team standing flat-footed and unprepared. Erin reacted too late, fisting the ball. It shot off to the right, out-of-bounds.

We all rushed to Luella who scrambled to her feet, a huge smile on her face. Sonja picked her up and swung her around. "Damn, girl! That was hot!"

Luella, pumped up on adrenalin, rotated into the serving position and chalked up the last four points we needed to win the match. We stomped and cheered. Sonja put Luella on her shoulder, marched up to the net and screamed, "Losers, huh? Well, guess what? I'm lookin' at the losers."

Miss Miller made us all shake hands before we went

into the locker room. When Nicole and I touched hands, she leaned close. I swear her nose quivered as she inhaled my scent.

She said, "You'd better hope you don't run into me after dark."

Spooked by the hostility in her voice and the fact she was memorizing my scent, I jerked my hand away, flashing on the image of her sparring match with Beck. The power in her punches. The vicious kicks. The speed of her movements. Nicole could put me in a world of hurt without breaking a sweat.

But my mouth got ahead of my brain, and I retorted, "You'll have to find me first."

In light of Beck's comments about the twins' extraordinary night vision and sense of smell, could I have said anything dumber?

"No problem," Nicole said, her eyes gleaming with anticipation.

While my teammates celebrated, I stood and watched Nicole walk into the locker room, thinking, *I've made a terrible mistake.*

Chapter Eleven

After school, I got off the bus at the diner, so I could ride home with Faye. I wanted to tell her about our counseling session with Miss Yeager before someone from CPS called. I hadn't had a chance to talk to Beck again. He'd been busy correcting papers during French class. I had a few things I wanted to run by him. Like, what had Mr. Hostetler said to him in his "little chat," and, oh yeah, did I mention your sister wants to kill me?

Beck did manage to slip me a note during the afternoon, saying, "Call you later."

It's true, Faye and I now had a telephone. Not that I wouldn't like to be talking, texting and snapping pictures on my cell phone like everybody else in the entire world. But, for Faye and me, having even a basic plug-in phone in the trailer was a giant step forward. We no longer had to trudge over to Manny and Mercedes' house to use theirs. Plus, certain people (like maybe Beck Bradford) could call me.

I'd had a cell phone once. Last spring, my newly-discovered father gave me one. He thought I needed one since I was supposed to save the world from evil. Faye thought differently. (About the phone, not the "saving the world" part)

She had glared at me and said, "I don't care if you're the next queen of England. Send it back. Does Mike Purdy think I can't provide a phone for my daughter?"

I knew better than to answer that question. When she got her job at Busy Bea's she'd made good on her promise to get us a phone, even though our phone was one of Brain Dead Roy's cast-offs.

I opened the door of the diner, practically empty at three in the afternoon. Only two tables in Faye's section were filled. A young guy wearing a Seattle Seahawks cap was having pie and coffee. Faye was deep in conversation with a couple she called *The Tweeners*, because they came in every day between lunch and dinner and ordered their meal before the price went up. She looked over and waved.

Bea, the diner's owner, paused from wiping down the counter to greet me. She turned and called through the serving hatch to the kitchen. "Hey, Harold, Allie's here."

Harold's face, dominated by a gigantic nose, appeared in the opening from the kitchen side. He winked a bloodshot eye and said, "How ya doin', kid? The usual?"

"Sure," I said, slipping off my backpack. When I plopped down on a stool next to the counter, I heard the sizzle of grease.

"How you been, doll-face?" Bea asked.

She crossed her arms and leaned on the counter, her piled-up hair shifting precariously. Bea, in keeping with the diner's bee theme, had what Faye called a beehive hairdo. It looked exactly like Marge Simpson's blue cartoon 'do, except Bea's was flaming red.

I smiled and sniffed the air, now filled with the delectable aroma of French fries. "I'm fine, Bea. How are you?"

"Could be better. My back's been bothering me and . . ."

Bea launched into a lengthy recital of her many ailments, all imaginary, according to my mother. I listened and nodded, my mouth watering in anticipation. Harold wasn't exactly a gourmet cook, but his fries were magnificent. Crisp, never soggy. Just the right amount of salt. Since I'd been too upset to eat lunch, I was famished.

"Order up!" Harold sang out, a plate of golden French fries appearing in the window.

"Here you go, honey." Bea set the plate in front of me. "This should meet your minimum daily requirement from the grease group."

I smiled my thanks and dug in, practically salivating in my eagerness. After one bite, I swallowed hard. Harold had forgotten the salt. Geez, you can't eat French fries without salt! Harold was watching me through the window and Bea was hovering nearby, both waiting for my reaction. The salt shaker was further down the counter, out of reach.

I didn't want Bea to know Harold screwed up, because she would rag on him for hours. But, I really needed the salt.

"Good, huh?" Harold called from the kitchen.

"Mmm hmm," I agreed.

I popped another fry in my mouth and looked longingly at the salt shaker, now bathed in an eerie, greenish light. Could it be . . .? Yes! I heard a loud buzzing sound like a colony of bees had flown in my ear and set up housekeeping inside my head. I knew what was happening. I stifled a shout of joy when the salt shaker jumped straight up in the air, plopped down and began to jiggle and dance its way down the counter toward me. Just the salt. Not the pepper . . . a small, but important detail unnoticed by Bea.

Her hands flew up and she screamed, "Oh my God! We're having an earthquake. Everybody out of the diner. Now!"

The Tweeners didn't want to leave their mashed potatoes and fried chicken. Faye, with a quick glance at me, herded them to the door. They grumbled as they exited, "What earthquake? I didn't feel anything. The siren's not blowing. They always blow the siren when we have an earthquake."

The pie and coffee guy threw some money on the table and left. Bea yelled at Benny the dishwasher to get out of the kitchen. We all gathered in the parking lot, where Bea scanned the sky (as if earthquakes came from the same place

as tornadoes) and used her cell phone to call 911. I wanted
to tell her earthquakes come from below, not above, but
since I was just a kid, I kept my mouth shut.

While we waited, I took the opportunity to check out
Benny the dishwasher. Faye mentioned him frequently, but
I'd never gotten a good look at him before. While I checked
him out, he was checking out my mother's backside, his
flat, gray gaze crawling over her like slow-moving spiders.
He was the type of guy who made me go "Eewww," which
meant, of course, Faye was attracted to him. His dark hair
was cropped short. He wore faded jeans and had a dirty
dish towel tied around his waist. Big, beefy shoulders
strained the fabric of a too-small, black, AC/DC tee shirt. A
fake-looking gold chain hung around his neck, the lower
portion tucked inside his shirt.

Suddenly, he lifted his gaze and caught me looking. His
lips were full and sensual. He smiled—more like a leer—
and winked. I was tempted to turn my back to him, but I
didn't want his eyes crawling over *my* butt, so I just held
my ground and stared over the top of his head.

After Bea summoned Sheriff Philpott, Peacock Flats'
only law enforcement officer, and demanded to know why
he hadn't blown the siren, we filed back into the diner. Bea,
still in a tizzy, had to go lie down in the break room, and I
got to salt my fries. The salt shaker sat right where it had
jumped on my psychic command.

And so I found out Beck Bradford wasn't just a hunky
half-demon whose main goal was to get in my pants. Okay,
maybe it was a secondary goal, but the healing thing was
for real.

My telekinetic powers had returned.

*

On the ride home, Faye said, "What got into Bea? Did

you feel anything?"

I shrugged. "Dunno. Maybe her big hair shifted, and she thought the earth moved."

Faye tried not to laugh. She shook her head sadly. "That mouth of yours. It will get you in trouble someday."

I thought about Nicole Bradford. *Yeah, like today.*

I'd decided not to tell Faye about the salt shaker. I knew she'd get all worked up and make me practice when we got home. Like use the TKP to lift up the couch so she could clean under it, or see if I could make the dishes fly out of the sink into the cupboard. I wasn't in the mood. Instead, I told her about our counseling session.

First, she made a pouty face. Then she looked over at me and winked. "I think the two of us can handle a school counselor. What do you think?"

"Right on," I said.

We slapped hands and that was that.

Turned out Faye had something else on her mind. "Roy's leaving tomorrow for a salvage job in Puget Sound. He wants to take me out tonight for a nice dinner. You okay with that?"

Was I okay with that? Other than my heart leaping with joy at the possibility of Roy having an unfortunate encounter with a giant octopus, I was very much okay. I tried to tone down my enthusiasm. "Sure. I hope you have a great time. You deserve it."

She steered the truck down the driveway and parked next to the trailer. "I won't be late. You've got Roy's cell number. Right?"

"Yep."

When Roy arrived, I decided I would make an effort to be nice to him. (A) I wanted Faye to enjoy her big night out. (B) I was feeling a little guilty about wishing Roy's death by giant sea creature.

Too bad he had to spoil it. He pulled up in his monster

four-wheel drive. It was so high, he had to practically throw Faye into the passenger seat. When he knocked on the door, Faye was still getting ready, and I was forced to make small talk.

I opened the door. "Faye's almost ready. Come on in."

"Hi, A.C. How's it hangin'?"

He thrust out his palms so I could slap them. Apparently I was supposed to congratulate him for this witty remark. I tapped his palms with my fingertips and stepped aside so he could enter.

"It's hangin' just fine," I responded, although I truly believed this remark was intended for the male gender. Really, at my age, nothing much was hanging.

Roy was wearing a leather jacket, a light-blue dress shirt and crisp black jeans. In the spirit of being a good daughter, I said, "You look nice, Roy."

If he'd had a tail, he would have wagged it. "Gee, thanks, A.C. How's school going?"

"School's okay. I hear you're leaving for a while."

I tried not to sound too excited.

"Yeah, got a gig over on the coast."

Fresh out of conversation, I was relieved when Faye threw open the sliding door. She looked hot in a slinky black dress, her blond hair pulled back in a sleek twist. She usually didn't wear her hair back because she didn't like her pointy ears. I thought they were cute—kinda elf-like—but cute. Poor Brain Dead Roy didn't have a prayer. When he saw Faye, the small amount of blood lingering in his brain immediately rushed south.

"You kids have fun now." I winked at Faye. "Remember your curfew!"

Faye gave me a bemused look. "Yeah, right."

My comment proved to be a real knee-slapper for Roy. I heard him ha-ha-ing all the way to the truck. After they left, I noticed Roy's Swiss Army knife on the chair.

Apparently, it had fallen out of his pocket while he was waiting for Faye. I picked it up and put it in the silverware drawer.

I closed the shades, locked the door and cranked up the heat. With Faye gone, I was free to give the TKP another test drive. I sat on the couch and focused on a dishrag hanging from a hook next to the sink. Dishrags weigh practically nothing. Should be a piece of cake. I gathered my scattered thoughts and focused on the dishrag, commanding it to lift. Lift! No aura. No buzzing. The dishrag didn't even twitch.

Aggravated, I glared at the thing and said aloud. "Stupid dishrag! Wouldn't you like to soar like an eagle?"

My disgruntled remarks were interrupted by the phone. When I answered, I heard a deep, male voice and the word, "Hey."

I thought it was Beck, but wasn't absolutely sure. Cautiously, I said, "Hey, yourself," praying I wasn't talking to some perv making an obscene phone call.

"What's up?"

Okay, it was definitely Beck. "Not much," I said. "Just homework."

"Need any help?"

Actually I did. The whole *etre* "to be" thing in French had me on the ropes. *Il est . . . Je suis . . . Nous sommes . . .* Swear to God, it was making me crazy! Beck was eager to help.

"The library's open until nine. We can hang out there."

He picked me up at 6:30. As we drove down Peacock Flats road toward the library, I told him about making the salt shaker move and my disappointing follow-up with the dishrag.

He glanced at me through his special glasses. "Remember, last night was just the first step."

I heaved an impatient sigh. "So, what happens next?

Do you have to anoint me again or something?"

"Probably not. But, I need more information about your use of TKP and, of course, the moonstone."

He sounded exactly like our science teacher explaining how litmus paper worked. For some reason, I found this hilariously funny and started laughing like crazy.

Staring straight ahead, he said, "Is something funny?"

"Oh, don't mind me," I said, gasping for breath. "It's just this thing I do when stuff builds up and, oh, by the way, your sister wants to kill me."

Beck shot me a quick glance but didn't respond. He pulled into the parking lot of our small, community library, turned off the engine and stepped out of the truck. In fact, he didn't speak again until we reached the door of the library. Before I could open the door, he put his hands on my shoulders and turned me to face him. "We need to talk about Nicole."

"Did she tell you about the volleyball match?"

He nodded.

"We kinda, uh, got caught up in the moment."

"Yeah, I figured that. But she doesn't want to kill you."

"She sure acts like she does."

"Nicole's afraid of you, Allie."

"No way! She could kick my butt with both hands tied behind her back."

"It has nothing to do with her physical abilities. She's afraid you'll tell people what she is, and she'll lose her friends."

"Well, that's just stupid," I scoffed. "I'm a little different myself, you know? It would help if she didn't act like such a drama queen."

"Yeah," Beck said, releasing me. "I'll talk to her."

"Good," I said, though I doubted it would help. I reached for the door.

Suddenly, Beck said, "Nicole is very talented. She's

experimenting with astral travel."

My hand floated away from the door handle. "Astral travel?" I repeated, dumbly.

Beck said, "It's like an out-of-body experience. In this case, the astral body separates from the physical body and travels to another place."

I had a sudden image of a pissed-off Nicole hovering outside our trailer, glaring at me through a window. I tried not to snicker. "So, if you do astral travel, does your body disappear?

"No, your physical body remains."

"That's not possible . . . is it?"

"It's possible."

I dithered a while, trying not to say what I was thinking, that Nicole was so shallow she couldn't possibly have an astral body. "Well, it's good to have a goal."

After I said it, I realized it sounded snotty. I opened the door, and Beck followed me to an empty table. I pulled out a chair and sat, satisfied we'd finally laid the subject of Nicole to rest.

Chapter Twelve

The library was buzzing with people. I'd forgotten it was Oprah Book Club night. I waved at Kizzy, who was sitting with ten other women. Charlie, her driver, was slouched in an easy chair, reading *Popular Mechanics*. One of the women in the Oprah group was sobbing. Kizzy looked over at me and rolled her eyes. Mr. Linde, the librarian, glanced at the sobber, then returned to what he was doing before, namely, leaning over a glass aquarium, admiring Buster, his pet snake. Mr. Linde loved reptiles and brought Buster to work with him every day. Kizzy said the snake creeped out the Oprah ladies. To tell the truth, Buster creeped me out too.

Beck removed his glasses, scanned the room and settled in next to me. His eyes looked almost normal in artificial light but I could still detect a slight glow. Once again, I noticed how ripped he looked. His brawny shoulders stretched the fabric of his tee shirt to the max. I was about to make a comment about his wardrobe challenges when he picked up on our previous conversation.

"You know what's even better than having a goal?" he said.

I lifted an eyebrow.

"Achieving it," he said.

Since I thought Beck was engaging in idle chitchat, I gushed, "Oh, yes. Absolutely! Like when I first learned to ride a bike and . . ."

When I heard him chuckle, I stopped, mid-sentence. Beck rarely chuckles. In fact, this was a first. A light bulb in the dim recesses of my brain flickered to life. He was still talking about Nicole. "You don't mean she can actually . . ."

"The astral travel thing?" He looked over at me and winked. "Oh, yeah," he said, "She can."

I'm not speechless often. But the notion that self-centered Nicole could bear to part with her physical body long enough to travel astrally, blew me away. Embarrassed, I studied the tops of my shoes. Finally, I mumbled, "I guess there's a lot I don't know about Nicole."

Beck scooted his chair next to mine. He brushed my hair back, put his lips against my ear and whispered, "You don't know the half of it."

An involuntary shiver ran down my spine. Whether it was from Beck's words or the warmth of his lips, I couldn't say. "Like what?"

He pulled back. "If she wants you to know, she'll tell you."

Okay, this was weird. On one hand, it was like Beck wanted to defuse the tension between Nicole and me. But, his comments and actions made her seem more mysterious, if not downright scary. Maybe he was using some sort of half-demon logic beyond the comprehension of a mere mortal. Of one thing, though, I was absolutely sure. I was sick of talking about Nicole Bradford.

I pulled my French book out of my backpack. "Let's hit it," I said.

We got down to business. Beck made me practice until I could respond rapidly to the following questions:

"Where did you go?" "*Je suis alle' en France.*"

"How's the weather?" "*Il fait beau.*"

"What nationality are we?" "*Nous sommes Francais.*"

We were about to wrap it up when the door slammed open. A hush fell over the library as a slim brown-haired woman scanned the room. Melissa Bradford, sparks shooting from her eyes, spotted us and marched toward our table, wearing her anger like a suit of armor. Beck groaned.

"Busted," he muttered. "Supposed to be in church."

I was watching his mother approach when Beck mumbled again, something that sounded like, "Don't worry. I'll use the Taser."

Say what? I glanced at his backpack. No way would Beck be carrying a Taser, much less use it on his mother. I'd heard him wrong.

Beck gave his mom a sickly grin. "Oh, hi. What are you doing here?"

"What am *I* doing here?" she repeated, hovering over Beck like an avenging angel. "Imagine my surprise when I stopped by the church and you weren't there!"

I cringed. Every person in the library was tuned in to our little drama.

I said, "Maybe we should go outside and talk."

Big mistake. Melissa's eyes narrowed, and she plunked down in the chair next to me. She shook a finger in my face. "You have no idea what you're dealing with."

Well, actually, I did, but I wasn't about to share that bit of info with her.

Moving quickly, Beck reached over and wrapped his hand around hers, holding it fast. "Mom," he said. His voice was deep and reassuring. "Look at me."

I watched, fascinated, as Melissa Bradford released me from her furious glare and looked into Beck's eyes. Just as they had the night before, his dark pupils grew until only a narrow rim of gold remained.

"Mom," he repeated. His voice was pitched low so only she and I could hear. "It's fine. Allie knows about us. She needed help with her homework. That's why I'm here instead of church. You always tell Nikki and me to help people."

I thought, *If she falls for that one, Beck's got some serious magic going.*

Melissa stared into Beck's eyes for a long moment then,

with a little shudder, she pulled away. The anger left her face and when she spoke, her voice was calm and reasonable. "Well, I guess it's okay just this once. I'll see you at home."

A collective sigh of relief swept through the library as we all watched Melissa Bradford's exit.

Astonished, I turned to Beck. "What did you just do?"

Looking utterly serious, he said, "I used my dazer."

A dark cloud of suspicion began to form in my mind. "Your *what*?"

"It's a little trick I have," he said. "If I touch people and look into their eyes, I'm able to absorb whatever emotion they are feeling and change it into something different. That's what I did with my mother."

I thought about the kiss we'd shared last night. How he'd manipulated me. Anger flared and set fire to my words. "You used it on me, didn't you . . . last night?"

He reached out, and I scooted my chair away. As it scraped across the floor, it made a horrible shrieking sound and, once again, we were the center of attention. I hissed, "Don't touch me."

Mr. Linde, the boa draped around his neck, approached our table. He peered at me over the top of his glasses. "Everything all right, Allie?"

"Yeah, everything's fine." I waved him away before he could get up close and personal with Buster in tow. I wanted to know more about Beck Bradford and his dazer, and I could only deal with one snake at a time.

Beck's eyes were pleading. I hardened my heart.

"It's not what you think," he whispered. "When I kissed you . . . ?"

He paused and waited until I nodded. "Your eyes were closed. No dazer."

"What about earlier?"

His gaze shifted away from mine.

"And don't lie," I said.

He looked me straight in the eye. "Yeah," he admitted. "I used it. You were scared. I needed you to relax. Do you remember what happened next?"

My mind sifted through the strange events of the previous night. "It was like you were sucking me into your mind." My face was hot with remembering. "Then I heard my mother's voice, warning me."

Beck's eyes flared with emotion. "That's what I'm trying to tell you. You blocked me. The dazer doesn't work on you."

"But, I definitely felt something."

Beck nodded. "It worked for a few seconds. When you threw up a block, it felt like you'd punched me. And you weren't even trying. Think what you could do if you practiced."

I glared at him. "Believe me, Mister, I'll practice." He smiled as the tension surrounding us vanished. I added, "So, watch it!"

I glanced around the room, relieved to see Mr. Linde had put Buster away and was scurrying from window to window, closing the blinds. The Oprah ladies, clutching handfuls of tissues, were listening to one of their members read a passage from the book.

Beck picked up his chair and moved it closer to me. I held my ground.

"Wanna practice right now? You're in a safe place."

"Gee," I said. "I don't want to hurt you."

"I'll risk it."

"Okay, then. Give me your best shot."

He took both my hands in his. "Look at me."

I felt the power of his touch humming through my body and saw my face reflected in the dark pools of his eyes. It felt so good, I smiled and enjoyed the moment. *That's how it works, Allie. He makes you feel good. Makes you forget.* My mother's voice again.

I gathered my strength, gritted my teeth and whispered, "No."

My resistance slammed into Beck and he recoiled, but still clung to my hands. What happened next was so unexpected, so surprising, I could scarcely believe what I was seeing. My French book rose in the air and hovered vertically between us, blocking Beck's eyes. Beck grunted and dropped my hands. I gave a startled squeak, and the French book fell to the table.

Wide-eyed, I scanned the room to see if anyone had noticed. Kizzy had. Under the guise of blowing her nose, she turned away from the group and gave me a thumb's up.

When I looked at Beck, his eyes were back to normal and he was smiling like crazy. "Looks like the old TKP is working just fine."

I shook my head. "Maybe, maybe not."

I leaned close to him and whispered, "It's like I had a power surge. I wasn't trying to make the book move. Geez, what if that happened in the middle of geometry class. Everybody would know I'm a freak."

Beck, taking care not to touch me, whispered back, "I think I know what happened. The air between us was charged, like a force field. You have strong powers. So do I. When they collided . . . well, you saw what happened. Don't worry about it. Okay?'

I nodded, hoping he was right, not just feeding me a bunch of bull so I'd feel better.

Beck extended a finger and touched the moonstone, tucked inside my shirt as usual. "Any change with the moonstone?"

I reached inside my shirt and moved the moonstone one click. "No. Nothing."

Beck thought for a moment then said, "Okay, that's our next challenge."

Suddenly, my head was pounding with pain, not

uncommon after a burst of telekinetic power. "Can't do it tonight, Beck. I'm fried."

"Soon?"

I nodded.

"Okay, people," Mr. Linde announced. "We're getting ready to close. If you have books to check out, please come to the counter."

Beck looked disappointed when I decided to hitch a ride home with Kizzy and Charlie. I hadn't seen her for a few days and, truth be told, I was a still a little ticked off about the whole dazer thing.

Kizzy, of course, was delighted she'd witnessed the return of my TKP. She chattered non-stop all the way home. Most of her conversation was centered around the theme, "I just knew that Bradford boy could help you."

When I unlocked the trailer and went inside, the message light on the phone was blinking. I pressed a button and heard my father's voice.

"Allie, call me when you get in. I don't care how late. It's about your field trip."

My pulse began to race, echoed by the pounding in my temples. *Field trip* was the code we'd agreed upon for moonstone. I knew my father wouldn't call me unless I was in danger. I reached for the phone.

Chapter Thirteen

Mike answered on the first ring. I heard a television blaring in the background and the murmur of voices. A burst of family laughter reminded me of the picture I'd seen on Mike's desk: a blond wife who looked a little like Faye and two blond daughters. Mike also had a son, a dark-haired boy who looked exactly like me. I knew the laugh I'd heard was his because it sounded like mine. A wave of regret swept over me. I didn't even know his name. We'd never met. I was pretty sure he didn't know I existed.

"Just a sec, Allie," Mike murmured.

He spoke to someone else. "Let's go in the den where it's quiet."

I heard the sound of a door opening and closing. Mike told me, "Remember the guy Larry talked about at the Star Seeker meeting? The Trimark informant?"

"Yes."

"He turned up again. Larry's here with me. He wants to talk to you."

"Allie?" I jumped as Larry's deep voice boomed through the receiver

"Hi, Larry."

"Everything okay over your way?"

"Sure, everything's fine," I said, thinking, *Other than the demon mark on my hand and a new boyfriend who enchants people with his dazer.*

Larry got right to the point. "We just found out there's a second prophecy."

I clutched the phone tighter. "So, maybe I'm not the

one who's supposed to have the moonstone."

"Oh, you're supposed to have it all right," Larry said. "The second prophecy follows the other line, the bad guys."

Trimarks. Something in his tone knocked the wind out of me. I sank down on the couch. "Maybe you better start from the beginning."

As I listened to Larry describe what an informant had told him, one of Mrs. Burke's vocabulary words of the week popped into my mind. *Surreal.* I'd experienced the same feeling when Junior and I stumbled upon the first moonstone prophecy. Like I'd been dropped into an alien world with no guide book, no map.

"According to the Trimarks' oral history," Larry said. "the second prophecy goes back to the Gypsy."

I knew from the original moonstone prophecy that the Gypsy had set the moonstone in silver and cleverly added the mechanism allowing it to move in its setting. I also knew he was the father of Magda, the Empath, and through her, an ancestor of Kizzy.

Larry continued, "Magda had a twin brother. His name was Mikhail and, according to our guy, he was the embodiment of evil. Early on, he discovered the moonstone's magic and used it to perform unspeakable acts. Mikhail truly enjoyed the havoc he created, whether it was wielding a bloody knife or watching a house burn to the ground."

"He used the moonstone to do that?" I was having a hard time with the whole concept of 'Moonstone equals evil.'

"There's more to the moonstone than we realized," Larry said. His voice was grim. "It seems that Mikhail used the moonstone *to stop time.*"

To stop time. Stop time? Cold prickles broke on my skin. "Okaaay," I said slowly. "So, what happened then?"

"Allie," Larry's voice implied I was missing a few toys in my attic, one of Brain Dead Roy's favorite sayings. "Imagine what would happen if you could stop time."

It's not like I didn't have a good imagination. I just needed a little help. I gulped air, trying to think. "Well, I suppose if time stopped for everyone except the person with the moonstone, it could be a real advantage."

Yeah, I was winging it.

Larry said, "You could walk into a bank, use the moonstone to stop time, clean out the vault and be gone before anyone knew what happened."

"Oh," I said, in a small voice. "I didn't think of that."

"Mikhail, who was obviously bent in some way, used it to fulfill his need for violence."

I could hear Larry breathing into the phone. I gathered what was left of my courage and said, "Tell me the rest."

"The Gypsy gave the moonstone to Magda. Mikhail was driven from their village."

"That's a good thing. Right?" I asked.

"In some ways, yes," Larry said. "But Mikhail knew the secret of the moonstone's magic. He wanted it back."

I felt a little sick to my stomach. My hand closed over the moonstone pendant against my chest.

Larry said, "You know, of course, that Magda came to America with the moonstone and used it to gain personal wealth."

"Yes," I said. "Do we know what happened to Mikhail?"

"Mikhail joined with others of his kind."

"By others of his kind, you mean . . . ?"

"Trimarks."

"And Mikhail told the Trimarks about the moonstone."

"Exactly," Larry growled. "According to our source, Trimarks meet in a room with a blood-red inverted triangle etched into the wall."

The image gave me cold chills.

"The second prophecy is exactly like the first . . . until it reaches *you*." Larry cleared his throat. I had the distinct feeling he was stalling for time. "At their meetings, each

Trimark stands, extends his right arm, fingers pointing upward, palm facing the inverted triangle on the wall. Together, they recite the original prophecy word for word, with one little addition. After they get to you—the 'Keeper of the Light'—they chant, 'It is our destiny to unleash the full power of the moon. We will not rest until the moonstone is joined with the dark crystal, and the world bows to our will.'"

Yikes! I definitely needed to find a better hiding place for the moonstone.

Larry was quiet, waiting for my reaction.

"That's it?" I asked, knowing he could hear the trembling skepticism in my voice.

"More or less," he hedged.

I knew there was more. He'd given me the edited version, so I wouldn't panic. Part of me was grateful I didn't have to hear what the Trimarks had planned for me. I'd already had one encounter with them. I knew their fondness for cruelty. On the other hand, I needed to know the whole story, so I could protect myself.

I swallowed hard. "So I guess I'm in more danger than I thought."

Larry didn't deny it. "That's why we're sending Ruth Wheeler to Peacock Flats."

I muttered "Uh huh," stalling for time, trying to match a face to the name.

"Ruth paid you a visit in the hospital," Larry prompted.

"Oh, *that* Ruth," I gushed, like I knew so many Ruths I couldn't keep them all straight. Ruth Wheeler was an FBI agent and a Star Seeker. In my own defense, I'd been under the influence of heavy-duty pain meds at the time.

"Yes, *that* Ruth." Larry barked. I got the distinct feeling he wasn't too fond of teenage girls . . . or he'd run out of patience. "Do you want to talk to your father again?"

Good question. Better yet, did he want to talk to *me*?

When I didn't answer, I heard a muffled sound and Mike's booming voice. "Allie?"

"Is Larry still there? I didn't get a chance to thank him."

"I'll pass it on."

Obviously uncomfortable, Mike tried to act like a concerned father, asking about my health and my grades while avoiding all references to Faye. After admonishing me to "be careful" (did he think I was an idiot?) he hung up.

I looked at the small notepad I'd set by the phone in case I needed to jot something down. I picked up the pencil and made a list.

1. Mikhail, Kizzy's uncle, was a psychopath and a Trimark.

2. The moonstone had powers far beyond what we'd formerly believed. It could stop time.

3. There were *two* moonstone prophecies.

4. The Trimarks wanted to kill me, get the moonstone and rule the world.

Okay, that last one scared me a lot. For the umpteenth time, I wished I could give the darn pendant back. I couldn't, of course. The moonstone was *my* destiny.

Even though I'd closed all the shades, I felt the night closing in around me, along with it, a panic attack that grabbed me by the throat and wouldn't let go. I did something I'd never done before. I picked up the phone, dialed Roy's cell and asked Faye when she was coming home.

Chapter Fourteen

"Nicole's trying to go to Versailles," Beck said as he walked me to class after lunch. Much to the disappointment of Donna Jo and Dora Jean, he hadn't joined us at our table. I'd seen him leave campus, probably to take care of some important half-demon business.

"Really?" I chirped, hoping to fake him out while I searched my tired brain for a clue. Was Versailles that new hot clothing store in Vista Valley? The one I couldn't afford?

Beck looked down at me and smiled. Oh yeah, he knew. He said, "Versailles was Louis XVI and Marie Antoinette's palace in France."

"Oh, *that* Versailles. Why does she want to go there?"

He shook his head in disgust. "Stupid reason. She saw some movie about Marie Antoinette and got fixated on the clothes and the servants, completely ignoring the fact that both the king and queen got their heads chopped off."

My brain suddenly kicked into gear. I stopped and looked around before whispering, "You're talking about astral travel . . . right?"

Beck nodded, his amber gaze sweeping over me. I felt a little tingle of awareness.

"You're not wearing the moonstone," he said with a frown. I started walking again. Beck caught up and threw an arm around my shoulders. "Why not?"

Last night, Faye and I agreed we had to hide the moonstone. We put it inside an empty baby food jar and buried it under the apple tree. Faye held the flashlight while I dug a hole directly beneath the crooked branch where

Trilby always hung her wind chimes.

"Too many bad guys want it."

Beck looked irritated, like I'd messed with his homework. "You'll have to wear it if you want me to figure out why it's not working."

It was then I realized I *had* messed with his homework. "Oh, yeah," I said. "Step two in the healing process. Right?"

"Right," he said.

"No dazer this time. Promise?"

"You worried about it?"

I smiled. "Not! Don't forget, buddy boy, I can block you any day of the week."

He gave me a crooked grin and a peck on the cheek.

Beck headed for Physics, and I followed Nicole and her friends into the room where we had Health class two days a week. I wondered if Nicole had made it to Versailles already, without telling Beck. Not that I was surprised she would want to go to an opulent palace in France where Marie Antoinette changed her clothes ten times a day and had servants hovering over her.

I slipped into a desk next to Mercedes, groaning silently when I realized Miss Miller was gone. Her substitute was Mr. Ted, a retire-rehire who should have stayed retired. *Decrepit* doesn't begin to describe Mr. Ted. He's almost totally deaf, but refuses to wear his hearing aids because the feedback keeps him awake.

After a long, painful session of roll-taking—the Hispanic names gave him fits—Mr. Ted shouted, "All right, you yahoos! Boys! You are to go to the other side of this here folding wall where you will be watching a film about examining your boy parts for testicular cancer. Young ladies! You will remain here and watch a film about cancer of the ta-tas. Any questions?"

Ignoring the raucous laughter, Mr. Ted fiddled around with the VCR, told me to press the *play* button and herded the boys around the folding wall. Once the films were underway, we knew he'd sneak off to the boiler room for a snooze.

"Cheap damn school," Sonja Ortega muttered. "Should have a DVD player, not this stupid VCR."

After a thorough round of bitching, the girls settled down and I punched *Play*. Silence reigned as we watched a hot guy, who looked a little like Beck, soaping up in the shower and probing his family jewels for lumps. Apparently, the boys hit *Play* about the same time because I heard Cory Philpott yell, "Titties! All right!"

Oops. Looked like Mr. Ted got the tapes mixed up.

Suzanne Maloney, the prissiest girl at J.J. Peacock H.S.—her socks always matched the ribbon in her hair—shrieked, "Oh my God! Don't look! I'll go tell Mr. Ted."

Nicole Bradford practically levitated out of her chair and hissed, "Oh-no-you-won't!"

Suzanne, who insisted we pronounce her name "Suzonne" which rhymes with "fawn" huffed, "We're *supposed* to be watching the film on breast self-exam. *I* don't want to get in trouble."

She started for the door, a door suddenly blocked by Sonja Ortega's body.

"Sit your butt down, *Suzonne.*" The menace in Sonja's voice was unmistakable.

Suzanne flounced back to her chair, turned it around and stared at the back wall, the very picture of righteous indignation. Sonja and Nicole tapped fists in triumph. We settled in to watch the film, not an easy task what with all the loud, nasty comments coming from the other side of the thin partition.

Ten minutes later, we heard Mr. Ted return to the boys' side and his roar of rage. I hit the *Off* button fast. When he barreled into the room, we were all sitting silently—except for Suzanne—staring at the blank screen.

"Young ladies," he yelled. "Obviously we have a mischief maker in the group. The boys assured me they did not tamper with the video tapes, so it must have been one of *you*."

Say what? We all knew Mr. Ted had been the one to screw up. I saw Sonja Ortega open her mouth, about to say what we all were thinking. I looked at her and shook my head, a silent warning. Her mouth always got her in trouble. For once, she snapped it shut.

Suddenly, Suzanne popped out of her chair, whirled around and pointed at Nicole. "It was her! I saw her do it. I tried to stop her, but she wouldn't listen."

Nicole jumped up. "No way!"

Mr. Ted raked Nicole with an angry glare. Her face was scarlet with embarrassment. "Young lady, you are in big trouble."

Nicole's so-called friends didn't say a word in her defense. They just sat there, taking care not to make eye contact. How chicken-shit is *that*? Okay, so Nicole and I weren't exactly BFF's, but this was beyond lame.

I stood and said, "Mr. Ted, it wasn't Nicole. Suzanne's lying. I know how the tapes got mixed up."

Mr. Ted, his jaw jutting in belligerence, glared at me through watery, bloodshot eyes. "Are you saying it was my fault?"

"Oh, merciful heavens, no! It was an accident."

I'd heard him say "merciful heavens" a bunch of times before and thought it was a nice touch.

He plopped his ample butt on the edge of the desk. "I'm waiting."

"Whoever watched the tapes before you picked them up, put them in the wrong box. It's as simple as that. Certainly none of us would dream of going to the principal to tell him it was your fault. You can count on that."

I looked around at my classmates for support and saw

heads nodding in agreement. I walked over to Suzanne and said, "Right, Suzanne?"

My back was to Mr. Ted. I narrowed my eyes and gave her my meanest look, the one I practiced in the mirror. She looked away and murmured a barely audible, "Mmm hmmm," through tightly compressed lips.

I turned and gave Mr. Ted a big grin. "Well, then, I guess that's settled. Can we try again? With the right tapes?"

Since we had a half-hour left in the class, Mr. Ted liked my suggestion, but this time, he stuck it out on the boys' side.

After class, Suzanne's boyfriend was waiting for her outside the door. Charles Raymond Atkinson Jr., was pale, undersized and equally as prissy as Suzanne, a match made in heaven. Suzanne grabbed his arm, talking a mile a minute. I gathered I was the topic of conversation, because Charles glared at me like I'd inflicted terrible trauma on his beloved. I smiled and waved.

I was headed for French when Nicole caught up with me. Her buddies were nowhere in sight. She slipped a hand through my arm and said, "Hey, Allie. Thanks a lot. You saved my butt back there."

"That's okay. I'm sure you'd do the same for me."

She had enough sense to look embarrassed. We kept on walking. Finally, she said, "Look, I know I've been mean to you. I'm not sure why you helped me, but I want you to know I appreciate it."

I stopped and looked at her. "I though Caitlyn or Lexie would say something."

She blushed and looked away. "Yeah, well, you know, they were afraid they'd get in trouble."

It ticked me off she was so willing to overlook their act of betrayal, but, like Beck said, she'd never had friends before.

"Uh huh," I said, pulling my arm free. "Well, glad I

could help."

As I walked away, she called after me, "I owe you, Allie, and I won't forget."

"Whatever," I mumbled. To tell the truth, I needed time away from the Bradford twins. I had other things to worry about. Like, when was Ruth Wheeler going to pop up in Peacock Flats? I needed her as back-up. Always good to know an FBI agent who's a fellow Star Seeker.

After school, I was on my way to catch the bus and noticed a new guy coming out of Miss Yeager's office. He was standing in profile, studying his schedule. Something about him looked familiar. I slowed down to get a better look. When he looked up and our eyes met, I knew exactly who he was and my brain screeched, "Danger! Danger!"

True, the rings and studs had been removed from his pierced flesh and he was dressed conservatively in jeans and a tee shirt, but he was definitely the guy I'd faced down last year outside Tom's Corner Market. The leader of the PWT's (Proud White Tuffs). He and his buddies had been pounding on Cory Philpott until I used a little magic to stop them. Don't ask me why, because Cory never even said, "Thanks."

The new guy smirked and sauntered over to me. I held my ground, even when he got right up in my face.

"Hey, I remember you," he said, looking me up and down. "You're the freak."

Ignore him, Allie. When I started to walk away, he said, "I'm Shane Boldt. Don't you want to shake hands? Since I'm new and all?"

He held out his right hand, palm up. At the base of his thumb, directly in the fleshy center of his Venus mound, was a partially formed inverted triangle.

I must have made a sound because he lowered his hand. "Oh, yeah. Now you know my little secret."

He grinned and strolled away, leaving me

hyperventilating with frustration. I marched into Miss Yeager's office. She was filing her fingernails into sharp, dagger-like points and humming. She looked up when I entered. "Allie. Just the girl I wanted to see."

I blurted, "You shouldn't let that guy in school. He's in a gang. The school district has a policy about admitting gang kids."

She set her nail file down and rolled her eyes at me. "I firmly believe people deserve a second chance. Shane no longer has gang affiliations. The boy wants an education. Was I supposed to turn him away?"

"There are things about Shane you don't know."

Miss Yeager leaned back in her chair and folded her arms. "Why don't you fill me in?"

Guess what? I just stood there looking stupid and didn't say a word. Pretty hard to explain the world of Trimarks and Star Seekers to a person like Miss Yeager.

"Oh, never mind," I muttered.

"Now, about that counseling session with you and your mother . . ."

"What about it?"

"Monday night. Seven o'clock."

"I'll check with my mom and let you know tomorrow."

I'd just turned to leave when she said, "Tell your mother it would be in her best interests to attend."

It sounded like a threat, and I felt my temper flare. But, instead of getting angry, I just smiled because I knew it would be in Miss Yeager's best interests not to mess with Faye.

Chapter Fifteen

Beck promised to call me after school. When the phone rang, Faye beat me to it. After she answered, she frowned at the phone then glanced at me. "So, you want to talk to my daughter. And you are . . .?"

I smothered a laugh, imagining Beck at the other end of the line, unable to touch my mother and daze her. Served him right! Faye listened for a long time, trying to look stern. She couldn't do it. After a few minutes of listening and murmuring, "Uh huh," the corner of her mouth twitched and her eyes softened. Whoa! Maybe Beck had a telephone dazer I didn't know about.

I held out my hand for the phone.

She waved my hand away and said, "Sure, come on over."

Oh, great! Beck, Faye and I crammed in a twenty-four foot trailer making small talk. I knew Beck had an agenda. If he had his way, we'd be under the apple tree with a flashlight, digging up the moonstone. After hearing about the second prophecy and running into Shane Boldt, I was totally freaked out and confused. I felt a sense of urgency I didn't understand. But, even girls with paranormal powers need a break once in a while. I couldn't handle Beck poking into my mind tonight. The evil doers would just have to wait.

I snatched the phone out of Faye's hand. Ignoring her glare, I said, "Hi, Beck. Tonight won't work for me."

As I said the words, they sounded phony, like I spent every night jet-setting from one party to the next. I felt my cheeks heat up at the lie. Faye rolled her eyes, walked back to the bedroom and turned on the TV.

After a long silence, Beck said, "Are you mad at me about something?"

"No, no," I said. "I'm just tired, that's all."

As I said the words, I realized they were true. I wanted to crawl into bed and go to another place until Ruth Wheeler showed up to help me out. Maybe she would know why Shane Boldt had enrolled in my school. I was positive it had nothing to do with getting an education.

We talked for a while, and it turned out I was right about his agenda. Before he hung up, Beck said, "We need to get together, so I can figure out what's happening with the moonstone. I helped you with the nightmares . . . right?"

I agreed they were gone. But, later that night, that statement proved to be wrong. My jumbled dreams featured Shane Boldt, who suddenly morphed into Magda's evil twin, Mikhail. It was like being in the middle of a horror movie except I couldn't get up and leave during the scary parts. Unable to escape, I watched Mikhail, dressed in a long, black coat, creep into a darkened house and stand over a sleeping couple, fondling a large knife.

I tried to scream, "Wake up!" but had no voice. After a long moment, Shane/Mikhail slipped the knife into his pocket. He stuffed a diamond necklace in his pocket, exited the house and set it on fire. When the couple ran, screaming, from the house, he reached under his coat and pulled out an automatic weapon and began firing. Powerless to stop it, I watched the blood bath, my throat aching with pent-up screams.

I awoke, sweaty and trembling. In my thrashing, I'd knocked the dreamcatcher off the wall. My little pouch of healing stones lay on the floor. I got up, drank a glass of cold water and tacked up the dreamcatcher. I slipped the pouch under my pillow and did some deep breathing to calm my racing heart.

Faye called, "You okay? Sounded like you were fighting demons out there."

"I'm okay." I smiled at her choice of words and thought about Beck, my own personal demon. I remembered the touch of his fingers as they brushed across my forehead and eyelids, leaving a trail of warm, scented liquid. As I drifted into that blissful place between consciousness and deep sleep, I heard his voice wash over me and the words, *Allie Emerson. Bathed in pure, white light, you are restored in mind and spirit. So, shall it be.*

*

The weekend passed without a peep from Ruth Wheeler. I wasn't sure what to do. Sunday night, Faye and I were eating waffles for dinner, our weekly tradition.

"Do you think I should call Mike and ask him?"

At the mention of Mike's name, Faye made a sour face and set her fork down. "What exactly did that man say . . . the one you talked to on the phone?"

"He said they were sending Ruth Wheeler to Peacock Flats."

"That's it?"

I nodded.

"Then she's most likely here, watching out for you. Maybe she's in disguise."

"I'd feel a lot better if I actually knew she was in Peacock Flats. What if something happened to her?"

"Don't borrow trouble," Faye said.

She finished her waffle, picked up a spoon and smeared a thin layer of syrup across her plate. She used the tip of the spoon to draw a heart and wrote *Roy* inside it.

Oh, geez, I wanted to gag.

"What are you, sixteen?" I sputtered.

"I can't help it. I miss him," Faye said.

I knew why she missed him, and it wasn't his sparkling conversation. I didn't want to think about Roy and my mother doing *that*. Eewww! At least she was taking birth control pills. I'd seen them in the medicine cabinet, which meant we wouldn't be adding Brain Dead Roy *Junior* to our little family circle. Thank God.

Faye gave me a wounded look. "I didn't have normal teenage upbringing like you do. I was very unhappy and ran away."

I couldn't believe my ears. "You think this is normal?" I didn't elaborate on the fact that we lived in a travel trailer next to a cow pasture. We'd covered that ground a bunch of times. Instead, I zeroed in on my less-than-normal life.

"Okay, let's start with the fact that I'm supposed to save the world from evil, and the very thing I'm supposed to save it *with* is buried under the apple tree because it's too dangerous to wear. And, oh yes, my super powers aren't exactly super at the moment. I've got bad people after me and the person who's supposed to be helping me is missing."

I popped out of the dinette and starting opening drawers. "You know what the worst part is?" Faye shook her head. "We buried the moonstone to keep it safe. But, what if it's the only thing that *can* keep me safe?"

I finally found what I was looking for and stuffed Roy's Swiss Army knife into the pocket of my jeans.

Faye shook her head in disbelief. "What are you going to do with that? Corkscrew someone to death?"

"Better than nothing."

I slid back into the dinette, feeling a little guilty. None of this was Faye's fault. Since the term "drama queen" had probably been invented for my mother, I had no idea how bad her life had been as a teenager. It might have been something minor, like she got grounded and decided to run away. Or, maybe something awful really had happened to her. I knew her mother died when Faye was ten and Grandpa Claude married Uncle Sid's mother. Maybe now was the time to give it another shot.

"How come you never talk about your family? All I know is you hate Grandpa Claude."

Faye's face closed up. "I have my reasons."

"Tell me."

"I don't want to talk about it."

I usually let it go at this point but her attitude ticked me off. I glared at her. "What if I get some terrible disease and the doctor wants to know my medical history? What am I supposed to say? 'Well, duh, I don't know 'cause my mom doesn't like to talk about it?'"

Faye folded her arms and glared right back at me. "If and when you get that disease, I'll make sure the doctor knows everything he needs to know."

I threw up my hands in disgust and snorted, "Whatever."

I picked up the dirty dishes and put them into the sink. Since Faye had slammed the door on her family history, I gave up. "Remember, we have to go for counseling tomorrow night."

Faye nodded absently. She'd been strangely silent on the subject. I didn't have a clue how she felt.

"I'm going to Kizzy's after school, so pick me up at quarter of seven. Okay?"

She nodded again. When the phone rang, her face lit up. Roy. She took the cordless phone back to her bedroom and shut the door. I cleaned up the kitchen and did my homework.

*

After school Monday, I got off the bus at Kizzy's house. She'd been after me to stop by. I was curious to find out what she knew about the Bradford twins. Sure, she thought

Beck was my healer, but did she know about the demon thing? I also wanted to talk to her about Mikhail.

We sat side by side on stools at the kitchen bar and sipped hot chocolate. Kizzy looked at me and smiled. "How are you getting along with the half-demon boy?"

My mouth dropped open, and I stared at her wordlessly.

Kizzy's sparkling turquoise eyes danced with delight. "You thought I didn't know Beck had demon blood?" .

I gulped. "Well, how *did* you know?"

"Allie, you know I saw them that night in the gym. Halloween night. I spoke with Beck and I could tell he was a healer. Good-looking kid, for a half-demon."

"You could tell Beck and Nicole were half-demons by *looking* at them?"

"Deductive reasoning, Alfrieda. I knew Melissa Bradford left the convent and went to Europe, then returned with twins that were surely conceived before she left. When I saw the twins, I knew."

"But how?"

"My dear, their eyes glow, a sure sign of demon blood. Surely you've noticed."

"Well, yeah," I sputtered. "Now that I know what to look for."

Kizzy smiled and sipped her hot chocolate. "I *was* looking for it. Since I know incubi often frequent convents, it was a simple conclusion. Really."

I shook my head in disbelief. "You're amazing."

Kizzy leaned closer and gave me a mischievous wink. "I think the half-demon boy is sweet on you."

I let that comment go by without a response. The fact that Kizzy knew about the Bradford twins made the next part of the conversation a lot easier.

"Beck thinks he can figure out the mind-reading thing with the moonstone," I told her. "We need to get together, but his mother doesn't exactly like me. Would you mind if we meet here?"

Always the gracious hostess, Kizzy said, "I'd be delighted." She hopped off her stool. "Now I have a special treat for you."

I slurped my hot chocolate and watched Kizzy bustle around the kitchen, pulling out pots, pans, a wooden cutting board and a huge meat cleaver, the kind you see in horror movies.

"I'm going to teach you how to make goulash," she announced as she extracted an amazing variety of vegetables from the refrigerator. Potatoes, green peppers, celery, tomatoes, onion, garlic and a couple of things I couldn't identify.

"My mother's special recipe," she said.

She set the recipe on the counter in front of me. The recipe was hand written in tiny, precise script on paper creased with age and splattered with tomato sauce. Across the top were the words "Magda's Special Goulash"

Magda. Mikhail. The moonstone. A shiver crawled down my spine.

I chopped vegetables and tried to decide what to do while Kizzy browned beef cubes. Finally, I made a decision. "Kizzy, did Magda ever mention a brother?"

Once again, Kizzy surprised me. She wiped her hands on her apron and looked over at me. "Are you talking about Mikhail?"

I nodded.

She frowned. "How do you know about Mikhail?"

I told her what Larry had learned, but made it sound like a fairy tale. In fact, by the time I finished the story, Mikhail wasn't the vicious psychopath described by Larry. He was the village bad boy. In my own defense, I was talking about Kizzy's blood kin, her uncle. If she knew he was a Trimark, she'd feel guilty about giving me the moonstone.

Kizzy covered the pot and turned the heat down. "That

sounds about right. Mother said he'd been banished from the village. That's when their father, the Gypsy from the prophecy, gave the moonstone to Magda."

I'd left out important stuff, like Mikhail hooking up with the Trimarks and the second prophecy. I could tell Kizzy was waiting for me to tell her more. When I didn't elaborate, she said, "Strange this Larry person would call and tell you about Mikhail. I wonder why."

Mental slap upside the head. I'd brought this up . . . *why*? I scrambled for an answer. "Well, uh, I guess he thought it was important."

I lifted my hands helplessly. "I have *no* idea why he thought I needed to know."

I was a terrible liar. Kizzy studied my face, but all she said was, "Hmmm."

At 6:45 p.m., stuffed to the gills with Magda's Special Goulash, I watched out the window for Faye. 6: 50 p.m. No Faye. At 6:55, I was officially worried. I called home. No answer. She showed up two minutes before seven and parked in front of Kizzy's house with the nose of the truck in the hedge and the rear sticking out on the road. I thanked Kizzy, grabbed my coat and backpack and dashed out to the truck.

"Here, you drive." Faye dropped the keys in my hand.

I smelled her breath and my heart sank. "You've been drinking."

She gave me a lopsided grin. "I was nervous about meeting Ms. Yeager."

Great. Now, so was I.

Chapter Sixteen

My mother's not an alcoholic. She only drinks when she anxious, bored, scared or celebrating something. Okay, maybe she has a little problem. But, she does go for days without drinking a drop. I know. I know. I shouldn't make excuses for her drinking. She already has an ample supply of excuses. She doesn't need my help.

When I saw Faye's condition, I was seriously freaked out, because when she drinks, she talks too much. I thought about all of the above as we drove to the school and came to the following conclusion: Our butts were in a sling!

"I only had two glasses of wine."

Faye was popping breath mints and peering at me through the dim dashboard light. "I think."

She couldn't remember how much she'd drunk. Great. Just great.

"Okay, okay." I tried not to hyperventilate. "We need a plan."

It was hard, but I reined in my anger. I knew from past experience, it would only make things worse.

"Let me do the talking, okay?"

Faye nodded solemnly.

"Don't offer to shake hands. The woman has a nose like a bloodhound. If she asks you something directly, stick to simple answers like, 'Yes. No. Just fine. I don't know.' Or . . . 'You should ask Allie that question.'"

For the remainder of our short trip, we practiced.

Me: "How is your relationship with your daughter?"

Faye: "Just fine."

Me: (sarcastically) "Oh, really! That's not what I heard."

Faye: "You should ask Allie that question."

I was feeling better when we pulled into the school parking lot. Faye was reciting her lines like a pro. The parking lot was deserted except for Miss Yeager's Honda SUV. I parked the truck, turned to Faye and repeated the first line of our silly little ritual. "I'm stickin' to you . . . Like Elmer's glue," Faye said, with a goofy grin.

We bumped fists and marched into the school, arm in arm. Drunken, screwed-up mother and freakoid daughter, ready and willing to do battle with the nosy school counselor.

Miss Yeager, looking extremely pissed, was waiting for us.

"Sorry, we're late," I said, a frozen smile stuck on my face. I was relieved to see she'd tossed the bean bag chair in the corner and replaced it with three chairs set in a circle. Hers, of course, had a big, cushy seat and padded arms.

I made the introductions. Faye, as per instructions, did not offer to shake hands.

Before Miss Yeager could start firing questions, I launched into my cover story. "My mother's on cold medicine. It makes her a little spacey."

Ms. Yeager stared at Faye, blinking rapidly. "Over-the-counter meds?"

Faye said, "Just fine."

Miss Yeager frowned at Faye's inappropriate answer so I gave a little cluck of amusement. "See what I mean? Of course, over-the-counter. What else would they be?"

Fortunately, Faye pulled it together and we plowed through the first painful half hour. I could see Miss Yeager was getting frustrated by my mother's repetitive answers, but that was *her* problem. We were racing toward the finish line when Miss Yeager came up with the one topic that pushed all Faye's buttons.

"I understand your father has a big house in Vista Valley

and would like you and Allie to move in with him," she said.

Faye snapped to attention, her body rigid with anger. "Why the hell are you bringing up my father? That topic is off limits. Besides, you should be counseling Allie, not me. She's the one with the nightmares. She's the one who's lost her powers."

All at once Faye realized what she'd said. She gasped and clapped a hand over her mouth.

"Hours," I said. "She meant to say I've lost *hours*. Oh my God, the hours of sleep I've lost from those stupid nightmares."

Miss Yeager's eyes reminded me of pictures I've seen of raptors spotting their prey. Her gaze darted back and forth between Faye and me like she was deciding which one of us to nail with her razor-like talons.

She picked me. "It sounded like your mother said *powers . . .* not *hours*."

"It's that damn cold medicine," Faye said. "Gets my tongue all tangled up."

I nodded my head vigorously, afraid if I opened my mouth it would make things worse.

Miss Yeager glanced at her watch. "Our time is about up. I believe I have enough information to compile a report for your case worker."

I grabbed Faye's arm and pulled her out of her chair. Before we stepped through the door to blessed freedom, I said, "What do you plan to say in this report?"

"Nice try, Allie," Miss Yeager said. "You'll just have to wait."

Now I was scared. "Be sure to say Faye was on cold medicine."

She gave me a smug smile. "Oh, yes. I'll be sure to mention *that*."

I didn't like her tone, but I'd done the best I could do,

considering the circumstances.

"Okay then," I said. "See you tomorrow."

Faye was silent on the trip home. When I pulled into the driveway and turned the truck off, Faye grabbed my hand. Her eyes were bright with tears.

"I can't lose you."

I kissed her cheek. "Lose me? Are you nuts? It will be fine. I promise."

Please God, I prayed, help me keep that promise.

*

The next day I was sitting in my keyboarding class when I was called to Mr. Hostetler's office. I knew why. I'd tried to see him earlier but, according to Alice, his secretary, he was in a parent conference. I wanted to tell him there had been another ass-pinching incident. I'd been stuffing my coat inside my locker when the assault on my buttocks occurred. After my shriek of pain, I'd spun around to see who was walking by and wrote down the names of everyone I saw. Ten in all.

List in hand, I presented myself to Alice, who gave me a strange look.

"Did you tell him I have suspects?"

Alice shook her head. "I don't think this is about the ass pincher, honey."

She picked up the phone and punched a button. "Allie Emerson is here, Mr. Hostetler."

Startled, I tried to think if I'd broken any important rules. Mr. Hostetler came out of his office and pulled the door shut. He took my arm and guided me a few steps away from Alice's desk. This was getting stranger by the minute.

When he spoke, his voice was low. "Allie, there's someone here who wants to meet you, but in order for that to happen, I need permission from your mother."

I heaved a sigh of relief. Ruth Wheeler had arrived. Finally.

"Well, sure," I said. "I'd love to see her again."

Mr. Hostetler's brows shot up and, like two fuzzy caterpillars, crawled together to meet over the bridge of his nose.

"Her who?" he said.

"It's not a 'her?'" I asked, still clinging to my dream of back-up.

"No, Allie," he said. "It's your grandfather, Claude Emerson."

The breath whooshed out of my lungs. I must have looked like a deer caught in the headlights because Mr. Hostetler said, "Your choice entirely."

My grandfather! The very person I'd been whining about when I accused Faye of keeping secrets. It must run in the family, because good old Grandpa Claude had pulled the ultimate fast one. He'd sidestepped Faye so he could meet me at school.

Mr. Hostetler was still peering at me anxiously. "Do you want me to call your mother?"

Oh, geez. Visions of Faye on a rampage, appeared in my mind like lead stories from the evening news, complete with soundtrack . . . "Stay tuned," said the anchor man in my head, "for the tragic story of a bloodbath at John J. Peacock High School . . ."

"Allie?" Mr. Hostetler spoke again.

"Absolutely not."

*

After French class, I spent a few minutes talking to Mrs. Burke, which meant I had to run like a maniac to catch the bus before it took off. Patti was just about to pull away when I ran up. It was then I spotted the black Suburban parked behind the bus. A man stepped out of the car and called, "Allie Emerson?"

He was dressed in a dark suit, pale blue dress shirt and tie. I stopped, dead still and watched him walk toward me.

"I'm Claude Emerson, your grandfather. I'd like to talk to you."

All my life, Faye had refused to talk about this man. I was caught in the jaws of a dilemma. I wanted to know more about my mother's family, but what if Faye was justified in protecting me from her father?

The doors of the school bus whooshed open. Patti yelled, "Get your butt in here, girl!"

My grandfather said, "I'll see that you get home."

No way was I getting into that Suburban. "That's okay," I said. "I should get on the bus."

"There's a taxi parked behind my car. When we're done talking, you hop in the taxi and catch a ride home."

I took a step back and peered around his car. Sure enough, a yellow cab was parked next to the curb.

"Allie!" Patti's voice had risen to a screech.

I had to make a decision. What if this was my only chance to learn more about mother's family?

"It's okay, Patti," I said. "I've got a ride home."

Patti peered out the door, her eyes narrowed in suspicion. "You sure?"

I nodded.

"Okay then, but I'll look for you on my second run. If you need a ride, you wait right here. Got it?"

"Got it," I said.

When the bus pulled away, I checked out my grandfather. He had an ax blade of a nose and eyes as black as coal. His clothes hung on him like he'd recently lost weight. I saw nothing of Faye in him. We studied each other silently.

"Is there someplace we can talk?" he asked.

He must have realized I wasn't about to jump in a stranger's car. I pointed to the little pocket park across the street from the school. "There's a bench over there."

We walked in silence to the bench. Dark clouds driven by a brisk wind scudded overhead. I shivered and zipped up my coat.

We sat on a cold concrete bench with two feet of space between us. He checked me out again, then shook his head in wonder. "Alfrieda Carlotta Emerson, I can't believe how much you look like her."

Since I'd been named for his mother, I assumed he was talking about her. Of course, my curly hair and green eyes were from my dad.

"Oh?" I said politely. "Well, maybe it's because we have the same name."

He looked puzzled for a minute. "No, I'm not talking about my mother. I'm talking about *her*. Faye's mother, Melia."

"Melia," I repeated, rolling the name around on my tongue. It tasted good, like sweet, dark chocolate. "I didn't know I had a grandmother named Melia."

Grandpa Claude continued to study me. His eyes were like pools of ink, so dark they didn't even reflect the light. The silence grew and I started to squirm, trying desperately to think of something to say.

I started babbling. "Uh, Faye told me her mother died when she was ten and that she doesn't remember her. I don't believe her, though 'cause I can remember all kinds of stuff from when I was ten."

He smiled, and the smile grew into a burst of choking laughter, painful to hear.

"You're a smart girl," he said. "Faye lies a lot. She's probably lied about me."

He waited to see if I'd respond. I didn't.

"Melia didn't die. She left," he said.

"She didn't die?" I repeated. "But why would Faye lie about it?"

"Have you ever wondered why your mother is so unhappy?" Claude Emerson said. "She drinks too much. Her relationships fail. She is unable to become an adult."

I'd never thought about it in those terms, but, in a sense, he was right. *I* was the functioning adult in the family.

I shrugged like it didn't matter. "It's just how it is. The way it's always been."

"What do you know about your mother's history?"

"Nothing!" burst from me before I could stop it. I lowered my voice. "Faye doesn't like to talk about it. I don't know why. Does our family have some horrible genetic disease?"

That really struck him funny. He started to laugh, but it turned into a spasm of uncontrollable coughing that scared the hell out of me. I clapped a hand over my mouth in horror. When he stopped coughing, I said, "Are you all right?"

He pulled a snowy white handkerchief from his pocket and held it to his mouth. When he could speak, he said, "To answer one of your questions, no, I'm not all right. That's why I'm here. I wanted to see my only grandchild before I die."

I must have looked as shocked as I felt, because he said, "It's okay. I know I'm dying. I've had time to get used to it, and I won't be kicking off for a year or so."

I didn't know what to say, so I stared at my feet.

"Your other question? The one about the horrible genetic disease?" he said, "I have cancer, plain and simple. The family history I was talking about involves your grandmother. Your mother needs to tell you about Melia."

She never will, I thought. "Would you tell me, please?"

"No," he said flatly. "It's up to her. But, until Faye accepts who she is, she will continue to be unhappy."

I was puzzled by his choice of words. "What do you

mean?"

He didn't answer my question. Instead, he stared at me for a full minute with those opaque, black eyes. Finally, he stood. "We'll meet again, Alfrieda."

"Almost everybody calls me Allie."

"Everybody but me," he said.

Chapter Seventeen

Confession time. I'm not above using emotional blackmail. Probably says something about my character. When dealing with Faye, I had to use all the weapons in my arsenal and pick my battles carefully. That's why I chose not to pester her with questions about the Grandpa Claude/ Grandmother Melia mystery. No way would I be able to guilt Faye into spilling it.

Instead, I'd use my leverage to let Faye in on the Beck/ moonstone/healing scenario. The stars were in the proper alignment for Faye and Beck to meet, because my mother was feeling bad about screwing up our session with Miss Yeager. With Faye, timing was important.

On Wednesday, Faye worked the early shift. I knew she'd be home after school so I asked Beck if he wanted to take a look at the moonstone. His eyes lit up with a flare of amber that told me he was *intensely* interested. He insisted on driving me home. I wasn't real happy about Beck seeing how we lived, but sometimes you have to separate the big stuff from the little stuff. How I lived wasn't a big deal. Getting my powers back . . . *that* was important. Especially now, when I wasn't sure if Ruth Wheeler was still in the picture.

Thank God for small favors! Faye was outside, bundled up in jeans and a heavy sweater, raking up leaves under the apple tree. Blaster the bull was grazing over the other side of the fence. She leaned on the rake and watched us get out of the Ranger, her gaze fixed on Beck. As we approached, Blaster lifted his tail and let loose with a thunderous fart.

Faye and I were so used to it, we hardly noticed, but Beck stopped dead in his tracks. "Was that the bull?'

I took Beck's hand, pulled him over to Faye and made the introductions. It went something like this:

"Hi, Faye. This is my friend, Beck Bradford. He's a healer. We need to dig up the moonstone so he can figure out why it's not working."

Faye's eyes widened in surprise.

"Hi, Ms. Emerson." Beck stuck out his hand for her to shake.

She waited a few ticks before wiping her hand on her jeans and placing it in his. I hid a smile as I watched Beck do his thing. He clasped her hand in both of his and looked down at her. "It's nice to meet you."

Faye stood motionless, gazing into Beck's eyes. After a few moments, I could tell the large dose of dazer was working its magic. Her lips curled in a smile.

"The mystery boyfriend." She freed her hand. "I wondered when I would get to meet you."

"Not my boyfriend," I mumbled.

Faye and Beck both looked at me like they were humoring a cranky child.

"Oh, right." Faye's voice was dripping with sarcasm. "Excuse the hell out of me."

My face was hot with embarrassment. "I'll get the shovel."

Faye pointed out the spot and Beck dug, taking care not to hit the jar with the shovel. I fished the moonstone out of the jar and slipped it over my head.

"We have to go to Kizzy's to do this," I told my mother.

"Hold it," Faye ordered. "Exactly what does this *healing* involve?"

Beck said, "First of all, I have to figure out how Allie was using the moonstone to read minds. Granted, she has special powers, but there has to be a scientific principle involved. I'll need to know where she was standing in relationship to the other people and . . ."

Beck droned on and on, using words like alpha particles, unpolarized light and photons. By the time he got to Kepler's second law, Faye's eyes glazed over and I was thinking, *"Please, God, make him stop."*

He paused to draw a breath. Faye flapped her hands in dismissal. "Okay, okay. Sounds harmless enough. Tell Kizzy 'Hi.'"

When we backed down the driveway, she returned to her raking. Thinking about what was in store for me, the idea of raking leaves seemed like a better way to spend the afternoon. Maybe I should stay home and help Faye, or maybe I should develop a killer headache and take to my bed. But, I couldn't bring myself to rain on Beck's parade.

Kizzy ordered pizza, delighted to have company for the evening. I could tell she was curious about Beck's personal history, but she refrained from asking too many embarrassing questions. He managed to daze her without making physical contact. His smile did the trick. Of course, Kizzy *was* still recovering from a head injury.

After we ate, Kizzy went into the living room to watch the news, leaving Beck and me alone in the kitchen. He pulled a physics book, paper and pencil from his backpack and put them on the table. I braced myself for more scientific gibberish, but he surprised me.

"Turn your chair to face me."

He pulled his chair close to mine. When our knees touched, he reached over and took my hands. His touch affected me like it always did. A river of sensation flowed through my veins, leaving its heated imprint on every cell in my body. It made me feel weird, out of control. I tried to pull my hands away. His grip tightened.

"Allie, your resistance is slamming me. I can't work with that."

I pulled my hands away. "You're trying to daze me."

"Call it what you want. You have to let me into your mind if you want this to work."

"What about the scientific principle? Or was that just a bunch of bull you told Faye to get her to trust you?"

"No, but first I have questions, and I need to touch you when you answer."

I was still suspicious. "Why?"

He glanced out the window into the growing darkness. A muscle jumped in his clenched jaw. When he spoke, he avoided my eyes. "Okay, you're going to make me say it. Since I'm not fully human, I can sense things beyond the spoken word. It's possible I might be able to pick up something you've forgotten."

Finally, he looked at me and held out his hands. "It's nightfall. My senses are keen. I need to touch you, Allie."

It wasn't his words that grabbed my heart. It was the sadness in his voice.

I nodded and placed my hands in his. He gripped them lightly.

"Tell me about the first time you tapped into someone's mind, Allie."

"I was in the back seat of Matt's Jeep. Matt is Faye's stepbrother's son, and I had a huge crush on him last year."

Beck's fingers tightened around mine. He frowned. "Why were you in the back seat?"

I grinned at him, enjoying his discomfort. "Oh, yeah, that sounded bad. I was walking home from the store when Matt and his girlfriend, Summer, drove by. Matt stopped to give me a ride."

"So Matt and Summer were in the front and you were in the back?"

When I nodded, he released my hands and made a sketch on the notebook paper.

"Then what happened?" He took hold of my hands

again.

"Summer was being a bitch. She kept making snotty comments, tossing her hair around and playing with her necklace. I decided to show her a real piece of jewelry. The moonstone."

Beck smiled and shook his head sadly. "Women."

"I know. Kinda silly, huh? Anyway, when I pulled it out of my shirt, I accidentally turned it one click clockwise."

He let go of my hands. "Show me."

I turned the moonstone in its setting, expecting to feel nothing. My right hand covered the moonstone, my left reached out for Beck's. I gasped as a strong current of power flowed between us. The moonstone was eerily warm, like it had responded to my hand touching his. All at once, the room exploded into a riot of color and sensation. Fragrance drifted from a bowl of oranges, flooding my senses with their heady aroma. Silver light danced on the surface of the knife Kizzy had used to cut the pizza. A red dishtowel hanging from a hook on a white wall throbbed with pulsating energy.

I looked into Beck's eyes and was drawn into their amber depths. This time, I didn't resist. A feeling of peace stole through my body. Maybe it was the moonstone. Maybe it was because I felt my strength matched his. I don't have a logical explanation or the words to describe my state of mind other than to say it *just felt right.*

My mind reached out and joined with his, open and trusting, connecting in a way we'd never done before. A brilliant blue aura danced above his head, a vaporous crown held by invisible hands. I leaned closer until I could feel the warmth of his breath on my face. We were bathed in blue light as Beck's aura swirled around both of us.

When, finally, I pulled away, I turned the moonstone back one click and released his hand, breaking the spell.

He looked puzzled. "What just happened?"

I smiled at him, trying to think how to begin. "You felt it, didn't you? The moonstone's power."

He nodded. His gaze was intense. "Your mind was reaching out to mine. Could you read my thoughts?"

This was the first time our relationship had been on an equal footing. I liked it.

"No," I said. "But I felt our connection. The colors were so bright I could almost taste them. Exactly the same thing happened in Matt's Jeep that day. The sky turned an unreal shade of blue. I could smell apples even though the trees were still in blossom."

Beck thought for a while, then took my hands and asked me a bunch of questions . . .where exactly was I sitting in the Jeep? Whose mind did I read first? Did I hear their thoughts out loud, or did I read them like a book? Finally, he dropped my hands, drew some more sketches and thumbed through the physics book.

He tucked the pencil behind his ear. "What about the second incident?"

We were off and running again. This time, the scene was Kizzy's hospital room. I'd walked in on Chris Revelle, who'd been about to smother Kizzy. Not only had I read bits and snatches of Revelle's thoughts, I'd seen a smudged aura hovering over him like a nasty thunder cloud.

More questions. Where was I standing in relationship to Revelle and Kizzy? Did I move closer or further away when I read Revelle's mind? More notes. More sketches. When I looked at the clock, I was surprised to see two hours had passed. Inky darkness pressed against the window panes, the stars and moon hidden by a thick blanket of clouds.

Some people get depressed when they can't see the sun. As long as I can remember, I've felt connected to the moon. When it's hidden, my world tilts slightly off-center. I get restless and out of sorts. Such was my feeling as I gazed out into a night so dark it made me think of my grandfather's eyes.

Beck looked up from his notes. "Something wrong?"

I forced a smile. "Nope."

The corner of his mouth quirked up in a brief smile. He didn't believe me. In the fullness of night, hunky Beck was back. He was dressed in a plain white tee shirt with a surfing logo. Earlier today, he'd looked like a typical, though extremely hot, teenage guy. But, now . . . whew! His eyes smoldered with intensity as he studied my face. His shirt clung to him like a second skin, skimming over the sculpted muscles of his chest and arms. His physical attraction was like a magnetic force field pulling me in.

To keep from giving into it, I gave myself a vicious pinch on the thigh and tried to figure out what Beck had that other guys didn't, other than the demon thing, of course.

My answer? Pheromones. Lots and lots of pheromones. He probably had way more of the stuff than the average guy. This reminded me of a film I'd seen in biology class, starring a studly male moth who used pheromones to attract every female moth within a six mile radius. Yeah, that Beck was a dangerous boy when the sun went down. Then again, he was part incubus, and daddy incubus *had* seduced a nun-in-training! Note to self: watch it, Allie!

The interest in Beck's eyes was unmistakable. "What are you thinking?"

Whoa! Maybe I wasn't the only one who could read minds.

"Nothing much," I lied. "Do you have a theory yet?"

His heated gaze cooled down, and Brainiac Beck reappeared. He shuffled papers until he found the one he wanted. "I have a working theory, but it will have to be tested."

"Tested how?"

"Do you know what a vortex is?" Beck asked.

"It's a swirly thing, like a tornado."

He gave me an indulgent smile, the kind parents give their kids when they say something cute but utterly stupid. "Yes, in its simplest terms."

"So, what now?"

He stared at me for a long moment then dug a cell phone out of his pocket. "Now, I call Nightwalker."

It took me a few seconds to remember who Nightwalker was. "Oh, yeah, the Indian guy who taught you how to heal."

I wondered out into the living room and found Kizzy snoozing in front of the TV. I'd just curled up on the couch next to her when Beck burst into the room. His smile was huge, his eyes sparkling with excitement.

"I figured it out," he said. "But it has to be tested. We need three people."

Chapter Eighteen

"Allie." Beck pointed to a spot on the kitchen floor. "You stand there."

I trotted to my appointed spot.

"Ms. Lovell?"

"Call me Kizzy, dear."

"Kizzy, would you please stand over here?"

Kizzy, still looking a bit groggy, walked to the place Beck indicated.

"And now," he positioned himself equidistance from Kizzy and me, "We have an equilateral triangle. Turn the moonstone one click, Allie."

I took a deep breath and did what he asked. Even though my senses sharpened, I was unable to pick up anyone's thoughts. Beck gazed at me expectantly. I shrugged.

"Nothing."

Instead of looking disappointed, Beck looked relieved. "Good. Turn it back to its original setting and, Kizzy, you move a couple of feet toward me so we're still forming a triangle but with unequal sides."

When he was satisfied with our arrangement, he turned to me. "Try it again."

With one click of the moonstone, I was inside a rainbow, a place of such unearthly beauty, I reached out a hand to watch the play of colors against my skin. I heard someone say, "Ooohhh." It sounded like my voice, but I wasn't aware I'd spoken aloud.

"Allie." Beck's deep voice invaded my mystical rainbow world. "Look at me."

With my right hand still touching the moonstone, I looked at Beck who was, once again, crowned with a brilliant blue aura. His lips didn't move, but I clearly heard the thoughts in his head.

In answer to the question I read in his mind, I smiled and said, "Yes."

He grinned and signaled thumbs up.

"Now, look at Kizzy," he said. "Move if you have to."

I didn't have to move. Kizzy's thoughts appeared as beautiful turquoise bubbles the exact color of her eyes. It was like looking into a simmering pot of turquoise fudge. A swelling bubble would rise to the smooth surface of her mind and burst, only to have another take its place. Every thought was the same. "I'm sorry the moonstone has caused you grief," she said. "Oh, Allie, I'm so sorry."

When I saw a tear slide down her face, I couldn't stand it. I clicked the moonstone back, closed the distance between us and hugged her, shocked at how fragile her body felt. My tears mingled with hers.

"Don't be sorry," I whispered. "I can handle it."

I smoothed the hair away from her face, patted her cheek and spoke loudly enough for Beck to hear. "If you hadn't given me the moonstone, Demon Boy here wouldn't have looked at me twice."

"Not true," Beck said, the air around him vibrating with excitement. I was pretty sure his happiness had nothing to do with our personal relationship and everything to do with proving his theory was right.

"Let's try it again," Beck said. "You feel okay?"

When I first got the moonstone, using it made me dizzy and disoriented. But now, I had none of the negative effects. If anything, my world seemed to be in sharper focus.

"I'm fine," I said. "This time, don't try to send anything. Just let your minds wander."

We tried it again. When I peeked inside Beck's mind, it

was like watching an armed conflict. The Body versus the Brain. He thought I was really hot. In fact, he could hardly keep his hands off me. But, his brainy part kept telling him, "Cool it! Deal with the facts, not the emotion."

There was definitely a downside to telepathy. I wondered if this was status quo for Beck, if he had to fight the duality of his nature on a daily basis. It would make me crazy.

I turned to Kizzy. She was wondering if Beck and I were an item and what would happen when Junior came back. Good question.

Both looked at me expectantly. No way was I going to blab about what I'd picked from their brains. All I said was, "Clear as a bell. Let's take a break."

Kizzy led us into the living room. She settled into her recliner. I sat next to Beck on the couch.

"So, how did you figure it out?" I asked.

Beck leaned forward, his elbows on his knees. "My original theory was based on the moonstone creating a magnetic field that resulted in a vortex. Once the vortex occurred, you were able to access the thoughts of another person."

"So, is that what just happened?"

"No," Beck said. "I knew there had to be more to it than that. That's why I called Jed Nightwalker. I described the physical set-up, the fact that three people had been present when it happened before. He said we needed to apply the rule of three."

Kizzy smiled and nodded.

I said, "Okay, I'll bite. What's the rule of three?"

Beck stabbed a hand through his hair and continued. "If three people form an equilateral triangle, the space between them is static. But, if you change to a triangle where all the angles are different, a dynamic interaction occurs."

"That's what happened when you told me to move closer to you," Kizzy said.

"Exactly," Beck said. "When we changed the angles, a vortex was created. In other words, the conditions allowed Allie to become a telepath."

"Nightwalker must have been a whiz in geometry," I muttered.

Kizzy snapped her recliner into an upright position. "Did he mention anything else about the rule of three?"

"Yes, he did. I wondered if you knew about that," Beck said.

Kizzy nodded. "Of course I do. In the world of magic, the rule of three means the actions you take affect you physically, emotionally and spiritually. It's a reminder that forces greater than ourselves exist. If we misuse power, the deeds will come back to us threefold."

"Yes," Beck said. "That's exactly what Nightwalker said."

Since I was the one with the moonstone, therefore the power, I couldn't help but apply the rule of three to my own past actions. Kizzy's words grabbed me by the throat and squeezed. When I spoke, my voice was choked with emotion. "That's what happened to me when I killed Baxter with the apple bins."

Kizzy and Beck stared at me, wide-eyed, as I enumerated my points. "Number one, the physical aspect: I was badly injured. Number two, the emotional aspect: I had killer nightmares. Number three, the spiritual aspect: I lost my powers. Does the rule of three mean I should watch out for falling apple bins?"

I meant the last statement as a joke, but it came out all wrong. To my utter embarrassment, hot, stinging tears welled up in my eyes. Kizzy popped out of her chair, sat next to me and took my hand.

"You saved your mother's life," she said, stroking my hand. "The man who died would have killed you both, and the moonstone would be in the hands of the Trimarks. Do you think they'd use the moonstone for the greater good?"

When I didn't answer, she said, "You did what you had to do. Don't waste one more second of your precious life worrying about Baxter." She gave me a little shake. "Are we clear on that?"

As I gazed into Kizzy's sparkling eyes, the puzzle pieces of my jumbled life clicked together to form a complete, perfect picture. Why, at that particular moment? I don't know. It's not like Kizzy hadn't said the exact same thing dozens of times. Maybe it was because Beck had blocked my nightmares. Or, had the moonstone made me more receptive? Whatever the reason, the time had come to let go of the guilt.

I squeezed Kizzy's hand. "Yes, ma'am, I'm clear on that. Thank you."

Beck looked at me, relief in his eyes. "I think Kizzy's a healer too."

I heaved a huge sigh. "Maybe it's better not to know what people are thinking."

Kizzy patted my hand. "You may be right."

Apparently, unseemly emotional displays by females did not hinder Beck's appetite, because he polished off the rest of the pizza before he drove me home. He turned off the truck when we pulled into the driveway. The weather had taken a turn for the worse. Driven by an icy wind, sleet soon covered the windshield.

"You want to come in?"

"It's late. I should get home."

He made no move to start the truck. He slipped an arm around my shoulders and pulled me close.

"You did it," he said, nuzzling my ear. "You actually read my mind."

I responded by answering the question I'd read in his mind. "Yes, I'd love to go to the dance with you."

He gave a little growl of pleasure and nipped at my

earlobe. I pulled away and flashed the moonstone at him. "Back off, demon boy. You've met your match."

My statement had the ring of truth and he knew it. He also knew I was drawn to him. I'd felt the pull of his physical attraction too many times to deny it. But, I could block his dazer. I could counter his magic with my own. I liked Beck a lot. Maybe I even loved him a little, but we had achieved a balance of power, and that was just fine with me.

He touched the moonstone, dragged his forefinger along the sensitive skin of my neck and tilted my chin back.

"You still have the demon mark, right?"

"Um hum." I knew where he was going and I was along for the ride.

"And you're wearing the moonstone."

"Right again."

"Remember my theory about the moonstone driving the demon DNA out of your body?"

I nodded.

"And wondering if the moonstone would block it if I kissed you again? Since we're testing theories . . ."

"Mr. Science Guy," I murmured before his lips touched mine. My arms went around his neck. Somewhere, in the back of my mind, Faye's voice was telling me I was a little *too* willing to test this theory. But, inquiring minds want to know.

His hand went to the back of my head. His lips were surprisingly soft with none of the heated urgency of our previous kiss. If anything, I was the aggressor, pulling him closer, wanting to feel the muscular strength of his body against mine. When his tongue slipped between my teeth, I forgot about demon marks and let out a little gasp of pleasure. Immediately, Beck pulled away, breathing hard. His hand was shaking when he turned on the dome light.

"Let's see your palm," he said, gulping in air.

I held my hand up to the light. The demon mark hadn't

changed. We looked at each other and slapped hands. The moonstone had worked as Beck predicted.

"Okay," I said. "Lesson learned. When we make out, I have to wear the moonstone. Too bad I have to bury it again, huh?"

His look of disappointment was so obvious, I almost laughed. Then, I remembered something I'd learned from one of Faye little "life lessons." She'd told me, "You may think the thing dangling between a guy's legs is his most sensitive part, but it's not. It's his precious ego. Never forget that, Allie."

Because Faye knows about these things, I kept a straight face when Beck said, "You could wear the moonstone Friday night. Nobody will mess with you when you're with me."

He was probably right, but the implication was that I couldn't take care of myself. I narrowed my eyes at him and opened the door. "I'll think about it."

He started the truck but didn't move. I'd only taken a few steps when his window zipped down. "Hey, Allie. Come here a sec. I want to tell you something."

I walked to his open window.

"Weird, isn't it?" he said. "You and me?"

What I really thought was weird was standing there, freezing my buns off and listening to my sleet-dampened hair go *boing* as it turned into a massive ball of frizz. But, bearing in mind Faye's caution about the fragile male ego, I leaned into the open window and touched my forehead to his. "I don't know, Beck. Maybe we just have to let it happen."

He put his warm hands around mine. "Yeah," he said. "Maybe we do."

The events at Kizzy's house and Beck's words would remain crystal clear in my memory for years to come. Something special happened to me that night. From that point on, I opened my arms and embraced my *otherness*.

I'd been fighting against the current too long. It was time to jump in and go with the flow. I'd been chosen to embark on an extraordinary journey. I was ready.

If Beck was part of my journey . . . so be it.

Chapter Nineteen

John J. Peacock High School has less than one hundred students, too small to field a regulation football team of eleven players. Instead, we played eight-man football in a special league for small schools. Friday night was the big game. The Fighting Peacocks were hosting the Georgeville Taters, a truly awesome team from the Columbia Basin. A lot of potatoes were grown in the basin, hence the name.

The game was painful to watch. Most of our students had jobs after school, which depleted the ranks of potential athletes to a pathetic few. Beck and I climbed up the ancient wooden bleachers to the top row. I warned him to sit, not slide, unless he wanted a giant sliver in his studly butt. Nicole was ecstatic because Joey Gregson, the team quarterback, had asked her to the dance. She sat front and center by the cheerleaders, most of whom were her best buds.

"Why didn't Nicole try out for cheerleader? All her friends are out there."

Beck, looking buff in a leather jacket, black silk tee shirt and pressed jeans, peered at me through his night-vision glasses. "Same reason I'm not out for football."

"With your strength and speed, you'd be an awesome football player. Is it the glasses?"

"No, it's not the glasses. You saw Nicole and me sparring that night."

I looked down at the cheerleaders struggling to lift a tiny girl onto their shoulders in order to form a pyramid and flashed on Nicole jumping over Beck's head.

"Couldn't she pretend to be like the others?"

A group of people climbed the stairs and sat gingerly on the bench directly below us. Beck put his mouth to my ear and whispered, "It's not that simple. When it's fully dark, our strength and speed is probably fifty times better that the average person. If I tackled a guy, I could kill him. If Nicole picked up another cheerleader, she might just throw her into the stands."

I giggled, imagining Nicole's best bud, Lexie, sailing into the stands like a Frisbee.

Beck frowned. "Think about the big picture. The cheerleaders and football team practice in the daylight when Nicole and I are like everyone else. The games are played after dark. Imagine what would happen when we got our full powers, not to mention a surge of adrenaline."

"You'd be the lead story on the network news."

"Right," Beck said. "We can't do that to our mother."

I sobered quickly. Being a half-demon definitely had its downside. At least I didn't have to worry when the sun went down. That thought reminded me I hadn't used TKP for a while. After the kick-off, Beck was absorbed in the game and unwilling to engage in idle chitchat. Bored out of my gourd, I decided to see if I still had the juice.

Nicole was leaning over the metal bar separating the bleachers from the cheerleaders section, gossiping with Lexie, whose pompoms hung loosely from one hand. I summoned my power and focused on the maroon and white pompoms. Gradually, the sights and sounds of the football game disappeared. It was just the two of us, the pompoms and me, joined by a brilliant shaft of dancing light. I sent the message, *Lift! Lift!* The pompoms flew from Lexie's hand and hovered in the air for a brief moment before plopping down on Nicole's head like a giant maroon and white wig. Lexie stared, open-mouthed.

The kid sitting in front of me cracked up laughing. "Whoa! Did you see that?"

Nicole snatched the pompoms from her head and handed them back to Lexie. She looked around until she found me in the crowd. I smiled and waved. She gave me a warning glance and turned back to the game. I looked over at Beck. He was staring at me, one brow lifted in an unspoken question.

I shrugged. "Must have been the wind."

He leaned close and murmured, "Give it up, Allie. You think I can't tell when you're up to something? You vibrate like you're running on a 220 current. The air around you changes. I can see it and feel it."

I figured offense was the best defense. "Did you tell Nicole I could move things with my mind?"

"Well, sure," he said.

Unspoken, but obvious in his tone was the question, *Do you even need to ask?*

Faye always says blood's thicker than water. Beck and Nicole had a stronger bond as twins than Beck and I had as boyfriend/girlfriend, fake or otherwise. Wake up call for Allie.

Thankfully, the lop-sided game was called late in the third quarter due to the "mercy rule," invoked when one team was ahead by forty-five points.

Beck and I joined the rowdy throng heading for the gym. As the crowd fell in around us, he wrapped an arm around my neck and pulled me close, our bodies pressed together and our strides matching. I smiled up at him, aware of the envious looks coming my way from the female population. I was thinking how nice it was to be going to the dance with my sorta boyfriend when I felt a cold chill brush the back of my neck. I glanced over my shoulder and saw a smirking Shane Boldt slouching along directly behind us.

He was with four other guys I recognized as habitual troublemakers. He smirked and grabbed his crotch in an unmistakable gesture. His buddies howled with laughter.

Before I looked away, I noticed he wore a silver chain around his neck. Whatever he'd hung on it was tucked inside his shirt. Since he was a Trimark, I was pretty sure it wasn't a cross. I must have tensed up because Beck asked, "You okay?"

Even though the brief encounter stomped all over my feel-good mood, I gave Beck a cheery smile and nodded. No sense asking for trouble.

Before we were allowed in the gym, we had to pass the Hostetler-Miller test. Mr. Hostetler, clad in jeans and a Green Bay jersey, manned the door with Miss Miller by his side. Margaret Miller's sense of smell was legendary. The test went like this: Mr. Hostetler greeted each student by name. When the student responded, Miss Miller leaned close enough to sniff his/her breath. Then, Miss Miller indicated Thumbs Up or Thumbs Down.

Thumbs Up people were sent into the gym. Thumbs Down folk had the choice of leaving or having their saliva checked with a little stick to see if they'd been drinking. Once we entered the gym, we were not allowed to go in and out. In other words, no drinking or drugging in the cars and re-entering the dance, which was okey-dokey with me.

Mr. Hostetler said, "Hello, Mr. Bradford."

Beck said, "Hi."

Miss Miller leaned in and sniffed, gave him a big smile and two thumbs up.

Same routine with me, minus the enthusiasm. Beck must have used his dazer.

The gym was packed, the music blaring. We got rid of our coats, and Beck pulled me into the crowd for a fast dance. Let me say, up front, I'm not the world's best dancer. My only other boyfriend, Junior, seemed to be missing-in-action whenever dancing was involved. We'd never had the opportunity to dance together. Sure, Manny, Mercedes and I danced around their tiny living room now and then, but their taste ran to Salsa. Consequently, I was a little nervous.

Fortunately for me, Beck was an awesome dancer. In the fullness of night, his body rippled with muscle. His movements were graceful yet powerful. He seemed not to notice the reaction of people around him. The girls were practically drooling. The guys looked resentful. Moving to the beat, I decided to relax and enjoy the moment. I saw Nicole and Joey at the edge of the crowd and waved. Nicole waved back, apparently over her pompom snit. Even though she wore her night vision glasses, she looked radiantly happy. She was getting a few envious looks of her own.

Suddenly, I was whapped by a wildly flailing arm. Knocked off balance, I stumbled forward. Without missing a beat, Beck caught me and spun me around. We kept dancing, both facing the same direction, and I found out who the whapper was.

"Sorry," Charles Raymond Atkinson Jr. said insincerely, glaring at me through his oversized glasses. He continued gyrating with his beloved, Suzanne Maloney. Whether or not the whapping was accidental, I couldn't say. Because of my confrontation with Suzanne the day of the video mix-up, I suspected not. But, after observing his enthusiastic but grotesque dance moves, it was obvious he had no control over his arms and legs. Suzanne was dressed in a fuzzy pink sweater, pink hair ribbon, pink jeans, pink socks and pink tennis shoes. She gave me a dirty look, like it was my fault her nerdy boyfriend practically knocked me over.

From my new vantage point I spotted Mercedes, who was with Roberto, one of her many cousins. She grinned and yelled, "Check it out! Manny and Sonja!"

I looked where she was pointing and sure enough, Manny Trujillo and Sonja Ortega were grinning at each other and moving to the music. Manny usually goes to the dances alone and dances with all the girls who don't have partners. But yesterday, when were eating lunch, we heard the thunder of Sonja Ortega's approach. She was stuffed into a pair of Spandex jeans, a belly shirt and four-inch, black patent leather heels. The gap between the shirt and the jeans was overflowing with too much Sonja. She stomped over to our table, stood over Manny and fluttered her mascara-thickened eyelashes.

Instead of calling him *Manny* like everybody else, she purred, "Hi, Mon-Well!"

Manny, looking trapped, said, "Uh, hi, Sonja."

She poked him in the arm with a blood-red fingernail, "You. Me. Friday night. How about it?"

Manny's face turned the color of ripe plums. His gaze darted frantically between Mercedes and me. Wisely, we held our tongues.

Sonja stood over him, hands on her ample hips, waiting for an answer. Finally, he looked up at her, licking his dry lips nervously, trying to formulate an answer.

Sonja smiled broadly. "I'll take that as a 'Yes.' Game starts at 7:30. Pick me up at seven. You know where I live . . . right?"

Totally struck dumb, Manny could only nod.

He and Sonja were dancing at the edge of the crowd. Manny was smiling broadly. Funny how things work out.

The song ended. The next one was a slow dance. Beck pulled me close, took hold of my wrists and wrapped my arms around his neck. With his body pressed to mine, I could hardly breathe.

I was wearing the moonstone tucked inside the blue silk blouse I'd borrowed from Faye. After checking the heated glow in Beck's eyes, visible even behind his special glasses, I was planning on an earth-moving, toe-curling lip lock before the night was over. Yes, Allie Emerson—along with the Boy Scouts—was a big believer in the motto: *Be prepared*. No more demon consequences for me!

The dance floor was crowded, but I easily spotted Shane

Boldt dancing with a skanky-looking girl wearing a crop top and a pair of jeans hanging so low on her hips she had to be going commando . . . very convenient for Shane, who had both hands planted on her almost bare buns. Before I could look away, he saw me and licked his lips in an exaggerated gesture. Once again, I had the feeling I should be doing something about Shane Boldt, but I didn't know what. He'd been eager to let me know he was a Trimark. Therefore, he had to be up to no good. I'd considered telling Beck about him, but I didn't want Beck to think I couldn't take care of myself.

An hour into the dance, I excused myself to go the ladies room. Beck wandered over to talk to his physics teacher, one of the chaperones.

"Allie! Allie!"

Oh, shit. Before I could change course, I was face to face with Miss Yeager, whose door I had not darkened since Monday night.

"I see you're with Beck Bradford," Miss Yeager gushed. She looked downright envious.

"Uh huh." I had nothing to lose so I said, "My mother and I haven't heard from our case worker. Did you send your report?"

"Oh, Allie, let's talk about school biz another time. It's Friday night. Time to party!"

She wriggled away and latched onto Mr. Hostetler from behind. Startled by Miss Yeager's sudden attack, he whirled around, practically knocking her down. I clapped a hand over my mouth to keep from laughing, then I meandered into the bathroom and checked myself out in the mirror. What a mess! My face was flushed, my hair turning frizzy. It took a while to get myself together and I dashed out the door, hoping Beck hadn't been cut from the herd and carried off by predatory females.

A large group of senior girls was approaching the

bathroom. Suddenly, something hooked my right ankle and I staggered forward. I hit the floor hard, chin first. Stunned, I lay sprawled on the floor, listening to the girls laughing their heads off. With the taste of blood in my mouth, I struggled to my hands and knees and looked up to see Shane Boldt and his punk friends enjoying my humiliation. Excitement over, the girls drifted into the bathroom. I scrambled to my feet and brushed the dirt of my clothes, trying to ignore Shane and his buddies.

"Way to go, Grace," Shane sneered.

"You tripped me! What's your problem, Shane? Trying to prove you're tough by tripping a girl?"

He moved closer, his face a mask of rage. I took a step back and glanced around to see if I could spot Mr. Hostetler, but he was out on the dance floor boogying with Miss Yeager.

Shane hissed, "You're a damn freak, Emerson. Don't think I've forgotten what you did to me and my friends. Payback is coming. Count on it."

I started to say he didn't scare me— big, fat lie—when I heard a low, feral growl, clearly audible in spite of the loud music. Beck stepped away from the shadowed wall next to the boys' bathroom. In a blur of color and movement, he was between Shane and me.

"I didn't quite hear you," Beck said. "Say it again."

Shane's mouth dropped open and he blinked. One step back and he was flanked by his buddies. Still full of bluster, he sneered , "It figures. Freaks always hang out together. What's with the goggles, Four Eyes? Your sister's a freak too."

Beck was as still as stone. When he spoke, his tone was icy and controlled. "Outside. Behind the gym. Now."

Chapter Twenty

Shane grinned at his friends. "Whaddya say, guys? Wanna kick some ass?"

Personally, I didn't think they looked too enthusiastic. I tugged at Beck's sleeve. "If we leave, we can't come back."

"Stay here. I'll meet you in the parking lot later."

Yeah, right. Like I was going to cower inside the gym while he fought my battles. I grabbed our coats and dashed out the door in time to see Beck following Shane and his gang around the corner of the gym.

"Allie!"

Manny was standing in the open doorway. "What's happening?"

"Nothing. Really. It's okay, Manny," I said and took off running. As much as I wanted Manny along for back-up, he'd get in trouble if we got busted by Mr. Hostetler. My breath hitched in my chest when I thought about the odds. Beck had only me. Shane was backed by four other guys. Sure, Beck was super quick and strong but . . . five guys? Should I go back for Manny or scream for help? My moment of indecisiveness ended abruptly when I remembered Shane most likely had a switchblade.

I rounded the corner of the gym. In the dim light I saw Shane and his guys in a loose semi-circle, facing away from the building. Beck stood about fifteen feet away, arms folded across his chest, a slight smile on his face, like he was observing the antics of monkeys in a zoo.

Shane stepped forward, hands held loosely at his side, fingers twitching.

"Knife!" I screamed as his right hand dove into a pocket. "He's got a switchblade."

The blade popped out on the knife. Shane gathered himself, knife blade thrust forward. "I'm over here, Four Eyes, in case you can't see me."

In my peripheral vision I saw Shane's buddies spread out, ready to move in on Beck. Tension hung in the air like acrid smoke. With my heart pounding in my throat, I looked around for a weapon. A stick. A rock. Anything! I wanted to scream at Beck, "Do something!"

It happened so fast, I'm not even sure what I saw. One second, Beck was perfectly still, the very next, he'd moved with blinding speed toward Shane. His leg came up in a roundhouse kick and the knife went flying. Shane yelled, "Shit!" and grabbed his hand. The rest of the guys stopped dead in their tracks.

Beck dropped back, crouched and ready to spring.

Still cradling his hand, Shane circled to the left and tried to rally his reluctant troops. "Get him! He can't handle all of us."

All five guys rushed Beck. They went in low, going for Beck's legs. The first guy to reach him sailed through the air. I found my weapon, a metal garbage can lid. I suppose I should have looked for the knife, but I was pretty sure I wasn't capable of using it. I would have to think it over, weighing the pros and cons and, by then, it would be too late. And the action was moving so fast I couldn't focus my mind enough for TKP. Instead, I grabbed the lid with both hands and waded into the battle.

Beck was doing okay without me. Two of Shane's guys dangled from his hands, where he held them by the back of their shirts. When Shane made a flying tackle for Beck's ankles, Beck side-stepped quickly and kicked Shane in the butt. I followed up with the garbage can lid, swinging it hard at Shane's head. Shane's roar of fury was almost muffled by the clang of the metal lid as it bounced off his head and struck the asphalt.

With casual indifference, Beck glanced down at the boys held in his iron grip. He tapped their heads together gently and launched them toward the building. They hit the wall with a thud and a moan. The one remaining member of Shane's back-up crew took off running. Shane struggled to his feet, backing slowly away from Beck, holding his injured hand. Bruised and battered, he had to get in one last shot. "You better watch your back!"

Beck shrugged. "Whatever."

He took my hand and led me around the corner of the building, where we came face to face with Manny, Roberto and four Trujillo cousins.

"Need any help, man?" Roberto asked.

"Nah, they're done," Beck said. "Stick a fork in 'em."

"Well, damn!" Roberto said, clearly disappointed. "Let us know next time, you hear?"

"Thanks, man," Beck said, bumping fists with Roberto.

Suddenly, my legs were shaking so hard I almost fell over. Beck clamped an arm around the waist and pulled me close, supporting my weight.

"This girl's a killer with a garbage can lid," he told the guys. "Couldn't have done it without her."

That comment got a big chuckle of appreciation from Beck's new fan club. I felt my lower lip tremble. *No, Allie, you will not cry,* I told myself. *Not in front of all these macho guys.* I don't cry very often, even when I get hurt. But, when I do, my timing sucks.

I didn't get a good look at my condition until we got to the Ranger. Life's not fair. Beck, who'd done all the work, was unscathed. Not a hair out of place, not a speck of dirt on his clothes. I pulled down the sun visor and almost screamed when I saw the wreck staring back at me in the mirror. Apparently I'd bitten my tongue when sprawled on the floor. Not only did I have a bloody chin, I'd bled all over Faye's silk blouse. Beck pulled a cotton tee shirt and a bottle of water out of the console between the seats.

I tried to snatch the shirt from his hand. "I can do it."

"Hold still." He daubed at my face.

My tongue hurt and I was mad at the world for ruining my perfect night. I was even a little ticked at Beck, because he'd enjoyed himself so much.

He finished cleaning my face and looked me over. "Are you hurt anywhere else?"

"No," I snapped, looking away.

"Don't be scared. Those guys won't bother you again."

"Shane's a Trimark," I said.

Beck narrowed his eyes and stared at me. "Are you sure? Have you seen his hand?"

"Oh, yeah, I've seen it. He couldn't wait to show me."

The amber flare of his eyes told me he wasn't happy. "What else haven't you told me?"

"I found out there's a second prophecy connected to the moonstone, one passed along by the Trimarks."

I paused to see how he was taking the news. His expression was stony.

"There's more," he said. It wasn't a question.

I nodded. "It's possible the moonstone has additional magical properties we—meaning the Star Seekers—didn't know about."

His lips barely moved when he spoke. "Such as?"

I drew a shaky breath. "It's possible it may be able to stop time."

Beck jerked like I'd poked him with a sharp stick.

"Holy shit!" he exclaimed, which made me think about his mother's Christian fiction series and her preoccupation with church-going. I chuckled.

"Something funny?" he said. "Or is this one of your hysterical moments?"

I sobered quickly and waved a hand. "Never mind."

"What did the second prophecy say?"

"Basically, the Trimarks won't rest until they get their hands on the moonstone." My hand flew to the pendant. "That's why I buried it."

Beck rubbed his chin and thought for a moment. "Anything else?"

"That's pretty much it except for Ruth Wheeler. She's a FBI agent who was supposed to be here a week ago. As far as I know, she never got here."

"Did you call your dad and let him know?"

"Not yet. My mom thinks Ruth's gone undercover."

Beck shook his head and started the Ranger. "You need to call him. Something might have happened to her."

"Shane was wearing a long, black coat at the football game," I said.

Beck backed carefully out of the parking stall. "Is that significant?"

I told him about my dream, the one where the Mikhail/ Shane guy, dressed in a long, black coat, set fire to a house then killed the occupants when they ran out. "Of course, it was just a dream," I finished.

Beck glanced over at me. "Allie," he said in an overly patient tone. "You have supernatural powers. Why are you acting like dreams don't mean squat?"

I bit my lip and looked at my hand covering the moonstone between my breasts. I had no answer. But of one thing I was sure. Beck was right. I needed to call my dad. Something bad may have happened to Ruth Wheeler.

When we got to the trailer, the lights were on and a big, old car I'd never seen was pulled up next to our truck.

"Oh, man," Beck breathed. "Check out the car."

It was white with a black top. The hood looked as long as a football field.

"Sure is big," was all I could manage to say.

Beck gazed longingly at the beast, his eyes glowing in appreciation. "You know what that is?"

"Uh, no. Should I?"

"It's a fully restored, two-door 1973 Monte Carlo. Muscle car, big time."

"Bet it's hard to park."

Beck frowned at me. "It's a classic."

I shrugged. I couldn't care less about the car, but I did care about its driver and why he/she was visiting Faye at this late hour. A jillion thoughts ran through my head. Did Faye have a new girlfriend I didn't know about? A new boyfriend? Were caseworkers from Child Protective Services making midnight calls in perfectly restored cars from the 1970's? Did it belong to Ruth Wheeler? Or—the thought made me shiver—did the car belong to a Trimark who was holding a knife to my mother's throat and demanding the moonstone?

I grabbed Beck's hand and dragged him into the trailer, where we found Faye and Benny, the dishwasher, seated at the dinette, drinking beer. I stared at them, goggle-eyed; relief mixed with outrage mixed with disappointment mixed with . . . whatever nameless emotion that made me wish I could turn back time and not walk into the trailer and see what I just saw. I made a mental note to check the moonstone for such a possibility.

"Oh, it's you," was all I could manage to say to Benny.

Faye introduced Benny to Beck. Benny didn't rise. He took a swig of beer, wiped his mouth with the back of his hand and said, "How ya doin', kid?"

Beck said, "Cherry car, man."

Benny said, "Thanks."

"Big block, huh? 454 engine?"

"Yeah," Benny said. "Pristine condition. 115,000 original miles. Hydramatic transmission. Power brakes. Power steering."

"Cool," Beck said.

Since I'd fully recovered my power of speech during this stimulating interlude, I put my hands on my hips and glared at Faye. "What's *he* doing here?"

Faye glared back. "We're just *talking*. Is that okay with you?"

I didn't back down. "What about Roy?" I asked . . . *like I really cared about Roy.*

Faye's angry eyes were barely visible through narrow slits. "I *said*, we're just talking. I needed company while I waited up for *you*. What happened to my blouse?"

Faye was a master at diverting the conversation to safer ground, at least for her.

"I had a bloody nose. Don't worry about it. If it's ruined, I'll buy you another one as soon as I get a babysitting job."

During this exchange, Beck gently extricated his hand from mine and sank down on the couch, his elbows on his knees, chin in his hands. Benny scooted his butt sideways so he could check me out. I hated the feeling of his creepy gaze sweeping over my body. Instead of glaring at Faye, I glared at him.

He stood and stretched. "I'd better get going, babe," he said, winking at my mother.

Babe? Eewww.

Faye slipped out of the dinette and continued to glower at me like I'd ruined her fabulous social life. "I'll walk you out," she told Benny.

I plopped down on the couch next to Beck and pulled my feet in to let them pass. Before Faye could slam the door, I said, "I need the calling card."

Faye stopped and looked at me. "Who are you calling this late?"

"Mike Purdy." I knew it would push her buttons.

Her lips compressed into a narrow line. Finally she said, "Can't it wait until morning?"

"No," I said.

"It's in my purse." Faye stepped out into the night.

I really didn't want to know what was going on between Faye and Benny, so I snagged the calling card out of her purse and dialed.

Chapter Twenty-One

I didn't like phoning my father, even though he'd given me his private cell number. Mike Purdy was a stranger. For the first fifteen years of my life he had made no effort to contact me, much less offer support, financial or otherwise. If Kizzy hadn't tracked him down on the Internet, we wouldn't have connected at all. Of course, once he figured out I was the *Maid whose palm bore the mark of the star*, he was all, "Oh, yeah. That's my girl."

Still, I had too many unanswered questions. Had he told his wife and kids about me? Did his wife know about the Star Seekers? And if she didn't, was she lying in bed next to Mike right this minute, listening to his end of the conversation?

Bottom line? The very second the phone went to voice mail, I was hanging up.

Beck must have picked up on my anxiety. "If he doesn't answer, leave a message."

"It's not that simple," I said.

"It's only hard if you make it hard."

Quite the philosopher, good, old half-demon Beck.

After six rings, a sleep-roughened voice croaked, "Yeah?"

"Mike?"

"Who's this?"

My words came out in a rush. "It's Allie. Sorry to wake you, but some stuff is happening here, and Ruth Wheeler hasn't shown up, at least I don't think she has unless she's like undercover or something because, well, I haven't seen her, and I do know what she looks like 'cause she came to see me in the hospital or maybe she's in disguise, but even if she is, wouldn't she somehow get in touch with me unless . . ."

"Hold it," my father said. I heard the sound of bedcovers rustling, footsteps and a door opening and closing. I looked over at Beck. He rolled his eyes and made the universal yakkety-yak sign by rapidly opening and closing his thumb and fingers.

"Oh, shut up," I said.

He grinned. "Didn't say a word."

"Allie." Mike's voice was sharp. "You say Ruth Wheeler hasn't contacted you?"

"That's right," I said. "Do you think something's happened to her?"

"I'll check with our guy first thing tomorrow. You said some other stuff is happening?"

I told him about Shane Boldt, how he flaunted the mark on his palm, how he'd tripped me and, since Faye was still outside, about the fight behind the gym.

When I finally ran out of words, Mike said, "Is the moonstone in a safe place?"

Would it have killed him to say, "Did you get hurt? Are you okay?"

"Yes," I said. "The moonstone's in a safe place. And, in case you're wondering, I'm all right too."

Beck shook his head in disgust and wrapped an arm around me.

I rested my head against Beck's shoulder and listened to my dad going, "Uh, er, um . . . "

Apparently, that's what he did when he screwed up and was trying to figure out what to say.

After a few seconds, he said, "When I find out what's going on with Ruth, I'll call you."

"If Faye answers, don't tell her about the fight. She'd freak out and never let me go to another dance."

Mike chuckled. "Got it. I'm glad you called, Allie. I hate to think the moonstone is putting you in danger."

Nice try, but a little too late.

Just as insincerely, I said, "Thanks, Mike. Talk to you tomorrow."

I put the phone back in its cradle just as Faye came in. Her face was calm, her anger gone.

She picked up the empties and tossed them into the garbage. "Get a hold of your dad?"

I nodded.

"Everything okay?"

I didn't want to worry her. "Probably. I wanted to let him know Ruth Wheeler hasn't made contact."

"You'd better bury that thing again."

I knew she was talking about the moonstone.

Beck stood. "Let's do it now."

"Now?" Faye and I said together.

"Now," Beck said.

Which is why, at exactly twelve forty-five a.m., I held the flashlight while Beck dug a hole and, once again, we buried the moonstone under the apple tree. After the burial, Faye went inside, while Beck and I said our goodbyes. Because the moonstone was no longer around my neck, and my tongue hurt like hell, no kissing was involved. I walked Beck to the Ranger and gave him a heartfelt hug.

I brushed my lips against his ear and felt his body react with a slight shudder. *Whoa, did I do that?*

"Thanks," I said. "The evening was . . . "

I searched through my memory bands for the perfect word from vocabulary lessons drummed into my head by Mrs. Burke.

"Unique!" I said, triumphantly.

Beck's body shook in silent laughter. He smoothed back my hair and cupped my face in his hand. He touched his lips against my temple and murmured, "Maybe some day we'll be able to go out on a date like everybody else and not have something weird happen."

The rumble of his deep voice vibrated against the delicate skin of my temple and sent a tidal wave of sensation surging through my body. I gasped and jerked like I'd been thrown into an electric fence, momentarily forgetting about my injured tongue and potential demon dust. I hauled him in and was searching for his mouth, when he grabbed my wrists.

He was breathing hard and his voice was husky. "You're not wearing the moonstone. You might not be protected from . . . you know."

"Yeah, you're right."

Reluctantly, I stepped away and looked up at him. "You got some other kind a dazer I don't know about?"

Beck took my hand and brought it to his lips. "Maybe we're just attracted to each other like normal teenagers."

"Ya think?"

Faye threw the door open and yelled, "Allie! Get in here before you freeze your butt off!"

Beck climbed into the Ranger and started the engine. The window zipped down. "Let me know what your dad says."

I promised I would and lifted a hand in farewell as he backed down the driveway.

*

My Saturdays had a predictable routine. First off, the weekly trip to Friendly Fred's Trailer Park to dump our tanks, a no-brainer in the summer, but a real chore when the weather was bad. If the roads were snowy, it involved putting chains on our old pick-up truck. More often than not, it resulted in a major Faye versus Allie screaming match. Fortunately, this particular Saturday, the roads were clear and dump day was a rip-roaring success.

Back at the ranch, our little house positioned in exactly the right spot, I'd just plugged in the electricity when I heard the phone ring.

Mike didn't waste time with small talk. "Nobody's heard from Ruth. She was using vacation days."

"Didn't she have to check in with somebody? Didn't anybody miss her?"

I heard the anxiety in my voice. I hated to think something bad had happened to Ruth Wheeler because of me.

"She wasn't on official FBI business, and she lived by herself. My contact talked to her mother, who hasn't heard from her lately, but apparently that wasn't unusual."

"Maybe she's here and watching out for me."

Mike's silence told me I'd been spinning the facts into my own little fantasy scenario.

I gulped. "Okay, assuming something has happened to Ruth Wheeler, now what?"

"Another guy in our organization is also an agent."

I noticed he took care not to mention the name of our "organization."

"Oh, that guy!" I'd been de-briefed by two FBI agents last June, because of the kidnapping issue. I'd liked Ruth, but the other agent, with his moist, lily-white hands and bad comb-over, gave me the creeps.

Mike said. "He's on another case now, but we're working to get him over there. Just make sure the moonstone is in a safe place."

"It is," I assured him.

Later, I was getting ready to go to the Laundromat— my other Saturday duty—when Beck called. I told him what my dad said and he reacted in silence. When he spoke, his words surprised me.

"Wanna go to church with me tomorrow?"

Chapter Twenty-Two

The way I figured it, why not? The moonstone was taking a dirt nap and, as I mentioned before, I wasn't sure what saved me that awful day in Junior's house when Revelle sniffed out my hiding place. Could have been the moonstone. Could have been Jesus. I needed all the help I could get. Might as well give the Catholic Church a shot.

I was thinking about all of this when Beck picked me up Sunday morning for mass. Not knowing what to expect, I was a little nervous when we pulled into the parking lot of the St. John the Baptist Catholic Church. Beck started to open the door.

"Hold it," I said. "If St. John was a Baptist, why is this church named after him instead of the Baptist Church?"

Beck sighed. "Gee, Allie, I really don't know."

Despite the note of sarcasm in his voice, I persisted. "What do I do during the service?"

"You don't have to kneel when I do. Just scrunch forward in your seat and bow your head. That way, the person kneeling behind you won't have his nose in your hair."

I tried to think of people I knew of the Catholic persuasion. Oh, yeah, Bea and Harold from the diner. I had a sudden visual of Harold snorkeling around in my hair with his humungous nose and lapsed into laughter.

I was still snickering as we exited the Ranger and walked across the parking lot. Beck, his forehead furrowed with worry lines, looked at me like I was a ticking time bomb ready to blow. As he led me to the pretty little stone church, he said, "I'm not sure what's funny, but you better get it out of your system before we go in."

"No problem," I said, desperately trying not to think about Harold's enormous quivering nostrils. "You may find this hard to believe, but I do know how to behave in church."

If I was trying to put him on the defensive, it worked. "Sorry. I thought the whole church thing was getting to you and you were, you know, kinda hysterical."

I assured him I wasn't hysterical. To prove my point, I told him about Harold's nose. He smiled politely. Apparently, he didn't find it as amusing as I did. Then, it occurred to me, Beck was probably nervous too. After all, he was bringing his semi-heathen girlfriend onto sanctified ground and, most likely, into the bosom of his family.

"One more thing," he continued. "During the Eucharist, just stay seated."

"Well, of course," I said, hoping I'd figure out what the Eucharist was once the program got underway.

"And, if you don't want to do the hug of Christian fellowship, just shake hands."

I squeezed his hand. "Your choice . . . hand shake or hug?"

This time, the smile reached his eyes.

We mounted the worn stone steps and followed two women I recognized from Kizzy's book club through the wooden double doors and into the lobby or, as I found out later, the *narthex*. A beaming middle-aged couple rushed over to us to bid us welcome. Beck introduced me to Milt and Maisie Duncan, today's official greeters. Milt winked and punched Beck in the shoulder.

"New girlfriend, huh?"

New? Geez, how many girls had he brought to church? I shot him a look while Maisie clasped both my hands in hers. "We're delighted you're here, Allie."

I murmured my thanks, and they dashed off to greet

another group of newcomers. Before we went into the sanctuary, Beck dipped his fingers into a bowl of holy water and touched his forehead. The sight and sound of his fingers dipping into the water evoked the memory of the night in his apartment. Once again, I felt the touch of his warm, wet hand against my skin . . . inhaled the sweet scent of sage and lavender . . . heard the deep, soothing sound of his voice.

Snap out of it, Allie, I told myself. You're in church. Thinking about pagan rites is probably the worst kind of sin.

Nevertheless, I reached in my pocket, wrapped my fingers around the healing stones and followed Beck down the aisle. As we slipped into the pew behind his mother and Nicole, I thought about Beck's strange existence. He was like the result of a bizarre science experiment. What do you get when you mix an incubus with a wannabe nun and add a generous portion of Native American shamanism? Beck Bradford, that's what. The very idea almost sent me to giggle-land again. Fortunately, at that moment, Melissa Bradford turned and gave me a tight little smile. I sobered immediately and arranged my face in what I hoped was the proper look of reverence.

I was doing okay until Nicole turned around, grinned at me, and then crossed her eyes. Taken by surprise, I disguised my snort of laughter as a cough. Beck kicked the pew beneath Nicole, and she turned around. Their mother hissed at Nicole, snapped her head around and raked both of us with a non-nonsense glare that clearly said, "Shape up!"

I glanced at Beck, who looked positively joyful. Was bringing me to church his little act of rebellion? Is that why we were sitting behind his mother and sister instead of alongside them? Was he using me to say, *In your face, Mom?*

The priest, Father Xavier Francis MacDougal, entered,

and I forgot all about family dysfunctions and immersed myself in the sights, sounds and smells of a Catholic Mass. I stood when others stood, sat when others sat and scrunched forward when it was time to kneel. I even figured out the Eucharist was the Catholic term for Holy Communion.

Because Thanksgiving was just around the corner, Father MacDougal's message was about appreciating what God had given us. Nicole began to squirm and fidget in her seat. Even her mother's warning glance had no effect. Beck was gazing off in the distance over the top of the priest's head, lost in his own little world. It seemed like Melissa and I were the only ones thankful for our blessings.

Suddenly, Nicole went utterly still, as still as the stone saints lining the sanctuary. Alarmed, I stared at her back. Was she even breathing? Was she about to have a seizure? A stroke? I was getting ready to poke Beck with my elbow when she finally took a breath. I counted, one thousand one, one thousand two, etc. I got all the way to one thousand twenty five before she took another. I stopped counting and gasped when the aura appeared, a radiant, dancing rainbow alternately flaring and subsiding over her crown of dark hair like an incandescent flame.

I tugged at Beck's sleeve until he came back from wherever he'd been. He inclined his head toward mine. I whispered, "Do you see it? The rainbow over Nicole's head?"

He studied his sister. "Yeah, I see it. It means she went somewhere else."

By "she went somewhere else," was he talking about astral travel? I stared at him, unwilling to believe he could be so casual about something so bizarre. I needed answers.

After the service, Melissa and Beck mingled and shook hands with other parishioners. Nicole took off down the hall, presumably to the ladies' restroom. I waited outside the door until she came out. She looked surprised to see me.

"Looking for the bathroom?" she asked.

"No," I said. "Looking for answers."

Her eyes narrowed with suspicion, but she didn't walk away. I waited until the hallway was clear and then asked, "Okay, how did you do it? The astral travel thing? Did you know you have an aura?"

Nicole scowled. "What's an aura?"

"Dancing lights shooting out of your head. Beck saw it too."

"Oh my God! How embarrassing! Do you think *everybody* saw it?"

Trust Nicole to miss the whole point. Since I wanted more information, I told her, "Just Beck and me. I guess you didn't know that happened during astral travel, huh?"

She gave me a dark look. "Apparently, my dear, sweet brother didn't think it was important enough to mention."

"So, where did you go?"

She ducked her head and looked up through her long, dark lashes. "I know I should have been listening to Father MacDougal, but he was just so *boring*, I had to get away. I went to the top of the Space Needle in Seattle, but it was foggy. Couldn't see a thing."

"Anywhere else?"

"I wanted to go someplace warm, like Disney World. But, then mass was over, so I couldn't."

I shook my head in disbelief. "You can really do that? Leave your body and go somewhere else?"

She nodded. "It's getting easier."

"So, it doesn't matter if it's day or night?"

"No," Nicole said. "Beck and I are different that way."

I waited, but Nicole had clammed up. I turned toward the narthex. "Guess we should go find Beck and your mom."

Before I could take a step, Nicole plucked at my sleeve. "You know what's weird?"

"What?"

She thrust out a hand and pointed at her demon mark. "I have no idea what I'm capable of doing. I'm only half-human. What if I do something really awful?"

Whoa, was Nicole developing a conscience? Of course, we were standing in a church. If reassurance was what she needed, I was all over it.

"You won't," I said. "It comes down to making choices, and it doesn't matter if you're fully human, half-human or. like me, some hick chick with a magic moonstone."

She managed a weak smile. "It's scary, ya know?"

I smiled back at her. "Believe me, I know."

*

That night, I dreamed of my long-missing grandmother, Melia. Dressed in a long, green dress, she hitched up her skirt and ran through the woods after a little girl with blond braids. Each time the woman caught up, the little girl squealed with laughter and scampered out of reach.

"Faye, stop!" Melia called. Her voice was high and sweet but layered with a note of panic. "Wait for Mama."

But, Faye wouldn't listen. She'd wait for her mother to catch up and then run ahead. Finally, she reached the edge of the woods and ran into a sunlit meadow. Melia stopped at the edge of the forest, her tangled dark hair wild and frizzy, her gown snagged with bits of moss and fern. Her face was streaked with mud, her eyes wild with grief.

"Come back," she cried, her voice escalating in fear. But, Faye didn't look back. She skipped through the meadow, stopping now and then to pick a wildflower.

I awoke from the dream, not screaming out in terror like I did with my Baxter nightmare (thank you, Beck) but with a sense of melancholy.

Melancholy. I snuggled under my faded pink comforter, smiling as I recalled how I'd added that particular word to my vocabulary. It was last year, in ninth grade English.

Mrs. Burke had said, "Melancholy. How many of you think it's a fruit?"

My hand shot up along with half the class.

Then, she said, "How many of you think it's a breed of dog?"

Everyone else in the class, minus one, raised their hands. The hold-out was Charles Raymond Atkinson Jr., who sneered and said, "It means sad."

Junior Martinez had been sitting directly behind me. He leaned forward and whispered, "What an asshole!"

Mrs. Burke must have agreed because she got a pained look on her face. "You're almost right, Charles. However, there's a bit more."

She paused and gazed around the class. "Have you ever seen something on TV, a movie that ends with a group hug? Or, maybe a Hallmark commercial that tugs at your heart and tears well up in your eyes?"

All the girls nodded. The boys stared at the floor.

"That's *melancholy*. A thoughtful sadness mellowed by a touch of hope."

I'd never forgotten it. My very next thought was, *Ask Faye about her mother and do not let her squirm away from an honest answer*. I swore I'd do that when she got home from work tonight.

Chapter Twenty-Three

Much to my relief, Shane Boldt and his buddies weren't at school Monday. The last thing I wanted was Round Two of the Friday night fight, especially at school. I was sure Beck would think he had to protect me even though I *was* "Killer garbage-can-lid girl." He'd offered me a ride home, but I'd promised Mercedes I'd help her after school. Our job was to keep four little Trujillos plus Rocky and Ricky, her twin two-year-old cousins, out of the kitchen while her mother, Juanita, and Tia Elena made tamales.

A little after six, weary beyond words, I trudged home, vowing I would never reproduce. My hair was sticky because Ricky decided to park his Tootsie Pop behind my ear while I changed his poopy diaper. My pristine white tee was splotched with crimson stains thanks to Rocky's cherry Popsicle, and the brown stuff on my jeans? Yuck! All I wanted was a quick shower, homework and bed.

After I unlocked the door, turned on the lights and flipped on the heat, I saw the message light blinking on the phone.

Faye's voice. "Allie. It's Mom. Call me."

She sounded, well . . . happy. Very strange, for Faye. So strange, in fact, I decided not to wait until the dinnercrowed thinned out before calling her back.

Her words came out in a rush. "Roy misses me. He sent me a plane ticket. Bea said I could take a few days off, and I called Kizzy. You can stay with her while I'm gone. Okay?"

"Sure," I said. "When are you leaving?"

"Tomorrow morning. Could you do me a huge favor and iron my good jeans, my blue blouse and . . . "

The list went on and on.

"Sure," I said, knowing Faye's aversion to ironing.

"You don't mind if I go? I'll be back for Thanksgiving."

I assured her I didn't mind at all. In fact, I was glad she was getting away from creepy Benny. Compared to Benny, Brain Dead Roy was the catch of the day. She was so excited, I couldn't help but be happy for her, at least until I asked who was driving her to the airport.

"Benny."

After my long silence, she added, "He's not so bad, you know. Give him a chance."

I let that pass. "I'll get the suitcase out from under the bed."

"Thanks, baby. Love ya."

"Love you, too."

I jumped in the shower, washed off the icky-stickies and ate a bowl of ramen before I retrieved the iron and ironing board from the storage shed next to the trailer. A bitterly cold wind was blowing in from the north. Beck had told me a snow storm was coming . . . he said he could smell it in the air. Not that I believed him. Blaster was nowhere in sight. He was probably in his heated stall. Nothing but the best for big, old stinky Blaster and his money-maker, the sperm Uncle Sid sold online. By the time I got back inside, my teeth were chattering, and I was actually looking forward to ironing because I knew it would warm me up.

In my world, ironing was a major pain in the butt because Faye wouldn't let me keep the iron in the house. I guess she thought I'd leave it on and burn the place down. I set up the ironing board—it took up the whole living room—plugged in the iron and turned on the TV. While I was ironing Faye's good jeans, I realized I couldn't spoil her day by hammering her with questions about Melia. I had two choices. I could wait until Faye came back, or I could take matters into my own hands.

I looked around for the phone book. *If I find the phone book, I'll call Claude Emerson. If I don't, I'll wait until Faye gets back.* I found the phone book. The little devil on my shoulder said, *Why not? It's not a long distance call and Faye won't tell you a thing. You need to know.*

Before I could chicken out, I dialed Grandpa Claude's number. After three rings, he picked up the phone and said, "This is Claude Emerson."

I opened my mouth but nothing came out. Oh, crap! Why hadn't I thought this through before I dialed?

After a couple of grumpy *Helloes*? and his mumbled curse words, I sensed he was getting ready to slam the phone down.

I gathered my courage and croaked, "Hi. It's Alfrieda."

He breathed into the phone—wet, raspy inhalations that made me cringe.

"Alfrieda," he repeated. "How's your mother?"

"Oh, she's fine. Actually, she's the reason I called. She won't tell me anything, and I really need to know about my grandmother, Melia."

"Oh, you do, huh? Did you ask her about Melia?"

His voice was sharp. I had the feeling Grandpa Claude was no dummy.

"I didn't actually mention her by name."

He chuckled into the phone. "So, now I'm supposed to fill in the blanks. Is that it?"

"Even a few of the blanks would be nice. Like, where did Melia go? Why did she leave her daughter? What did you mean when you said Faye is unhappy because of *who* she is? And, why did . . . ?"

"Hold it! You said 'a few of the blanks.' Pick one."

Chastised, I was silent for a moment. "Okay, the one about Faye."

More raspy breathing. Finally, Grandpa Claude said, "Faye needs to tell you why she's unhappy, but here's something for you to chew on. I'm going to ask you questions. Just think about them. Don't answer. Ready?"

"Yes."

"Have you ever wondered why you have, shall we say, special abilities?"

I froze. How did Grandpa Claude know? Maybe he didn't. Maybe he was fishing for information.

"Special abilities? Like what?"

He roared into the phone. "Don't try to fake me out, Alfrieda. I know about the moonstone. I know about the apple bins."

He scared me so bad I almost dropped the phone.

"Oh," I said, feeling like an idiot. I wondered how he found out, but was afraid to ask.

He continued, "And why, of all her boyfriends, did Faye choose Mike Purdy to be the father of her baby . . . Mike Purdy, who has major mojo of his own?"

Whoa! Faye *chose* Mike Purdy? Definitely not the story she'd given me.

"Still there, Alfrieda?"

I gulped loudly. "I'm here."

"Think about it. Combine Mike Purdy's DNA with . . ."

He paused.

"With what?"

"Never mind. Let's just say, you're unique in a number of ways."

I didn't know how to respond, so I said nothing.

Finally, he said, "Have you ever heard the phrase, *To thine own self be true?*"

"Is it from the Bible?"

"William Shakespeare. Food for thought."

"For me or Faye?"

He sighed heavily before he answered. "Faye, of course. You, Alfrieda Carlotta Emerson, are on the right path."

"What about Melia?"

"Melia's my problem," he said, and slammed the phone down. I stared at the receiver, my brain whirling in confusion. *Are you happy now, Allie? Did you get your questions answered? Do you know more about Melia? Do you know why Faye hates Grandpa Claude?*

No, no, no and no!

*

"I thought Beck was driving you home," Mercedes said as I plopped down on the seat next to her. I'd almost missed the bus. Patti was pulling away from the curb when she spotted me in the rear-view mirror.

I slung my backpack to the floor and crossed my legs. Tight. Trying not to think about my bursting bladder.

"He was going to, but Mrs. Burke asked him to stay and correct papers. We talked for a while. When I looked at the clock, I had to hurry to catch the bus, which left me no time to go to the bathroom, and I'm about to pee my pants."

Mercedes shrieked with laughter. Cory Philpott, seated across the aisle, shot me an evil, interested look. Since our previous encounter on the bus, when I'd almost snatched him bald-headed, he'd left me alone. I glared at him until he turned and stared out the window.

I lowered my voice and spoke to Mercedes. "Beck's picking me up later. I need to pack my stuff 'cause I'll be staying with Kizzy while Faye's gone."

"Oh, yeah," Mercedes said. "I forgot."

Just then, Patti hit a huge bump. I squeezed my legs together and muttered. Mercedes giggled. When we finally reached our stop, I grabbed my backpack and sprinted to the front of the bus. I danced in place while the doors hissed open slowly.

Patti said, "Gotta go, huh?"

"Big time," I said as I dashed down the steps. "See ya

tomorrow."

Nature's insistent call must have driven everything else out of my mind, even my instinct for survival. Probably why I fell for the oldest scam in history. Normally, I have the house key in my hand before I get off the bus so I can unlock the door, step inside and toss my backpack on the couch. Today, I'd been so intent on not wetting my pants, I'd forgotten about the key.

I dumped my backpack on the ground and unzipped the pocket where I kept the key. Oh, crap! Not there. I was seriously thinking about squatting behind the barn when Benny pulled in the driveway in the black and white monstrosity Beck found so fascinating.

Before I could form another thought, he jumped out of the car and hustled over to me, a look of panic in his eyes.

"Thank God, you're here, kiddo. It's your mom. She's been hurt."

An icy hand closed around my heart and squeezed. My mouth opened and closed but no sound came out. When I was finally able to speak, my voice sounded like it was coming from a faraway place. I plucked at his sleeve with a shaking hand. "Where is she? Is she okay? Did the plane crash?"

Benny grabbed my arm and led me to the car. "No, the flight was delayed because of fog. She was driving back to Peacock Flats and got rear-ended. She's at Vista Valley Regional Hospital. I'll take you there."

He opened the door to the passenger side, tossed me onto the vinyl seat where I sat, dazed, while he turned the car around and headed for the road. Later, I would remember little things that didn't add up. The car had a strange smell, a smell I couldn't identify, and the panic in Benny's eyes vanished rapidly, replaced by his usual expression of indifference.

Even numb with fear, I knew I was screwed when Benny

reached the end of the driveway and turned right. The car fishtailed violently on the icy road as he accelerated away from Vista Valley and the hospital. My heart jumped into my throat as I scrabbled for the door handle. "Stop! You're going the wrong way. What . . .?"

I heard a sound coming from the back seat. As I glanced behind me, a dark, looming presence reared up. A gloved hand reached out, clamped my hair in an iron grip and yanked my head back at a painful angle. With my upper body held fast against the seat back, I yelled and kicked out at Benny, hitting him solidly in thigh. He swore and whacked me across the face with a vicious backhand.

"For Christ's sake, get the stuff. What's your problem back there?" He snarled at his back seat accomplice.

The stuff? Fighting panic, I kicked, screamed and swung my fists wildly at my unknown assailant. As I gathered myself for another assault on Benny, an arm encircled my neck and squeezed. I was still able to breath, but almost immediately, starbursts began exploding behind my eyes, and my world turned fuzzy around the edges. I was desperately fighting to hang onto consciousness when I felt the jab of a needle in my arm and then . . . it was lights out for Allie.

Chapter Twenty-Four

Imagine waking up with your wrists and ankles bound with duct tape and Shane Boldt sneering down at you? Could anything be worse? Oh, yes. To all of the above, add soggy, cold, wet jeans. My first rational thought was, *Oh no, I peed my pants!* when it should have been, *You stupid ass! Your life is in danger!* Instead of being scared out of my mind, I felt like a little kid who'd wet her pants in Sunday school. Ashamed and embarrassed. The last person I wanted to witness this spectacle was Shane Boldt.

I was in a position Mrs. Burke would call *untenable* (lacking the sound reasoning or high ground that make defense possible). Too dizzy and disoriented to use TKP, the only weapon I had was my mouth, which I did not hesitate to use, even though I was curled up on a stinky carpet looking up at two Trimarks. Shane stood over me and Benny was a few feet away in a straight back chair pulled up to a wooden table. He had an open can of beer in one hand and a cell phone in the other.

"There are people looking for me right now. I can name three. Wanna know who?" I blustered.

Benny ignored me.

Shane said, "Yeah, right."

Trying to ignore my roiling stomach and pounding head, I repeated, "Yeah, right. Let's start with an FBI agent. Did you know I have one watching over me?"

Shane glanced over at Benny, who smiled and said, "Didn't do a very good job."

Okay, it's possible my mind wasn't working well. I tried

another approach. "I'm supposed to be at my friend's house. If I don't show up, she'll call the sheriff. Shouldn't be too hard to find you guys, especially since you drive a creepy old car."

Benny shot up and set the beer and cell phone on the table. Two strides and he was on me, his hand clutching my pony tail. He jerked my face close to his. I bit my lip to keep from crying out. Geez, if I survived this, I'd be lucky to have a single hair left on my head.

"Listen, kid," he hissed. "And listen well. I'm only going to say it once."

When he spoke, spittle flew from his mouth and ran down the side of my face. I recoiled and tried to look away from his unfeeling gray gaze.

He gave my hair another yank. "Look at me!"

This time, I couldn't hold back a whimper of pain. Reluctantly, I met his hate-filled eyes.

Benny said, "Nobody, I repeat, *nobody*, is looking for you. Your friend, Kizzy, got a call saying your mother's flight was delayed and you wouldn't be staying with her tonight. Your mother, by the way, is out of the picture. She's probably screwing her boyfriend as we speak."

In spite of his nasty comment, I heaved a sigh of relief. At least Faye was okay. Now, all I had to do was get myself out of this mess.

Benny gave my hair another little tug. "Oh yeah, the FBI agent. Whaddaya think, Shane. You scared of the bad old FBI guy?"

"Naw," Shane said, but shot a worried look at Benny. "Ya think there's really an FBI guy?"

Benny released my hair and shoved me down on the carpet. "Of course not, you dumb shit!"

He returned to his chair and sucked down some beer. Shane slouched over to a ratty-looking couch covered by a dingy crocheted coverlet. When he plopped down, the couch gave an ominous shriek and engulfed his body like it was trying to eat him. He shifted uneasily, his knees up by his elbows.

"Can I turn on the TV?" he asked Benny.

Benny shrugged. "Be my guest."

Shane heaved himself out of the carnivorous couch and turned on an old, black-and-white TV setting on a metal stand. While he channel-surfed, I checked out my surroundings. We were in the living room of what looked to be an extremely old, extremely small house. The worn carpet smelled like cats had been using it for a litter box. I was in a position to know since my cheek was pressed against it. The high, narrow windows were covered with tightly-pulled, filthy shades. A single light bulb burned in the high ceiling. I rolled onto my back so I could see the other side of the room. I saw two closed doors. Closet? Bathroom? The air inside was frigid as if the house had been unoccupied for a long time. I shivered in my wet pants, grateful I was wearing my coat.

After a blast of static and muttered curses from Shane, he finally settled on a game show I knew came on at six p.m. Shocked, I realized I'd been out cold for a couple of hours. I wondered what they'd shot me up with and hoped I wouldn't barf. It was bad enough I'd wet my pants.

Shane returned to the couch. "How long do we have to stay here?"

He sounded pouty, like he had really important stuff to do. I was quite sure it wasn't homework.

Benny glanced at the cell phone. "Not much longer."

"When is she gonna call?" Shane whined.

"Shut up!" Benny snarled.

Hmmm. Benny didn't want me to know a *she* was involved. *Why not?* I wondered, scrolling through my mind for possible female Trimarks. When the cell phone chirped, Benny pounced on it.

"Yeah," he said.

He listened for a while, without comment, glancing over at me from time to time. The look of anticipation in his eyes was unmistakable. I fought against the terror rising deep within me and considered my options. Most of the fuzziness in my mind had dissipated. Could I use TKP like I had against Baxter? I was outnumbered, two to one. Not good. But, lacking other options, it was worth a try. I looked around for possible weapons. Before I could settle on a plan, Benny clicked the phone off and gave me a cruel smile. He set the phone down and walked over to me.

"Don't even think about doing that thing with your mind."

I thought I saw a flicker of fear in his eyes and pushed harder. "You're a Trimark, probably a low-level one. I have way more power than you."

Benny spoke to Shane over his shoulder. "Get over here."

Shane climbed out of couch and joined Benny.

"Open the closet," Benny ordered.

Shane walked to one of the closed doors and pulled it open, revealing its pitch black interior.

This wasn't going well.

"Hold on," I yelled and tried to roll away.

Benny grabbed me around the waist, hoisted me in the air and tossed me into the closet. My head bounced off the wall. I landed on my left arm and shoulder, gasping with pain.

Benny looked down at me with a smirk. "Yeah, you're real powerful all right."

Shane joined him. They stood side by side, blocking my view of the living room. I was still breathless from battling the pain in my shoulder. When I was able to speak, I said, "What do you want?"

"The moonstone, of course. What else?"

Okay, Allie, focus. Imagine pouring gasoline on Benny and Shane. I shut my eyes to concentrate. I was getting ready to strike the match when Benny reached out and grabbed my face, his fingers digging in to my cheeks.

"Ow! Let go!" Funny thing about pain. It blocks everything else from your mind.

I tried to wrench away from Benny's vicious grasp, but he clung to my cheeks like a bulldog with a steak bone.

"Listen up, bitch," Benny snarled. "Here's the deal. You have until eight o'clock tomorrow morning to tell us where the moonstone is. If you don't . . ."

He paused and looked over at Shane, who grinned down at me. "A whole lot of people will be dead, and it will be your fault. You and only you can keep that from happening."

Still clutched in his pincer-like fingers, I gasped, "If I give you the moonstone, you'll kill me. No reason to keep me alive once you have it."

His eyes flicked away, then back. "Not true. Once we have the moonstone, we'll let you go."

I knew he was lying, but said nothing. What *could* I say?

"One more thing," Benny said. "You tell anybody about this, that person plus one more dies. You tell two people about it, four die. Get the picture?"

"Yeah," I said. "I get it."

Finally, blessedly, he released my face.

"Have a good night, sweetheart. See you in the morning."

He stepped back and slammed the door, leaving me in utter darkness. Bitterly cold darkness.

I heard them leave the house and start the car. Filled with dread, I listened until the sound of the motor faded away ,and all I could hear was the pounding of my heart. Then the panic I'd been fighting earlier rose up like a giant tidal wave and crashed over me. Plain and simple, I lost it.

I fought against my restraints and screamed for help until my throat was raw. Finally, exhausted physically and emotionally, I lay, whimpering, on the closet floor.

Okay, Allie, that didn't work. How could it? Do you think Benny was dumb enough to park you in the middle of a crowded neighborhood? Think. Breathe.

I began to breathe deeply, counting as I sucked air in and out. Breathe in, one-two-three-four-five. Breathe out, one-two-three-four-five. My racing heart slowed to a steady thump-thump-thump and my wits returned. First order of business: get free. I shoved Benny's ultimatum about the moonstone to a little compartment in the back of my mind and labeled it *Future Business. Don't think about it now, Allie. Just figure out how to get out of this deep freeze.*

My arms were bound behind my body. My ankles were immobilized. I'd seen a woman on TV flexible enough to crouch down and pull her body through her bound arms. If I could get my hands in front of my body, I might be able to pull myself up, open the door and hop out the front door. There had to be a road leading to the house, but I hadn't heard a single car. Would I have to hop ten miles down a country road hoping for someone to drive by?

After a few painful attempts to contort my body and pull my butt through my arms, I crossed that one off my list. My only other option was TKP. Just last Friday, I'd caused a cheerleader's pompoms to float through the air. I still had the juice. But, could I do it, here in the dark, shut in a closet?

I took deep breaths and focused my mind. The darkness was complete, but I'd landed facing the door. No trace of light at all. Benny must have flicked off the overhead bulb before he left. If I could open the door, maybe I could somehow get to my feet. A glimmer of hope sprung to life somewhere in the vicinity of my heart.

I summoned my strength and tried to visualize the door.

I traced its perimeter in my mind and began filling it in from top to bottom, then back up until I got to the doorknob.

"Open!" I whispered. "Open."

I heard a rusty squeak that had to be the doorknob turning

"Yes!" I shouted. "Do it, you sucker! Open!"

I heard a click as the doorknob released its latch.

Taking another deep breath, I concentrated on using my mind to push the door open. *Hard. Harder!* I tried to ignore the throbbing pain in my shoulder and rolled over until I was touching the door. I nudged it with my head and felt it move a few inches. Practically giddy with joy, I bumped it again, harder this time. This time, the door banged against an obstacle, bounced back and slammed shut again. My heart sank down to the top of my soggy socks. Benny had blocked the door with something heavy, damn him to hell!

Could I move it out of the way? I tried again and again until my head was pounding with pain and I felt bitter bile rise in my throat. I did manage to get the door open again, but I couldn't budge whatever was blocking it. My strength was completely sapped.

With no hope for escape, I was forced to think about Benny's threat. If I didn't give him the moonstone, a firestorm of death and destruction would rain down upon innocent people, most likely my friends and family. Could I live with that on my conscience? On the other hand, if Trimarks had the moonstone, the result would be violence on a much larger scale. It was a decision nobody should have to make, especially a fifteen-year-old girl. Part of me prayed for morning. Another part wished morning would never come.

Cold, miserable and sick at heart, I pressed my forehead against the door I couldn't open and sobbed.

Chapter Twenty-Five

Let me tell you, spending the night in a freezing cold closet is no walk in the park. I wouldn't recommend it, not even for building character. Whatever Shane shot into my arm gave me freaky, weird hallucinations and nightmares. I couldn't tell which, since I didn't know if I was awake or asleep. Strangely, at one point, I thought Nicole was with me. She looked kinda frazzled—unusual for fashion diva Nicole—but in my trance, or whatever, she said, "Oh, so this is where you are." Swear to God.

When it's pitch black and you're in an altered state, time means nothing. I'd agonized a while about the impossible situation Benny had put me in, but then the head trip kicked in. *Muddled* is too mild a word to use for the way I felt.

The action started when I was deep in conversation with Marie Antoinette whose head, in case you don't know, was chopped off in 1793. She had her head tucked under one arm, which made it really hard to concentrate, because I wasn't sure where to look, and it seemed like she didn't know her head was supposed to be on her shoulders. And, oh yeah, her head was also speaking French.

Since I'm in first year French, I only picked up about every fifth word. I was about to ask her to slow down, *sil vous plais*, when I heard a tremendous racket outside the closet and a thin strip of light appeared beneath the closet door. A male voice yelled, "Allie! Allie! Where are you?"

I said, "*Excusez-moi*," to Marie's head and called, "In the closet!"

My voice sounded all quavery and weak, like Kizzy's when she was in the hospital. In the next instant, I heard the same male voice cursing and the sound of something heavy crashing to the floor. The closet door flew open and Beck filled the open doorway, his shadowy figure outlined in weak yellow light from the overhead bulb. Before I could tell Marie Antoinette "*Adieu*," he scooped me off the floor, pulled me close and buried his face in my hair.

"Allie," he whispered. A shudder wracked his body and his arms tightened around me. "I thought I lost you."

When he raised his head, I saw a single tear crawl down his cheek.

"No way." I snuggled into his chest, reveling in the warmth of his body. "I was about to bust out of here. But I had to wait until Marie left."

He looked at me strangely, his forehead creased with worry wrinkles. "Marie?"

"Yeah, Marie Antoinette. Her head was under her arm and . . . "

"Let's get you out of here," Beck interrupted. "Nicole's in the truck. You can tell us about Marie Antoinette on the way home."

"Where am I, anyway?"

"Twenty miles south of Peacock Flats in an abandoned house. I dug up the moonstone then Nikki used astral travel and the moonstone to find you."

I smiled up at him. "Yeah, I saw her in the closet. She said, 'Oh, so this is where you are.' I thought I was dreaming."

Still holding me pressed against his body, Beck stepped through the front door he'd kicked in and slogged through about a foot of snow to the truck.

When he reached the truck, the motor was running, plumes of exhaust visible in the cold night air. Nicole threw the door open. She looked up at Beck, a huge smile on her face. "I did it! I found her!"

Beck grinned down at her. "You sure did. Now, scoot over. You're driving."

"No way!" she screeched.

Beck held me tightly to his chest. He glared down at his sister, his eyes flashing dangerously. "I put chains on the tires. You'll be fine."

Still grumbling, Nicole stepped out of the truck and flounced around to the driver's side. Still grumbling, Nicole stepped out of the truck and flounced around to the driver's side while Beck stripped the duct tape from my arms and legs. He cranked the heat to its highest setting. The blast of hot air felt so good, I wanted to express my thanks, but waves of exhaustion slammed into me with such force, I could barely stammer, "Fe-fe-feels good."

I was aware of the truck moving as Beck shook me, none too gently. "Wake up, Allie."

"So tired," I mumbled. "Wanna sleep."

"No!" Beck said sharply and pinched my cheeks, which annoyed the hell out of me.

I sat up so I could glare at him, but he ignored me and spoke to his sister. "I need to keep her awake until we get her warmed up. Hypothermia."

Suddenly, I was very angry at Beck for not letting me sleep. My words came out slurred and in the wrong order. "Mean, you are . . . don't like!"

Two things happened to snap me out of my lethargy. Beck gave my hair a vicious tug and managed to hit the very same spot as Benny, and Nicole said, "Eewww, what smells?"

"Ow!" I slapped at Beck's hand. He relaxed his steely grip and smiled. "I wet my pants. Okay? Couldn't help it. Una-una-unavoidable."

Beck nodded solemnly. "It happens."

Nicole, who never took her eyes off the road, simply

nodded.

"There's a convenience store up ahead," Beck said. "Pull in. She needs coffee."

I glared at him. "I hate coffee."

He patted me gently. "I know."

I bitched and moaned and carried on, but drank the coffee. I really didn't have a choice. My hands were so shaky, Beck held the cup to my lips, making sure I swallowed every single drop.

As we approached Peacock Flats Road, the caffeine kicked in and the fuzziness lifted. The illuminated clock on the dashboard flashed 3:58. My dormant brain sprung to life, shifted gears and zoomed directly into overdrive. "Oh my God!" I yelled.

I startled Beck so badly he banged his head against the back window and swore a blue streak.

"Eight o'clock," I said. "That's when Benny and Shane are coming back. I won't be there, so they'll know."

Nicole glanced over at me. "Shane was there?"

I nodded.

Beck's arms tightened around me. "What is it they'll know?"

"That I won't give them the moonstone. And there's a *she*—a she somebody—who called and told Benny and Shane what to do. They said if I don't give them the moonstone a bunch of people will be killed, and it will be my fault."

The enormity of the situation crashed down on me and, much to my embarrassment, I started to cry. Beck patted my back like he was soothing a sleep-deprived toddler. It ticked me off. I stopped blubbering and pushed him away.

"I need to figure what to do."

My teeth were chattering so hard I could barely get the words out.

"First we get you warmed up," Beck said. "Then, we'll

figure it out together."

After another thirty minutes of Nicole creeping down the snowy road at a snail's pace, me trying to sleep and Beck not letting me, we arrived at the Bradford house, blazing with light.

Beck and Nicole both groaned.

"I guess Mom woke up," Nicole said. "Grounded until hell freezes over."

"Maybe you should have dropped me off at home," I said.

Beck's face darkened. "Are you nuts? That's the first place they'll look."

To their credit, the twins had left a note saying an emergency had come up and not to worry. Not that it helped.

Dressed in a long royal blue robe, Melissa Bradford was standing in the middle of the living room, her arms folded across her chest. She was way beyond anger. Her face was white with worry, but the look in her eyes was anything but gentle. She glared back and forth between Beck and Nicole then simply said, "Spill it."

Since this was my fault, I wanted in on the conversation. Maybe I could divert some of Melissa's anger. Still clasped in Beck's arms, I struggled to free myself.

"Put me down. Now!"

Beck set me down. My knees promptly buckled and I plopped down on the floor, my humiliation now complete.

Beck reached out a hand to help me up. I waved him away, gathered my strength and managed to stand. When my head started spinning, I grabbed the back of a chair to steady myself.

Melissa stared at me, her brows drawn together in dismay, like she was wondering how a wounded animal got into her living room. Beck and Nicole watched her face anxiously.

Finally, Beck said, "Mom, Allie's been kidnapped, beat

up and she's got hypothermia. Maybe it's time for one of those acts of kindness you're always talking about."

At his words, Melissa flinched. Her expression softened slightly.

"You were with Beck that night at the library. Right?"

I nodded, unable to summon the strength to speak.

Melissa stepped close to me and touched the bruise Benny had inflicted. She drew a deep breath and let it out. "Who did this to you?"

"It's a long story," I said, sagging against the chair.

Suddenly, the anger left Melissa's face. She turned and spoke to the twins.

"Don't just stand there like dummies. This girl needs to get warm. Nikki, go upstairs and fill the bathtub. Beck, take Allie to my bathroom, then go make coffee. We'll sort this out later."

I groaned and mumbled, "Not more coffee."

Nicole scampered away to do her mother's bidding. Beck was only too happy to carry me up the stairs. By the time we got to the bathroom, clouds of fragrant steam rose from a huge, free-standing bathtub setting on strange, claw-like feet. When he plunked me down on the toilet seat in Melissa Bradford's bathroom, my only thought was, *I must be dead because this has got to be heaven.*

I inhaled deeply and looked up at the three Bradfords hovering over me.

"Heaven," I said, smiling.

"We need to get her out of those clothes and into the tub," Melissa said.

Beck's eyes flared with interest. His mother glared at him and pointed at the door. "You. Out!"

I fumbled with the zipper on my coat but couldn't seem to grasp the little tab and pull it down. Melissa pushed my hand away and, before I could protest, she and Nicole stripped off my clothes and helped me into the tub. In hot water up to my chin and a bath pillow behind my head, I sighed with pleasure.

Swear to God, I tried to listen to the little voice in my head, the one saying, *Allie, you've got things to do, people to warn*, but fatigue robbed me of my ability to function.

The last thing I heard before sleep bore me away was a conversation between Nicole and her mother.

"Beck said not to let her sleep."

Melissa answered in a surprisingly gentle voice. "She'll be fine, Nikki. I'll watch over her. Go put her clothes in the washer."

She woke me when the water began to cool. Assisted by her capable hands, I climbed out of the tub. She toweled me dry and helped me into a fluffy terry cloth robe.

Beck must have been hovering directly outside the door. When his mother called him, he popped in immediately.

"She's been drugged. There's a needle mark in her arm," Melissa told him. "We should get her to a hospital."

"No!" Beck and I said together.

"Why not?"

I studied Beck's face and was ninety percent sure he intended to use his dazer on Melissa again. Somehow, that didn't seem fair.

"Beck!" I said sharply. "She needs to know what's going on."

Melissa's gaze flicked back and forth between Beck and me. "Yes," she said. "That would be helpful."

She sounded a little sarcastic, but with all that had happened tonight, I'd say sarcasm was the least of our worries. I caught sight of my battered face in the mirror and collapsed on the toilet seat in horror. Beck frowned and leaned against the bathroom wall. Since he'd gone silent as a tomb, it was up to me.

"Okay," I said. "I'll start."

Melissa perched on the edge of the tub and listened while

I told her about my paranormal abilities, how I'd acquired them. I spoke of the moonstone and the struggle between the Star Seekers and Trimarks. She blinked rapidly, but didn't say a word.

Beck finally jumped in when we got to the healing part. I noticed he skipped over a couple of important items, like his fight with Shane and Benny's threat to slaughter a bunch of innocent people. Minor details. When we finished, I tried to figure out what was going on in Melissa's head Her expression gave nothing away. Was she mad? Glad? Sad?

I tugged a comb through my wet hair and peered over at her, wishing she would say something. Anything.

Finally, I said, "Kind of a weird story, huh?"

A glimmer of amusement flickered in Melissa's eyes. "Allie. I have twins fathered by an incubus who impregnated me in a convent. My son and daughter have abilities far beyond that of mere mortals. Even though I have half-demon children, I'm a deeply religious woman and make a living by writing Christian fiction. Are you getting the picture here?"

I smiled at her. "Yeah, your life is a little weird too."

"Exactly," she said.

Melissa stood and turned to her son. "Now, Beck, I have a question for you. When you found out Allie was missing, why didn't you call the sheriff?"

Beck pushed away from the wall and grabbed Melissa's hand. "Mom," he said, staring into her eyes. "You're upset."

I staggered over and stepped between them. "You think I'm too weak to block you, Beck? Wanna put money on it?"

Beck looked startled and dropped his mother's hand.

"Talk to your mother," I ordered and retreated to the toilet seat once again.

Melissa said, "What on earth is she talking about?"

Beck ignored her question and launched into his story.

When he went to pick me up after school, he found my backpack lying in the yard. He looked inside the trailer and checked with Mercedes, who told him I'd ridden the bus home. When he discovered I wasn't at Kizzy's, he figured something bad had happened.

"By then, it was dark," he said.

He stopped talking and gave his mother a charming smile.

Melissa snapped, "That's it? It was dark? That's why you didn't call the sheriff?"

"Well, yeah," he said, rolling his eyes. "Think about it, Mom. If I reported her missing, it would be hours before anything happened. A lot of bad stuff can happen in a few hours. I knew Nicole and I could track her better than any sheriff. They wouldn't have a clue where to look for her."

Melissa shook her head in disgust. "So you take off in the middle of the night, on icy roads, without telling your mother . . . unbelievable!"

Beck flushed. He leaned over and kissed her cheek. "Sorry, Mom," he mumbled. It sounded sincere. Worked for me.

I smiled.

Chapter Twenty-Six

Five a.m. More coffee followed by breakfast. Bacon, eggs and toast with blackberry jam. I couldn't eat a bite. If Benny's threats were real—and I believed they were—the people I cared about were in terrible danger. My mother. Kizzy. Mike Purdy and his family. As soon as I expressed my fears, Beck handed me his cell phone.

I called Charlie, the limo driver, and asked him to go to Kizzy's house. Charlie had a permit to carried a concealed weapon and was devoted to Kizzy. When I told him she might be in danger, he said, "Don't you worry, honey. I'll keep her safe and sound."

I promised I'd stop by later to tell them everything.

Then I called Roy's cell phone and asked for Faye. Even at her best, Faye is not a morning person. She is definitely not a 5 a.m. person. It took a while for her to wake up and another five minutes to comprehend what I was saying. Then the hysterics began. I kept saying, "Faye, please. Just listen! Faye!"

Melissa, a sea of calm in the midst of a storm, said, "Let me talk to her."

I handed her the phone. By the time their conversation was over, she'd convinced Faye I would be safer staying with them, and that Faye and Roy should move to a different motel and stay put until further notice. Melissa also promised Faye I'd call her every two hours to let her know I was okay.

"Thanks," I mumbled. "Sometimes Faye gets a little, uh, unreasonable."

Understatement of the century.

Mike Purdy turned out to be a piece of cake. Once he was fully awake, he instantly grasped the big picture. "Don't worry about me, kid. You're preaching to the choir. I can take care of my family. Just make sure you take care of yourself."

Once again, Melissa grabbed the phone to assure my father I'd be snug as a bug in a rug in the bosom of her family. She listened for a moment, then handed the phone to me.

"I've been wondering about something," my dad said. "Has anybody tried to take the moonstone from you? Physically remove it from your body?"

I thought about his question. Revelle and Baxter wanted it. Ditto, Shane and Benny. But when I was wearing it, nobody had ever tried to take it from me. I was alone a lot. How easy would that be? I'd often wondered about that myself.

"No, never," I said.

"What have you learned about the settings? I assume you've checked them out."

Of course I had. What kid with a magic moonstone wouldn't? I knew it had four settings.

"Yeah, I have. The first click is the mind-reading thing," I said. "The other three . . . nothing."

"It's possible one of the settings might make it impossible for someone to physically remove it," Mike said. "Maybe the Trimarks know about that, and we don't."

Whoa! If he was right, I'd wasted a lot of time and energy burying the darn thing.

"That would be so cool," I said, and meant every word of it. "I'll check it out. Thanks, Mike." I clicked off. "Okay, where's the moonstone?"

Beck said, "Nicole's got it."

Nicole snapped, "Do not. I gave it back to you."

I tried not to panic when Beck left the room to search for it. After a few minutes, he returned with the moonstone in his hand.

"It was in my coat pocket," he said, with a sheepish grin.

I slipped the chain over my head and turned the moonstone in its setting. The first click, to three o'clock, was the mind-reading setting. I clicked it to six o'clock.

"See if you can take it off me," I told Beck.

He could. Quite easily. We tried all the other settings. Same result. So much for Mike's theory.

Melissa said, "Let's try something else. Beck, are you wearing your silver cross?"

He nodded.

"Give it to Allie."

He pulled the cross from the neck of his shirt and slipped it over my head. While his face was next to mine, he gave me a quick kiss. Unnecessary, but nice.

"Now, try it again," Melissa ordered.

Twelve o'clock. Nothing. Nine o'clock. Nothing. Six o'clock. Bingo!

He reached for the moonstone and *wham!*

When his hand was approximately six inches from the moonstone, it reacted with a flare of radiant blue light and zapped him, but good.

"Ouch! That hurt!" Beck exclaimed, glaring at me like I'd been responsible.

"Yes!" I said, raising a fist in the air.

Beck gave me a grudging smile, and we slapped hands.

Even Melissa looked happy. "Has to be the cross. Let's try it again."

"Nikki's turn," Beck said.

Nicole gave it a try, first without the cross, then with. Same result. Six o'clock. Blue flare. But Nicole was smart enough not to get zapped.

She smirked at her brother, "And you think *you're* the one with the brains."

If I hadn't been so tired, I'd have danced around the kitchen. This was huge!

"It does make sense," I said. "Trimarks are repelled by a crucifix."

"So the cross, a symbol of the crucifix, must have a similar effect," Melissa said.

"When the moonstone's turned to six o'clock," I finished.

Nicole said, "Kizzy gave it to you. Right?"

I nodded.

"Why didn't she tell you how it works?"

"She doesn't know how it works. In the original prophecy, Kizzy was The Keeper. Her job was to keep it safe until I came along."

Nicole's eyes lit up. "So, it could do *lots* more stuff we don't know about."

"Yeah," I said, trying to stifle a huge yawn.

Despite the overload of caffeine coursing through my veins, I was fading fast. I slumped over my plate of food, my chin dipping perilously close to congealing egg yolk.

Melissa noted my condition. "Sleep first. Then, we'll figure out what to do next."

She ordered the twins to bed. Nicole headed for the stairs.

Beck didn't move. "I'm staying with Allie."

"No way," Melissa said.

They engaged in a stare-down not unlike Faye and me in one of our epic battles. Melissa caved after the third time Beck said, "I'm not leaving."

She patted his cheek. "Guess I don't need to worry. Allie's dead on her feet and Beck, in spite of what you think, I do trust you. I know you won't take advantage of her."

Oooh, sneaky, I thought. Must be how normal mothers operate instead of yelling.

Melissa led me to the couch in the living room and tucked me under a fluffy down comforter. Beck sprawled in a nearby recliner. Melissa reached for the lamp to douse the light, her hand hovering over the switch.

My eyelids drooped even though I still felt Melissa's presence. Semi-conscious, I wondered if I was breaking some cardinal rule of hostess-houseguest etiquette. Was she waiting for me to say good night? Say my prayers? Engage in conversation? What? Too weary to think about it, I pulled the comforter up to my nose and closed my eyes.

"Allie." Melissa's voice was low and right next to my ear. "Are you still wearing Beck's cross?"

I pried my eyes open and nodded.

"Do you mind if I give it back to him? I have another one for you. Might as well cover all the bases."

With great effort, I lifted my head. She removed Beck's cross, then fastened another one around my neck.

She rose, crossed to Beck and dropped a kiss on his forehead before leaving the room. Just before I tumbled into a deep, dreamless sleep, I clutched both the moonstone and cross in my hand. A surge of energy not unlike a mild electric shock shot through me, and I visualized my body wrapped in an impenetrable force field. My last conscious thought was, *Allie, you are safe.*

Chapter Twenty-Seven

Ba-Bump . . . Ba-Bump . . . Ba-Bump. Wonderfully, blissfully warm, I awoke slowly to the sound of a slow, steady heartbeat. Mine? Struggling upward through thick layers of sleep, I became increasingly aware that I was not alone in my bed. I opened one eye and found I was snuggled up against Beck's body, my head tucked under his chin. The heartbeat I heard was his, not mine. I must have made a sound because Beck croaked, "You awake?"

"Yeah," I said. "Awake and wondering why you're in bed with me."

Since my face was pressed against his chest, my words came out muffled. Reluctantly, I pushed away from him and sat up. Beck sighed, threw back the comforter and planted his feet on the floor. I was relieved to see he was still fully clothed. He stood and stretched, scrubbing a hand across his face. "I wanted to keep you safe."

"Yeah, well, as you can see, I'm perfectly safe," I said. "Good thing I woke up before your mom came in."

He gave me a wicked grin. "Yeah, I don't think she'd understand."

I thought about how easily he dazed Melissa that night in the library and concluded Beck was pretty much the king in this castle. He did as he pleased with few consequences. Thankfully, I had some magic of my own to counter his. Last night, he'd looked shocked when I'd forced him to level with his mother. Whole new concept for Demon Boy! As long as I was around, I'd try to keep him honest.

Beck headed out to his little bachelor pad to clean up,

and I went in search of my clothes. I found them clean and
neatly folded, setting on top of the dryer in the laundry room
next to the kitchen. By the time Melissa got up, I'd used the
bathroom downstairs to put myself together.

The mirror did not lie. I looked like crap. Benny's blow
had blackened my left eye and raised an ugly welt on my
cheek. My mind, however, was crystal clear and drug-free.
Gazing into the mirror, I wondered what happened when
Benny and Shane returned to the house to find me gone.
Were they looking for me now? Since they failed to get the
moonstone, would they leave Peacock Flats? And who was
the mysterious woman calling the shots?

One by one we wandered into the kitchen. Nicole,
looking tired and grumpy, was uncharacteristically quiet.
Beck slipped in through the back door with wet hair and a
piece of toilet paper stuck to a razor nick on his chin.

Melissa stood at the stove, spatula in hand, flipping
pancakes. She said, "While you were sleeping, I called the
diner and asked for Benny. Bea said he called in sick."

"What about Shane?" Beck asked.

"No listing in the phone book," Melissa said. "I called
the school, told them I was a newspaper reporter doing a
story on drop-outs returning to school and wanted to
interview Shane Boldt."

"Oooh, sneaky," Nicole said.

"He checked out of school yesterday," Melissa said.
"Said his family was moving. My guess is, since Allie can
identify them both, Benny and Shane will run."

Melissa didn't know about Benny's threat to kill people
if I blabbed, so I wasn't free to elaborate, but I did say,
"They're going to be pretty ticked off. They might do
something awful to force me to give them the moonstone."

"I'll call the sheriff," Melissa said.

"No!" Beck and I said together.

She stopped and turned to face us. "Why not? Allie

knows who kidnapped her. There has to be evidence tying Benny and Shane to the abandoned house and . . ."

Beck held up a hand. "Are you ready to explain how Nicole located Allie using astral travel? Or why Allie has the moonstone, not to mention why Benny and Shane would do anything to get it? Think of the lies we'd have to tell. They'd question all of us separately. Someone's bound to mess it up."

Nicole raised her head from her cocoa and shot him a dirty look.

Beck stood and stared down at his mother. "Don't you see? They'll think we're a bunch of nut jobs. Besides, I can protect Allie."

"Hold it!" I said. "I can take care of myself."

While Melissa thought it over, I carried my dirty dishes to the sink, rinsed them off and put them in the dishwasher. Leaning against the counter, I watched the silent interaction between Melissa, Beck and Nicole.

Melissa nibbled a fingernail, her gaze traveling back and forth between the twins. Nicole shrugged and looked at the ceiling. Beck folded his arms and rocked back on his heels.

Finally, Melissa said, "Since you didn't call and report Allie missing last night . . ." she paused and glared at Beck. "It's possible calling the sheriff at this point might complicate matters."

Melissa poured herself a cup of coffee and crossed to the table. She collapsed into a chair with a heavy sigh. Her face was pale and she had dark circles under her eyes. I wondered if she'd slept at all.

"What about school?" I said. "Can we go?"

All three of the Bradfords stared at me like they'd forgotten I was in the room.

Melissa rubbed her temples. "The question is, will you be safe?"

"School is probably the safest place for us right now," I said.

"I think Allie's right," Beck said. "We've warned Kizzy and Allie's parents. We should just try to act normal."

Melissa caved after Beck and Nicole promised to call their mother after every class. I made sure the moonstone and cross were tucked inside my shirt and that the moonstone was turned to the *stun* setting. We left for school.

*

"I *told* you twice already. I slipped on the ice. Nobody hit me!"

I stood in Miss Yeager's open doorway, staring down at her, willing her to believe me. I'd refused to climb into the damn beanbag chair and, when she closed the door, I'd opened it again.

She rolled her eyes and sighed. "Really, Allie, do you expect me to believe that story? You have knuckle marks on your face."

Desperate now, I practically shouted, "That's because I fell into a bush. The branches hit me in the face. I can't help it if it looks like somebody punched me."

She turned and stared out the window as if deeply pondering my answer. The last place I wanted to be was in the counseling office. When we'd arrived at school, Alice had barely glanced at the note I'd faked from Faye. Instead, she studied my face, reached for the phone and punched in three numbers. "Miss Yeager? I'm sending Allie Emerson to your office."

Things weren't going well. I hadn't had time to strategize, and Miss Yeager wasn't quite as gullible as I thought. After shaking her head sadly at my "falling in the bush" story, she pulled out the big guns.

"Fine," she said, reaching for the phone. "You can talk

to me or to Child Protective Services. Your choice."

Oh, crap! Faye and I'd had dealings with CPS last spring and hoped to never see them again. I plopped down on the bean bag chair, my mind busy spinning another story. What she said next shocked me.

"Did your mother hit you? Everything you say in here is confidential. You can tell me."

I practically levitated out of the bean bag. "Faye? No. Never!"

Her fingers were poised over the keyboard of her computer. "I'm writing your report as we speak. I know your mother drinks, Allie. It's not exactly a state secret. I have to be honest. I'm leaning toward having you removed from your home."

I rolled out of the chair and scrambled to my feet, trying desperately to get a look at her computer screen. It conveniently morphed into a screensaver featuring a basket full of kittens.

"Okay," I said, defeated. I leaned against the wall. "Here's what really happened. You're right. Somebody hit me but it wasn't my mother."

I told Miss Yeager I'd sneaked out of the house, unbeknownst to Faye, attended a party and met a college guy named Rico who became so infatuated with me, he dragged me into the bedroom with the intention of doing the dirty deed. When I resisted, he smacked me in the face. My lust-filled imaginary lover was, of course, using a fake name and vanished into the night without a trace.

Miss Yeager's eyes narrowed in suspicion as I spoke. When I finished, she said, "Is your mother at work?"

Double crap! If she knew my mother was out of town, she'd know I was lying about last night.

I edged toward the door. "It's her day off. I think she went shopping."

"Are you sure she's not home?"

"I'm sure."

"Is it possible she's out of town?'

A shiver of apprehension crept down my spine. Why had she assumed Faye was out of town?

"Out of town? Oh, no, she's in town all right. I'll have her call you."

I didn't like Miss Yeager's expression. She had that smug *Gotcha* look.

I threw the door open. "Talk to you later. Gotta go. Geometry."

I scurried away before she could stop me. Geez, did I need her on my case right now? Of course, if Benny and Shane had their way, Miss Yeager would be the least of my worries.

Chapter Twenty-Eight

Beck and I stopped by Kizzy's on the way home. Charlie peered through the peephole before he opened the door. After I explained the situation, Kizzy agreed it would be better if I stayed with the Bradfords.

"However," she said. "As much as I like Charlie, it's not necessary for him to stay here. I'm in no real danger. I don't have the moonstone."

"You didn't have it last spring either and look what happened. Please, just let Charlie stay, so I won't worry."

Loose ends tied up, all we could do was wait. The next day, Thursday, passed without incident. It was awful. Tense and on edge, Beck and I began snapping at each other. The weather, always iffy that time of the year, had turned unseasonably warm. A Chinook wind swept through the valley, melting the snow, leaving behind a soggy, muddy mess.

Thursday night I slept fitfully, my fingers wrapped around the moonstone and silver cross. My dreams were filled with dark closets and talking heads . . . faceless monsters giving chase . . . me trying to run but unable to move. I'd wake up disoriented and shivering in the dark, even though I was safe and warm, sleeping on the daybed in Nicole's room. I made sure the moonstone's defensive barrier was turned on.

Benny and Shane. I knew they were out there. Without a doubt, they'd want to get even.

*

Friday morning, sick and tired of thinking about Trimarks, I decided to focus my energy on another issue, namely, Miss Yeager's report. I had a little surprise in store for Miss Gotcha, but I couldn't do it alone. Mercedes was out of the question. She'd freak out. It had to be Nicole.

It was eleven forty-five, almost lunch time when Nicole and I stepped into the counseling office. Miss Yeager stood at the window looking out. She jumped slightly when we entered and turned to face us, her hand covering her "J for Jeanette" pendant.

Her eyes bulged in surprise. "I didn't know you two were friends."

Instead of trying to decipher that remark, I said, "Oh, yeah. We're tight, Nicole and me. That's why she's here. I'd like to see a copy of the report to my social worker."

Miss Yeager frowned and perched on her chair. I leaned against the door frame. Nicole edged a few feet away until the three of us formed an uneven triangle. On our way to the office, I'd turned the moonstone to the three o'clock setting. Immediately, my senses had sharpened. No dizziness. No nausea, although some of the thoughts I picked up on while walking down the hallways were pretty gross. Mostly, they involved guys thinking about my various body parts and what they'd like to do to them.

"Allie." Miss Yeager's tone was long-suffering and exasperated. "You know that report is confidential. I couldn't possible reveal its contents in front of Nicole. That would be a breach of professional ethics."

Things were going as I'd planned. Before long, I'd know exactly what was in her mind. She blabbed a while longer. I glanced at Nicole who, as coached, played her role perfectly.

With a stifled sob, she placed a hand over her heart. "But Allie and I are like *sisters.* We know everything about each other. There's no reason . . ."

While Nicole elaborated on our sisterhood, I nibbled my fingernails and fidgeted, trying to look distraught. In the process, I edged back and to the right, then forward until I felt a flow of energy humming between the three of us. I swiped at my eyes and stared at the floor while Nicole babbled.

What I heard in Miss Yeager's mind made my heart skip a beat.

Kill zone. The words were crystal clear and spoken without emotion.

I jerked in surprise, which took me out of the loop. I knew my face would give me away, so I kept my eyes down and shifted my feet until I picked her up again. Her thoughts were racing at warp speed. It was like trying to make sense of a movie on fast forward.

Nicole stopped talking. Miss Yeager's jumbled thoughts faded into white noise. I looked up. She was staring at me curiously.

"So you see, Allie. What you're asking is not possible."

"Okay, fine," I said, inching toward the door. "Let's go, Nicole."

Miss Yeager followed us out, closed and locked her door and strode toward an exit.

We joined a throng of students heading for the cafeteria. Nicole looked at me, a big smile on her face. "That was cool. We should do it again sometime. Did you read her mind while I distracted her?"

When I didn't answer, Nicole plucked at my sleeve. "Well, did you? God, you're white as a ghost. What's wrong?"

Panicky, I broke into a run, Nicole scurrying to keep up.

"We need to find Beck," I said.

Nicole grabbed my arm and pulled me to a stop,

practically giving me whiplash. I'd forgotten how strong she was.

"Beck's not here. Remember? His car insurance is due today. He went to pay it. He said it wouldn't take long."

I groaned. "Oh, yeah. I forgot."

"Tell me what she was thinking," Nicole demanded.

I told her.

Nicole's eyes narrowed. "That's it? *Kill zone*? She was probably thinking about some TV show she watched last night."

"Yeah, but . . ."

"But, nothing. Shut up. Eat your lunch. I'll see you later."

She wandered off to join her friends. I sat at my usual table and forced a smile while Mercedes and the Hoffman twins chattered. I had a feeling I'd missed something important. But what?

Too worried to eat, I watched as Sonja Ortega, clutching an enormous boombox, approached Mrs. Burke, who'd drawn lunch duty. After a few minutes, Mrs. Burke raised her hands in surrender and loud salsa music blasted through the cafeteria. A bunch of people groaned. Others fled the room. Hips swaying, Sonja danced her way over to Manny and crooked a finger in invitation. Though he looked like he'd rather drown himself in a river, Manny obliged.

They were actually pretty good. The crowd got into it, stomping, cheering and clapping. What with the loud music and crowd noise, my mind barely registered the sound coming from outside.

Somebody was screaming.

Mrs. Burke heard it too. She rushed to the boom box and hit the *off* button. I ran for the door leading to the courtyard. Just as I reached it, it flew open and a group of girls, all sobbing and screaming, stumbled through, knocking me to the floor.

I heard Mr. Hostetler yell, "Get inside! Everybody get inside."

I scrambled up and pushed my way through the crowd pouring into the cafeteria. When I stepped outside, I froze in horror.

The images, now indelibly burned into my brain, will remain with me always. Dazzling sunshine. Moans and screams. I'd heard no gunshots, butMr. Hostetler was on the soggy ground, writhing in pain. There had been no guns involved at all. Two girls crouched behind a bench, their lips moving in silent prayer. A car parked in the alley, its motor idling. Behind Mr. Hostetler, more crumpled figures. An ashen-faced boy trying to crawl toward the building. Puddles of melting snow.

Three people, spaced about forty feet apart, stood watching the chaos. Shane Boldt. Jeanette Yeager. Benny.

Clutching his left arm, Beck lay on the ground, a few feet from Shane Boldt. The sleeve of his long-sleeved tee was soaked with blood.

"Beck!" I screamed and started running toward him.

He yelled, "Allie, no!" right before I slammed into what felt like a concrete wall. The impact knocked me into the ground with such force, I lay there, stunned, unable to draw a breath. My chest convulsed. I prayed for air. Then, finally, my diaphragm relaxed and air, blessed air, rushed into my lungs. I struggled to my feet, my eyes on Shane, totally confused about who or what had blocked me.

He held a bloody knife in his right hand. Smiling like he'd just won the lottery, he said "Oh, good, you're here. It's only fair since you're the one who caused all this. Boyfriend isn't so tough now, huh?"

I had to get Shane's focus off Beck. I had to buy some time.

I took cautious steps toward the perimeter. "You want the moonstone, Shane?" I called. "You can have it." *Just try and take it off me, you jerk.*

As I drew closer, I could see Shane was wearing a pendant in the shape of an inverted triangle. The light dancing on its surface was more than the sun's reflection. A scarcely visible beam of light, shot from the Shane's pendant and intersected with the one worn by Jeanette Yeager. Benny must have been wearing a pendant too, because the beam of light shimmered between the three of them, forming a perfect triangle, the invisible barrier I'd bashed into.

What I really needed right now was a big old spray can of *Whup Ass*. Unfortunately, I had only my wits and whatever magic I could summon.

"It's all yours, Shane. Come and get it." I said, stepping closer.

"Don't be stupid, Shane," Benny yelled.

Okay, at least Benny knew they couldn't take it from me.

I heard sharp inhalation behind me and a voice I recognized as Nicole Bradford's yelled, "Snakes!"

When I jerked my gaze away from Shane, swear to God, I think my heart stopped. An enormous, mottled, brown *rattlesnake* slithered around the base of a concrete bench. Shaking its rattles in warning, the snake advanced toward the two girls trapped between the bench and one side of the triangle. The snake's head bobbed and weaved as it tracked its prey, forked tongue flicking the air. White with terror, the girls began inching sideways.

Two more thick-bodied snakes crawled from Jeanette Yeager's corner. I wasn't surprised.

It takes one to know one. Had she released the snakes or conjured them up using magic? It didn't matter, because the sight of Miss Yeager and the snakes filled me with such rage, all traces of fear vanished. I would and could kick some Trimark butt!

Okay, Allie. Time for some serious magic. A few months

ago I'd made Blaster the bull trot backwards. Would my telekinetic power work on snakes? I focused on the snake, coiled and ready to strike one of the girls. I summoned my power, gratified when the familiar aura appeared, bathing my snake friend in a pink glow.

I'm not sure if I yelled the words "Stop! Back off!" or just thought them, but the snake suddenly stopped swaying and slithered back toward Miss Yeager.

One down, two to go.

Before I could focus on the next snake, a small voice behind me said, "Oh, no!"

Reluctantly, I reined in the TKP and shook my head to banish the aura. Nicole grabbed my arm and pointed at the puddles of melted snow that were now caldrons of steaming, bubbling mud. "Look what Benny did."

No, this couldn't be happening! We watched in horror as each small puddle grew in size. The boiling-hot mud spread outward and began oozing across the ground toward the people trapped inside the triangle.

Panic erupted. Those who were able to move danced this way and that, trying to avoid danger. Even more pathetic were those immobilized by previous injuries, victims of Shane's wicked knife or stunned by the triangle's electrified perimeter. All they could do was scream out their terror.

I saw a blur of movement as a snake arched its head to strike. Boiling mud began to spew. In a matter of seconds, the trapped would have to make an awful choice. Death by rattlesnake bite or third-degree burns. Their screams tore at my heart.

Nicole wailed, "We have to do something."

"Allie!" Beck's voice was tight with pain. "It only takes *one.*"

Shane snarled, "Shut up," but made no move toward Beck. A quick glance told me the Trimarks were having trouble holding the perimeter while unleashing their magic.

Shane was shaking uncontrollably, his face ghost-white and beaded with sweat.

Suddenly, I understood what Beck was trying to tell me.

If I took out Shane, Miss Yeager or Benny, the triangle would collapse. *You can do it, Allie. You're a Star Seeker. Now! It has to be now!*

"Shane!" I screamed as a blast of power surged into my mind. "You're toast!"

A jolt of pure psychic energy arced between my body and Shane's. He gave a hoarse scream and flew backward. I cried out in relief as the triangle collapsed.

The snakes slithered backward and disappeared.

Boiling pools of mud were once again puddles of melting snow.

All three Trimarks ran for their getaway car, Miss Yeager's Honda. Nicole made a flying tackle for Benny and missed. After Benny and Shane dove into the back seat, Miss Yeager gunned the motor, and the car shot out of the alley just minutes ahead of the sheriff.

I sat in the mud, cradling Beck in my arms and watched the paramedics running toward us.

I held his hand while they applied a tourniquet and loaded him onto a gurney. Before they wheeled him away, he squeezed my hand. "This isn't good."

My heart stuttered in my chest as I scanned his body for more injuries. "Did a snake bite you?"

He managed a faint smile. "No, no, it's not that. It's just that now I owe you one."

I touched his face then leaned close and whispered. "You're wrong. Now, we're even."

Chapter Twenty-Nine

I sat on the floor outside Vista Valley Regional's emergency room with my head buried in my arms, listening to the moans and cries of pain coming through the wall. Melissa was with Beck. I'd been sitting at my post for over an hour as distraught family members and a bunch of people in hospital scrubs rushed in and out. The press, clamoring for information on the strange knifing incident at Peacock Flats High, had been banished to a nearby waiting room. I was trying to keep a low profile, so I wouldn't be kicked out, too.

I'd hitched a ride with Beck in the ambulance. When the medics inserted an IV tube in his arm, I got worried. Beck was only half human. Maybe he was like a Vulcan, maybe his blood was different, and whatever they were pumping into his veins would hurt him.

I told one of the guys, "He has a cell phone in his coat pocket. I should call his mother."

After Melissa recovered from the news her son had been stabbed, she said she'd meet us at the hospital and not to worry about the IV situation, adding, "But, you better believe I'll have him out of there before night fall."

I'd imagined Beck, muscles bulging, bursting out of his hospital gown surrounded by fascinated female medical personnel.

My reverie was interrupted by the squeak-squeak-squeak of a nurse's cushioned shoes coming to a halt directly in front of me.

"You!"

My gaze traveled upward and stopped at the top of the starched white nurse's hat perched on the head of A. Haugen, boss nurse. She and I had history.

She peered down at me. "Why am I not surprised to see *you* here? You were there, huh? The school incident?"

I scrambled to my feet, biting my lip to hold back the tears. I nodded, unable to find my voice.

She inclined her head toward the ER. "Someone special inside?"

In a quavering voice, I said, "They won't let me in."

She grabbed my arm. "Well, guess what? If you're with *me*, you can go anywhere you want."

She marched me through the swinging doors, still keeping a firm grip on my arm. Suddenly, overwhelmed by the sights, smells and sounds of medical personnel laboring over people I knew, I dug in my heels and lurched to a stop.

Nurse Haugen looked me over again. "If you pass out, you're on your own."

I knew she didn't mean it and managed a wan smile. "Yeah, right."

She pulled me out of the way as a guy rushed by us pushing a metal cart loaded with medical equipment.

"Who are we looking for?"

"A friend of mine," I said. "His name's Beck Bradford."

The large room held a series of cubicles, only partially screened by half-drawn curtains. As Nurse Haugen pulled me along, I spotted tough little Luella Hoptowit, the hero of our volleyball match, glaring through a curtain crack.

I poked my head through the opening. "Oh my God, Luella! I didn't realize you'd been hurt."

Her left arm was bandaged, but she was sitting straight up in the bed, her dark eyes snapping with anger. In other words, she looked perfectly normal. "No biggie," she said. "That stupid Shane Boldt was waving his knife around. I tried to get away, and he cut me."

I suddenly realized she'd been one of the two people I'd seen lying on the ground behind Mr. Hostetler. "I'm really glad you're okay."

After wishing her well, I followed Nurse Haugen to Beck's cubicle. He was naked to the waist, and two guys were working on his left arm. Melissa stood on the other side of the bed, holding his right hand. Nicole was at the foot of the bed, her eyes puffy and red from crying.

"Behave yourself," Nurse Haugen told me and squeaked away before I could thank her.

Nicole took my arm and whispered, "I should have listened to you. It's my fault my brother got hurt."

I'd been down that road before and knew what it cost in pain and guilt. "No way," I whispered back. "Shane's the one who hurt him. Shane, Benny and Miss Yeager. Trimarks. All of them. That's who you should blame."

We stood side by side, clinging to each other and watched the doctors work on Beck. Their voices were low, but I caught bits of their conversation.

"Paramedics said his left arm was slashed to the bone . . . not!"

"Yeah, that's weird . . . just needs stitches."

Nicole whispered, "We half-demons are fast healers."

I remembered Beck's left arm dangling limp and helpless in the ambulance. "No kidding."

A nurse popped through the curtain. "Which one of you kids was responsible for chasing away the bad guys?" Without waiting for an answer, she said, "CNN called. Whoever it was, they want an interview via satellite."

"Not me," I said.

The nurse's eyes danced with excitement and she told Beck, "There you go, stud. Your fifteen minutes of fame."

"Not me," Beck said. We made eye contact. This wasn't good. The CNN anchor fired questions like she was throwing poison darts. When she didn't like the answer, she'd squint into the camera and, in a voice dripping with sarcasm, say, "Oh, really?"

We needed to get our stories straight. After the docs left, we had to wait for Beck's discharge papers. We agreed to the following: Mr. Hostetler was the hero. Injured and lying helpless on the ground, he'd saved lives by ordering students into the building. Shane, a gang member, had a grudge against Beck as the result of their fight after the football game. He wanted payback, and if a few other people got injured in the process, so what?

My role? Seeing my boyfriend in danger, I threw caution to the wind and tried to help him.

We went on to say that Shane's two accomplices released poisonous snakes in order to create havoc and facilitate their escape. The boiling mud and resultant burns were impossible to explain. Beck simply shrugged and shook his head. I faked a fit of hysteria and screamed, "Please don't make me talk about it. I can't bear it!"

As far as Miss Yeager was concerned, we would imply her relationship to Shane was more than student and counselor, knowing the press would be all over it like ants on a discarded Pop Tart.

As the nurse wheeled Beck out of the ER, we passed Mr. Hostetler's cubicle. His arms and legs had been badly burned when he tried to break through the triangle and lead kids to safety. His ex wife, tears running down her cheeks, watched silently as their daughter and son leaned over the bed rails, looking confused and upset.

I left Beck and ducked in for a quick word. When Mr. Hostetler spotted me, he lifted a hand. "Come closer, Allie."

His voice was hoarse, his face etched with pain.

I leaned over the railing and whispered, "Thanks for what you did today. You were so brave."

He said, "You're the hero, kid. You broke the triangle. I don't know how you did it, but thanks."

I whispered back, "Our secret . . . okay?"

He smiled and winked. "You got it."

I straightened up and smiled at the kids. I'd seen them hanging out after school in Mr. Hostettler's office. The daughter, probably twelve or thirteen, was a carbon copy of her mom. The boy looked entirely different, not surprising since it was common knowledge he'd been adopted. The rumor was he'd been tossed in a dumpster. I really hoped it wasn't true. Nobody should start life in a trash can.

The daughter gave me a shy smile. The boy stared at me, wide-eyed and unblinking. Undersized with lank, dark hair falling across his forehead, the kid was the whitest person I'd ever seen. A pulsating blue vein in his temple was clearly visible through his pale, almost translucent skin. His eyes were huge and the palest possible shade of blue. He continued to gaze up at me with an expression I can only describe as *wonder*. Trust me, it was weird.

"Uh, hi," I said.

Finally, the kid blinked. "You're the one."

"Excuse me?" I said.

Mr. Hostetler said, "Yeah, Chad, she's the one. She helped me out today."

Chad shook his head violently. "No, no, that's not what I meant."

His dad turned his face away and sighed.

Time for Allie to split.

"Well, gotta go. Good luck, Mr. Hostetler. I'll come visit you real soon. Bye, kids."

I felt Chad Hostetler watching me all the way to the elevator.

I caught up with the Bradfords outside. Melissa was parked in front of the door with the motor running. A hospital aide, with a firm grip on Beck's good arm, helped him into the car.

I was just about to walk to the other side of the car and

get in the back seat with Nicole when I heard, "Allie, wait!"

I looked up to see Chad's slight figure framed in the doorway. He walked toward me slowly. I met him halfway. He handed me a folded piece of paper, turned and ran back inside.

Printed in block letters, the words jumped off the page.

They are all around you. I can see them.

He'd signed it "Your friend, Chad," followed by his phone number.

I swallowed hard and stuffed the note in my coat pocket. Later. I'd think about it later.

Chapter Thirty

Wracked with guilt, Faye returned the next day and refused to let me out of her sight. She was making me nuts . . . so nuts I was almost happy when the FBI came calling. I'd been expecting Ruth Wheeler or her partner, the creepy guy with the bad comb-over. But the man who knocked on the trailer door was a complete stranger. Maybe sometime soon I'd figure out what was up with Ruth.

Apple-cheeked with laugh crinkles framing merry blue eyes, he was dressed casually in jeans, boots and a green parka. He flashed his ID and introduced himself. "I'm Dennis McCarty. Can I come in?"

I glanced around at Faye, who was peering over my shoulder. Her eyes became glittering slits of fury, her hands fisted at her sides. I knew an explosion was coming and braced myself.

"Where the hell were you when my daughter was in danger?" she yelled. "And now you want to come in and talk about it? You people are unbelievable!"

She flung herself onto the couch and folded her arms across her chest, one eye twitching ominously.

I whispered to Agent McCarty, "No problem. She'll get over it."

He whispered back, "Maybe I'd better not tell her your dad's in the car."

I glanced at the dark blue sedan and, sure enough, Mike Purdy was in the passenger seat. He lifted a hand. I waved back. All at once, the situation struck me as hilariously funny, and I lapsed into a fit of giggles.

"This is no laughing matter, Allie," my mother said.

I clapped a hand over my mouth and stepped back so the agent could enter our tiny living room. Rest assured, I checked his hand before I let him in. He had a star smack dab in the middle of his Venus mound.

Still snickering, I pointed him toward the dinette. "You can sit over there. Do you want coffee? Where's Ruth Wheeler? What took you so long? Why are you here?"

My barrage of questions seemed to puzzle him. He settled himself in the dinette, his brows drawn together in confusion.

Faye, apparently over her snit, crossed to the stove and poured a cup of coffee. She set it on the table in front of McCarty. "For God's sake, Allie, you just asked him four questions. Give the man a break."

I sat across from the agent. Faye slid in beside me.

"What happened to Ruth? She was supposed to be here a long time ago," I asked.

McCarty's blue eyes lost their twinkle. He cleared his throat and gripped the edge of the table. "Ruth is dead. Her car was recovered from Lake Keechelus two days ago."

"Oh, no," I said, shaking my head in denial. Faye grabbed my hand and held on tight.

McCarty continued, "When you called your dad and told him Ruth was a no-show, we started looking for her. As near as we can figure out, she was driving over Snoqualmie Pass on her way over here when her car went into the lake. She had no ID on her, so her body was unclaimed until now."

"Was it an accident?" Faye said.

"We'll know more after the car's been examined. She may have been forced off the road."

"But who would have known her plans?" I demanded. My voice was shrill with anxiety. I didn't need another death on my conscience.

He shook his head sadly. 'I'm sorry, Allie. I wish I knew. I just don't have the answers right now."

We sat quietly for a moment, remembering Ruth Wheeler. A fellow Star Seeker, she'd generously offered her assistance whenever I needed it, no questions asked. And now she was dead.

McCarty stared out the window a while and then took a big slurp of coffee. "Actually, kiddo, I'm here about another matter."

"Oh, yeah," I said. "The incident at school."

Outside, a car door slammed. Faye's head swiveled to the left, and she peered out the window. Her mouth dropped open and she shot out of the dinette. She planted her hands flat on the table and leaned over until her face was just inches from poor Dennis McCarty. He recoiled and moved closer to the window. There was no room for retreat. Such is life in a small trailer. His cheeks were an alarming shade of red.

"Is-that-who-I-think-it-is?" Faye enunciated the words carefully.

McCarty lifted his hands in surrender and gave Faye an ingratiating smile. "Yeah, it's Allie's dad. He wanted to ride along. What could I say?"

Faye stared at him for a long, uncomfortable moment. When the agent started to squirm, she whirled and marched out of the trailer.

McCarty exhaled loudly and swiped a hand across his forehead.

"Sorry about that, Mr. McCarty," I said. "Faye's not too fond of my dad."

"Call me Dennis," he said.

I glanced out the window and, for the first time in my life, saw my mother and father together. Mike leaned against the car with his hands in his pockets, looking amused. Faye was tearing into him, gesturing wildly, her chin thrust out in anger.

Finally, Mike pushed away from the car and held up a hand. The fight went out of Faye. Her shoulders slumped, and her head went down. Mike put his hands on her shoulders and turned her around. Surprisingly, she didn't pull away. My dad pointed at the trailer, leaned close to Faye and said something that made her smile. Were they talking about me? I looked away then, because I wanted to remember that image . . . my parents standing together, both smiling, both looking my way.

Turned out that Dennis McCarty had lots of questions. Since he was a Star Seeker, I didn't have to lie . . . at least until I got to the part about the Bradfords. Even though Dennis McCarty believed in the existence of magic, it would be wrong to reveal the Bradford half-demon secret. I glossed over Beck and Nicole's rescue of me, saying simply that they followed some clues I'd left.

Dennis said, "What clues?"

I examined my fingernails and said, "Gee, I can't remember. Whatever they drugged me with must have given me short-term memory loss."

He frowned. "That's strange. You seem to remember everything *else* with amazing clarity."

I pretended I didn't understand and fast-forwarded to the day of *the incident.* When I told him how I made the snake crawl backward and knocked Shane out of the triangle, McCarty grinned and pumped a fist in the air. "Yes! Our girl is back!"

When I ran out of words, Dennis filled in the blanks. Jeanette Yeager's counseling certification was phony. Her goal was to earn my trust and figure out how to get her hands on the moonstone.

"Along with Benny and Shane, she was undoubtedly a Trimark," Dennis said. "Probably had the mark on her hand removed with laser surgery."

I told him about Faye accidentally letting it slip that I'd

lost my powers.

He nodded. "Yeah, they must have thought getting the moonstone would be like taking candy from a baby."

"I guess they were wrong."

He offered a fist. I bumped it with mine and grinned.

I sobered quickly. The whole Jeanette Yeager thing was so bizarre; I simply couldn't wrap my head around it. I told Dennis. "Here's the weird part. The day it happened, she asked me all kinds of questions . . . like what happened to my face . . . and was my mother out of town. Why did she do that? She already knew the answers. I guess she was just yanking my chain. Right?"

He shrugged. "If she was the one calling the shots, she knew. It's possible more people are involved. Hopefully, we'll catch up with her, but Trimarks have a way of disappearing."

The rest of the story was chilling. We'd been lucky. Even though several people were badly injured no one had died. In addition to Luella and Beck, a couple of kids had been slashed by Shane's knife. Beck's was the most serious injury, but like Nicole said, they were fast healers.

Benny had vanished. Yeager's Honda had been found, abandoned, on the outskirts of Peacock Flats. The FBI was on their trail but not hopeful.

Dennis asked a bunch of questions. He even had me draw the pendant I'd seen up close . . . Jeanette Yeager's.

"Are you sure there was a rim of black around the stone?"

"Positive. Why?"

He didn't answer right away. "What about the one Shane was wearing?"

"I was sorta busy doing other stuff, but, yeah, I think it did."

"Remember the Star Seeker meeting when Larry talked about Trimarks and the dark crystal and their use of triangulation?"

I nodded. "Yeah, the informant said the dark crystal gave Trimarks supernatural powers."

"We won't know for sure unless we get our hands on one, but I'm willing to bet their pendants have been infused with magic from the dark crystal."

I shook my head in wonder. "Makes sense. Shane, Yeager and Benny formed a perfect triangle with their bodies and used the dark crystal in the pendants to do magic."

Something else had been bothering me. "But, what was their purpose? Were they still trying to get the moonstone, or were they punishing me for not cooperating?"

Dennis said, "My guess is they were hoping you'd hand it over, but if they killed a few people in the process, no problem."

I pulled the moonstone and cross from the neck of my tee shirt and clicked the moonstone to six o'clock. I grinned at him. "Try to take it off me."

His mouth quirked up in a half smile. "And I'm doing this . . . why?"

"Just try it."

The look on his face was like, *Okay, she's just a kid. I'd better humor her.*

He reached out for the moonstone. *Zap!*

He jerked his hand back and, if I'm not mistaken, said a few choice words under his breath.

I howled with laughter.

"You could have just told me," Dennis said in a wounded tone.

"I thought a demonstration would work better. Spread the word, okay? The kid can take care of herself."

"Sure will." He stood and offered his hand, making sure he was nowhere near the moonstone. We shook and he headed for the door. "Talk to you soon, kid."

When he reached for the door, Faye threw it open. He

jumped about a foot and flattened himself against the wall so she could pass.

Faye stepped into the trailer without saying a word. She stopped at the dinette, dropped a kiss on top of my head and walked into her bedroom. Before she slid the door shut, she said, "Go talk to your dad."

I did.

Chapter Thirty-One

We didn't return to school until the Wednesday before Thanksgiving. I guess they had to secure the crime scene, wash away the blood or whatever. Counselors were brought in from other school districts and set up in the community center. We were encouraged to drop in for a counseling session during our two days off. In spite of Faye's nagging, I refused to go.

"Why not?" she demanded. "You know you'll have nightmares again."

"I'm fine," I said. "No nightmares."

Strangely enough, I *was* fine. When I told Nicole not to blame herself, it was like I'd come full circle. I believed my own words. How weird is that? The way I saw it, I had two choices. I could take on the burden of guilt. Ruth Wheeler probably died because of me. Beck was most likely stabbed because of me. Innocent people were injured and traumatized because evil people wanted the moonstone, and I wouldn't give it to them. A person can only carry so much guilt without collapsing under its weight.

On the other hand, I could see the big picture. I'd managed to save a few lives as well. And, unlike most fifteen-year-olds, I already knew my destiny. Even though I wasn't sure how it would play out, my life was bound to the moonstone. I needed to be at the top of my game. I am Allie, hear me roar!

Two unlikely and unrelated events happened on Wednesday, both involving my friend, Mercedes. The first occurred in a crowded hallway between second and third periods. Sweet, happy Mercedes Trujillo, who didn't have a mean bone in her body, caught the ass pincher.

She filled us in during lunch.

"Oh my God, Allie, it was so cool! I can't believe I did that!"

She stood and looked around to make sure everyone at the table was listening.

"Here's how it went down. I opened my locker and saw my algebra book had fallen off the shelf and smashed my lunch, so, right away, I was pissed off, ya know?"

We all nodded.

"I bent over to pick it up and he nailed me…the ass pincher!"

She made a face and rubbed her butt cheek. "Oh, girl, did that ever hurt!"

Donna Jo sighed hugely. "We know it hurts. Get on with the story."

Mercedes shot her a dirty look. "Okay, okay, I'm just setting the scene. Here's what happened: I grabbed the algebra book and whirled around, quick like a panther and whapped him. He fell down, his glasses flew off and it was game over."

She extended her arms over her head. "Winner: Mercedes Trujillo. Loser: Charles Raymond Atkinson Junior! Yes!"

That's right. The ass pincher was none other than Suzanne Maloney's sneaky little boyfriend, Charles. Swear to God.

Mercedes bowed. We applauded.

"What's going to happen to Charles?" I asked.

"Suspended until Mr. Hostetler gets back," Mercedes said. "And he has to take a class on sexual harassment."

We all got quiet for a minute, thinking about how strange it was that the ass pincher turned out to be someone as nerdy as Charles. Guess you can never tell about people.

The second incident happened after school. I was sitting at the dinette conjugating French verbs when I heard Mercedes screaming, "Allie! Allie! Come quick! Hurry!"

My heart leaped in my chest as visions of horribly injured little Trujillos danced through my head. Gushing blood . . . broken bones . . . grease burns . . . tamales lodged in tiny windpipes. Scared to death, I burst through the door and ran through mud and melting snow in my socks to where Mercedes stood, waving her arms.

"What? What?" I screamed back.

Then, I looked at her face. She was smiling, big time. Mercedes grabbed my arm and dragged me across their little yard and through the front door of their mobile home.

"Can't tell you," she said. "You've got to see for yourself."

The whole Trujillo family was gathered around a fifty-four inch television set, tuned to a Spanish speaking station. When they saw me, they all started talking at once and pointing at the screen. Since they were speaking Spanish, the only word I picked up was *Junior.*

Puzzled, I looked back and forth between Mercedes and the TV. "Did your mom just say *Junior?*"

Mercedes was jumping up and down with excitement. "Wait 'til the commercial's over. Do the words Mexican soap opera mean anything to you?"

"Duh . . . no," I said. "Why?

"Look!" Mercedes shrieked, pointing at the screen. The whole Trujillo family burst into applause as Junior Martinez (my Junior) strolled out of a bedroom with a satisfied grin on his face, his arms around two scantily dressed bimbos.

A strangled sound burst from my throat. "Aaarrgh!" My knees buckled and I plopped down on the floor, totally ignored by the Trujillos who were mesmerized by Junior's every word and gesture. Looking buff in faded jeans and a tight brown tee that emphasized his pecs and biceps, his hair was tipped with blond highlights and skillfully tousled.

During a close-up, his clear gray eyes looked right at me and I sighed, remembering our scorching farewell kiss.

Mama Trujillo sighed too and fanned herself by flapping her blouse up and down. " *Que tipo tan bueno!*"

Mercedes giggled. "Mama just said, 'What a babe!'"

When the show ended, Mercedes said, "Can you believe it? Junior's a star. That's why he didn't come back. Do you have his cell number? Maybe you could call him, and he'd send us autographs."

Mama clapped her hands and said, "*Si! Si!* Allie, get autographs."

I assured them I'd try and scampered home in my wet, muddy socks.

Later that night, after Faye went to bed, I sat cross-legged on the couch and thought about the strangeness of my life. My former boyfriend, Junior, was starring in a Mexican daytime drama. I'd probably never see him again. My current boyfriend wasn't fully human. As a result of kissing him, I'd acquired a demon mark on my palm that meant . . . who knew? His sister could leave her body and travel to faraway destinations.

So many questions without answers. Grandpa Claude. My missing grandmother, Melia. Faye's mysterious past. Mr. Hostetler's spooky little kid. And, the moonstone . . . could it really stop time?

I turned out the lights, opened the blinds and looked for the moon, my nightly ritual. It was easy to find. Scudding clouds raced across the moon's surface, now in its last quarter. In all honesty, the ritual wasn't truly mine. Faye had started it years ago, before I got too old to tuck in bed. Bits and pieces of the song she used to sing drifted through my mind, and I hummed the melody. When the words came back to me, I sang aloud,

"I see the moon

The moon sees me."

Faye's voice rang out from the back of the trailer,
"God bless the moon
And God bless me."

We sang it again, louder this time then laughed like lunatics. When the trailer got quiet, I sat in the dark and gazed at the rising moon, so predictable in its cycle . . . so utterly different from the chaos of my life.

I lifted the moonstone toward the window, watched the light play across its surface and made a decision. Just for tonight, I would put my problems aside and let unanswered questions remain unanswered. Instead, I would capture this tiny, fleeting moment of pure joy and hold it close, like the gemstone in my hand.

Feeling blessed, I smiled at the moon.

How Allie Emerson's Story Began . . .

MOONSTONE
Book One in The Unbidden Magic series

Excerpt

Prologue

I've been wondering . . . is there a normal way to become paranormal? Like, go to Google, type in "Make me magic," click on a website and wait for a list of rules to pop up? I really need a list of rules. How else can an almost fifteen-year-old girl living in Peacock Flats, Washington learn to deal with special powers? Here's how it started . . .

Chapter One

One minute, I was on a ten-foot ladder adjusting the TV antenna on the twenty-four-foot trailer behind Uncle Sid's house, where I lived with my mother, Faye. The next minute, I sailed off the ladder, grazed an electric fence and landed face down in a cow pie.

Swear to God.

Though groggy and hurting, I rolled onto my back. A window in the trailer cranked open and I heard my mother scream. "Allie! Ohmigod! Somebody call 911!"

I was surprised Faye managed to open the window. She'd spent most of the last two years in bed since, at age thirty one, she Retired From Life. But really, call 911? We had no phone and I was the only other person in the area. Who was she talking to? Blaster the bull? I smiled weakly at the thought of Blaster in a phone booth, punching in 911 with one gigantic hoof.

Okay, technically, I landed in a bull pie, not a cow pie. The mess dripping off my face was compliments of my Uncle Sid's prize bull, speaking of which . . .

It was then my wits returned. I felt the ground vibrate, heard the rumble of hooves. I reared up to see a half-ton cranky bull racing toward me, head down, mean little eyes fixed on my prone body.

Faye continued to scream shrilly. I moaned and crawled toward the fence, looking over my shoulder at Blaster who bore down on me like a runaway train. When I tried to stand, I slipped in the wet grass and landed on my belly. Oh God, he was just inches away. I wasn't going to make it! I rolled into a ball and screamed, "No, Blaster! Go back! Go back!"

Laying on the wet grass, trembling with terror, I watched

as Blaster stopped on a dime, blew snot out of his flaring, black nostrils and released a thunderous blast of flatulence—that's what my teacher, Mrs. Burke, calls farting—and, of course, is the reason Uncle Sid named him Blaster.

"Back off, Blaster," I said between shallow, panicky breaths. "Good boy."

I hoped the "boy" comment wouldn't tick him off, what with his fully-developed manly-bull parts dangling in full view as I lay curled on the ground looking up. Yuck!

Suddenly my vision narrowed and grew dark around the edges. It was like looking down a long tunnel with Blaster front and center, bathed in light. A loud buzzing filled my head. The next moment, Blaster took a tentative step backward, then another, walking slowly, at first, then gradually picking up speed until he was trotting briskly backwards like a video tape on slow rewind.

Mesmerized by the sight, I sat up and watched Blaster's bizarre retreat back through the tunnel. At that precise moment, I should have known something strange was going on. But hey, I was a little busy trying to save my life.

As I crawled under the fence, my vision returned to normal and the buzzing faded away. I stood and swiped a hand across my sweaty face. At least, I *thought* it was sweat until a trickle of blood dripped off the end of my nose. Surprised because I felt no pain, I touched my face and found the blood was oozing from a puncture wound in the center of my forehead.

I glanced up at Faye, who continued to peer out the trailer window, her pale face framed in a halo of wispy blond curls, her eyes wide with shock. She inhaled sharply, and I knew another scream was on its way. I held up a hand. "Come on, Faye, no more screaming. You're making my head hurt."

"But, but, the bull . . . he, he . . . " Faye began.

I wasn't ready to go there. "I know, I know."

I staggered around the end of the trailer and banged through the door. Two giant steps to the bathroom. I shucked off my clothes and stepped into the tiny shower.

"You okay, Allie?" Faye asked.

She peered through the open doorway, paler than usual. Her right hand clutched the locket that held my baby picture, the one that makes me look like an angry old man. The only time she took it off was to shower.

"I'll live," I muttered.

"Weird, huh? Blaster, I mean. I heard you yell at him. Bulls don't run backward, Allie."

When I didn't answer—what could I say?—she waited a beat. "Use soap on your forehead. Did it stop bleeding?"

"Yes, Mother." I reached over and slid the door shut.

Deep sigh. "You don't have to be snotty. I told you to be careful."

The TV blared suddenly. Oprah. Not that I'm a spiteful person, but I blamed Oprah for my swan dive off the ladder. Late last night, a sudden gust of wind knocked over our TV antenna. When I got home from school today, Faye insisted she had to watch Oprah. Like that was going to change her life. I finally got tired of hearing about it and borrowed Uncle Sid's ladder. Moral of story: Never wear flip flops on an aluminum ladder.

I turned on the water, stood under the weak stream and checked for damage. Other than a slight tingling in my arms and legs and the hole in my head, I seemed okay.

I toweled off my curly, dark-brown hair and pulled it back into a messy ponytail. When I wiped the steam off the mirror, I saw a dark-red, dime-sized circle the size in the exact center of my forehead. I touched it gingerly, expecting it to hurt. But it didn't. Instead, a weird sensation shot through my head, like my brain was hooked up to Dr. Frankenstein's machine, that thing he used to make his monster come alive. I must have given a little yip of surprise because Faye said again, "You okay, Allie?"

"I'm fine," I said. "Just a little sore."

"Did you check the mail?"

"The first's not until Friday. Today's the twenty-ninth," I said.

"Sometimes it comes early."

The welfare check *never* came early. The state of Washington was very reliable when it came to issuing checks.

"Yeah, okay," I said, not wanting to burst her bubble.

Wrapped in the towel, I took two steps into the living room/kitchen, reached under the table and pulled out the plastic crate containing my clean clothes. I dug around and found clean underwear, a tee shirt and a pair of cut-off shorts.

I slipped into my bra, once again thinking how cool it was I finally needed one. Though I hoped for peaches, I'd managed only to grow a pair of breasts roughly the size and shape of apricots. Oh, well, apricots are better than cherries. Our valley is called "The fruit bowl of the nation," hence, my obsession with naming body parts after produce.

I slipped into my treacherous flip flops, headed out the door and spotted Uncle Sid darting behind the barn. Faye says Uncle Sid is not a people person but I thought he was just trying to avoid Aunt Sandra and her constant nagging. That woman's voice could make a corpse sit up and beg or mercy.

I trotted down the driveway, stopping suddenly when I spotted a pair of denim-clad legs sticking out from under the Jeep Wrangler parked next to Uncle Sid's house. Legs that belonged to Matt, Uncle Sid's son and older brother to spoiled brat, Tiffany.

How can one kid—Tiffany—be so annoying and the other—Matt—so totally hot? I tried to avoid Matt because of the way I got when I'm around him. Though I'm normally loquacious (last Wednesday's vocabulary word that I copied and vowed to use at least three times,) one look at Matt and I lost my power of speech. My jaw dropped and my mouth went dry. There's just something about him—sleepy blue eyes, light brown hair that usually needs combing, a crooked grin and a sculpted, rock-hard body.

It wasn't some creepy, incestuous thing since Matt and I weren't real cousins. Sid was Faye's step brother. Nope, we didn't have the same blood coursing through our veins. Matt's was probably blue, while mine came from the mystery man Faye refused to talk about.

I tiptoed past the Jeep to spare myself further humiliation. I'd almost made it when he rolled out on one of those sled thingies and grabbed my ankle. "Hey, kid, how ya doin'?"

The warmth of his hand against my bare skin turned my normally frisky brain cells to mush. Sure enough, my lower jaw was heading south. "Uh, just great, Matt," I said, averting my eyes and licking my suddenly parched lips.

He released my ankle and stood up. "Good," he said. "Your mom still got that . . . whaddaya call it?"

"Fibromyalgia." As I said the word, I felt my upper lip curl in a sneer. "So she says."

"She getting better?"

"She's trying to get social security benefits, you know, the one for disability."

The words tasted bitter in my mouth.

"Oh yeah," Matt said. "I saw Big Ed's car here the other night. He's her lawyer, right?"

My hands automatically curled into fists. I narrowed my eyes and studied Matt's face, looking for a smirk or maybe a suggestive wink. Even though I didn't want to punch him, I could and I would. I knew how to punch. Faye had made sure.

No problem. He'd moved on. Wonder of wonders, he was looking at me. I mean, really looking at me with those sexy blue eyes. His gaze lingered for a long moment on my chest. Whoa! Was he checking out my 'cots? I was suddenly aware I'd outgrown my shorts and tee shirt. Not knowing what else to do, I shoved my hands into the pocket of my cut-offs and took a step back.

"Well, hey, I gotta go check the mail. See ya, Matt."

His voice followed me as I headed down the driveway. "Hey, kid. If you ever need a ride somewhere, let me know. I got the Jeep running real good."

Because my mouth had fallen open once again, I settled for a casual wave of acknowledgement even though I wanted to pump a fist in the air and scream, "YES!"

As I trotted to the mailbox, the late April sunlight warm on my shoulders, I pondered this strange turn of events. Even though he called me "kid," clearly Matt had noticed a couple of new bulges on my formerly stick-like body. Hmmm. Had my tumble off the ladder, followed by the electric fence zapping, released some sort of male-attracting hormone?

In spite of my mini-triumph, Matt-wise, a dull headache began to throb painfully at the back of my skull. I opened the mailbox and, as predicted, Faye's check had not arrived. There was, however, a familiar tan envelope from the Social Security Office of Adjudication and Review. Probably another form for Faye to fill out asking questions like, "Are you able to push a grocery cart?" And, "Can you walk up a flight of stairs?" Questions Faye had already answered "No" and "No."

When I handed her the envelope, Faye sighed and dropped it, unopened, onto the pile of similar tan envelopes stacked between the bed and wall.

"Big Ed's coming tomorrow. I'll let him deal with it." She looked pointedly at her watch.

I took the hint. It was time for Fay's nightly ritual, two slices of peanut butter toast and two cans of Busch Light. The menu varied only on Thursday night. Big Ed night. He always brought burgers, fries and a fifth of Stoli. Not that I'm around on Thursdays. No way. But, when I come home on Friday, the place smells of grease and vodka.

Let me make this crystal clear. Big Ed was Faye's lawyer, not her boyfriend. That was what Faye said. He'd been working day and night on her case for two years. That was what Big Ed said. Me? I had my doubts.

Later that night, I heard the sound of Faye's rhythmic breathing and tiptoed back to the bedroom. I gathered up the empties and the plate littered with peanut butter-smeared crusts and tossed them in the garbage.

Tomorrow was Thursday, Big Ed night. I'd be staying with Kizzy Lovell, the town witch. That was what a lot of kids called her. Since I wouldn't be home until Friday, I made sure I had clean underwear in my backpack.

As the evening wore on, my headache grew steadily worse. At ten, I turned out the light. I pulled the curtains back so I could see the night sky, a brilliant canopy of far-flung stars and a full-faced moon. I held my hand up to the window. Bathed in moonlight, my palm looked washed in silver, its tell-tale lines carved in dark relief by the unknown maker of my fate. I thought about the times Kizzy studied the lines on my palm and said, "You're a special girl, Alfrieda. Like it or not, you have the Gift."

Every time I'd say, "What gift?" Kizzy would smile mysteriously and say, "You'll see," which really irritated me because, clearly, the only gift I had was the ability to get all-A's on my report card. Even that wasn't a gift, since I hated Algebra and had to work my butt off.

I had no sooner wrapped up in my faded pink quilt and snuggled into the couch bed when I remembered the aspirin and glass of water I'd placed by the bathroom sink before I brushed my teeth. I groaned and switched on the light. The bathroom was only a few steps away. But in my present state—cotton-mouthed and head pounding with pain—the distance seemed as vast as the Sahara Desert. I swung my feet to the floor and turned my head slowly toward the bathroom. I could see the glass of water perched on the counter like it was taunting me, "Come and get me, Allie."

I reached out a hand, thinking, *It would be a whole lot easier if you came to me,* and it happened again. The whole dark-around-the-edges, tunnel-vision, buzzing-in-the-head thing. The glass teetered back and forth, danced a little jig across the counter and shot into the air for a moment before it slammed onto the floor and shattered into about a jillion pieces.

"What the hell's going on, Allie?"

I looked up to see my mother standing in the narrow hallway. My hand, still extended toward the glass that wasn't there, shook violently. "I dropped it. That's all," I said. "Go back to bed. I'll clean it up."

Faye's eyes narrowed in suspicion but finally, she turned and trudged back to the bedroom. When I opened the door and stepped outside to fetch the broom, I was greeted by a symphony of night music. Strangely, the pain in my head was gone. The soft spring air was alive with a chorus of crickets backed by a full orchestra of spring peepers, their mating songs accompanied by the tinkle of wind chimes.

But, hold on. We didn't have wind chimes. We'd never had wind chimes. I walked to the back of the trailer and stared up at the gnarled old apple tree next to Blaster's pasture. Nudged by a gentle breeze, long silver tubes bumped together, creating a melody with subtle variations as the air around them ebbed and flowed. It was stabilized by a dangling iridescent glass ball whose surface caught and held the moonlight.

Must be some prank of Matt's. Vowing I'd figure it out in the morning, I grabbed the broom, opened the door and froze. A woman sat on my couch bed. A woman with flowers in her long, dark hair, wearing a pink-and-yellow, tie-dye dress embellished with a blazing purple sun. A woman, smoking what looked and smelled like weed. I opened my mouth, preparing to scream so loudly and shrilly the shards of glass on the floor would shatter into even smaller pieces.

The woman said, "Hi. I'm Trilby, your spirit guide. Guess what? You just passed your first test. Isn't that groovy?"

Lightning Source UK Ltd.
Milton Keynes UK
25 November 2010

163472UK00001B/23/P